Sorry for Your Trouble

Sorry for Your Trouble

Stories

Richard Ford

HARPER LARGE PRINT
An Imprint of HarperCollins*Publishers*

This is a work of fiction. Names, characters, places, and incidents are products of the author's imagination or are used fictitiously and are not to be construed as real. Any resemblance to actual events, locales, organizations, or persons, living or dead, is entirely coincidental.

 For information, address HarperCollins Publishers, 195 Broadway, New York, NY 10007.

HarperCollins books may be purchased for educational, business, or sales promotional use. For information, please e-mail the Special Markets Department at SPsales@harpercollins.com.

FIRST HARPER LARGE PRINT EDITION

ISBN: 978-0-06-299910-8

Library of Congress Cataloging-in-Publication Data is available upon request.

20 21 22 23 24 LSC 10 9 8 7 6 5 4 3 2 1

Kristina

Contents

Sorry for Your Trouble

Nothing to Declare

All the senior partners were having a laugh about a movie they'd seen. *Forty-Five Years.* Something, something about the movie taking forty-five years to sit through. The woman McGuinness thought he recognized was into it with them at the far end of the table—leaning in, as if hearing everything for the second time. "Miss Nail!" they were calling her. "What do you say, Miss Nail? Tell us." They were all laughing. He didn't know what it was about.

The woman wasn't tall, but was slender in a brown linen dress, a tailored dress that set off her tan and showed her well-drawn body. She'd glanced past him twice—possibly more. A flickering look asking to be thought accidental, but could be understood as acknowledgment. She'd smiled, then looked away, a smile that said possibly she knew him, or had. So peculiar, he thought, not to remember. Eventually he would.

They were at the Monteleone, the shadowed old afternoon redoubt with the bar that was a carousel. It wasn't crowded. Outside the tall windows on Royal a parade was shoving past. *Boom-pa-pa, boom-pa-pa.* Then the trumpets not altogether on key. St. Paddy's was Tuesday. Now was only Friday.

At his end, the younger associates were talking about "contracts for deed." People were getting rich again, they said. "Help the banks out," one of them said. "The first fish to go ashore. *Gut und schlecht.* Man would rather will nothingness than not will . . ." Theirs was the old Poydras Street Hibernian firm Coyne, Coyle, Kelly, McGuinness, et al. Friday was the usual after-hours fall-by with the juniors. Give them a chance to find their place, etc. McGuinness was there to be congenial.

The woman had arrived *with* someone. A Mr. Drown. Someone's client who'd left. She was drinking too much. Everybody ordered the Sazerac the moment they arrived in New Orleans. The guilty taste of anise. She'd had three or more.

Her eyes passed him again. Another smile. She raised her chin as if to challenge him. The old priest was to her left—Father Fagan in his dog collar. He'd fathered a child, possibly two. Had diverse tastes. His brother was a traffic judge. "Why would sex with me be better than with your husband?" he heard the woman say. The men all laughed—too loud. The priest rolled his eyes, shook his head. "What did Thomas Merton say . . ." Old Coyne said. The priest put his hand to his brow. "What're they saying now?" someone said where he was sitting—one of the young women. "Nothing new," was the answer. "Coyne thinks he's a priest when what he is is a son of a bitch."

"Miss Nail! Miss Nail! What do you say about *that*?" They were shouting again.

They had traveled to Iceland together thirty-five years ago (though to be here now was shocking). Both students in Ithaca. They'd known each other only slightly, which hadn't mattered. A Catholic-school boy from uptown. Her mother, a rich landscape painter living in the Apthorp; her father on a yacht in Hog Bay. Both parents were colorful drunks. Minor exotics.

They'd first decided on Greece for spring recess—again, knowing little of each other, but ready for an adventure. Mikonos. The limpid water. The little bleached houses you rented for pennies. Each day the natives caught a fish and cooked it for you. However, there was money enough only for Iceland. Their trip wasn't being advertised at home. She was then called "Barbara." A name she disliked. He was simply Sandy McGuinness. Alex. A lawyer's son. His mother was a school teacher. Nothing about them was exotic.

With their pooled money they took a package flight to Reykjavik and the bus to the far western fjords. Ten hours. There'd be hostels, they believed; friendly Icelanders, wholesome, cheap food, cold Scandinavian sun. But there'd been none of that. Not even a room to let. A fisherman who tended a cod-drying rack far out a dirt road, and who spoke little English, offered them a sod house with goats asleep on the roof. Free of charge. Sandy was in love with her before the flight departed.

In the sod house, they slept cold together, talked, smoked cigarettes, sat beside the fjord in what little sun was available. He made unsuccessful efforts to fish, while she warmed her legs and read Neruda on Machu Picchu, Ken Kesey, Sylvia Plath. She told him she had Navajo blood on her father's side. He was a blacklisted director. Her mother was in essence a courtesan and half-French. About herself, she said she wished to acquire repose—the inner resolve (elusive) she'd read about in Fitzgerald. She told him she'd loved women.

The fisherman provided them cod, hard soda bread,

herring, yeasty homemade beer, blankets, candles, kindling for the March chill. One night he invited them. There was his wife, and two children who spoke English but were shy. The wife scowled at Barbara. They visited only once. They were twenty. It was 1981.

Sandy McGuinness did not know, really, what to think about what he was doing. When they talked, Barbara punctuated her phrases with small, audible intakes of breath, as if these were conversations they neither would forget—though in his view they didn't seem very important. What he *did* think was that she was beautiful and intense and unfathomable, but possibly not as smart as he was. Often, as their week idled past, he would see her watching him as he performed his homely duties required to keep them warm and dry—moving wood, airing blankets, sweeping. She was assessing him, he knew, as prelude to some decision. He didn't know what needed to be decided about him. And then she told him, unexpectedly, she was intending to stay on after he left—to learn to read the sagas, which she believed would help confer the repose she so badly wanted.

To which Sandy McGuinness thought: Yes. Loving her did not mean more than how he felt at that moment. He would go happily back. Perhaps he would see her again, or not. He was thinking about veterinary school. She could read her sagas. He also felt he could easily marry her.

On their last day, they'd gone into the little town for Sandy to find the bus, after which she was returning to the sod house. She'd arranged to do domestic work for the cod dryer's wife—a victory, she said. She also said—to him, smiling into the glinting sun, looking luminous and foreign in her big blue sweater—"You know, sweetheart," she said, "we don't want anyone else once we've learned who we are. It's a very hard choice to make."

"I don't know anything about that," he said. His cheap, black-nylon bag sat beside him at the bus stop. She had the smile. Radiant. Caramel-colored eyes. The shining mahogany hair she dried in the sun. They had made love that morning—not very memorably. She had begun to talk with fewer than the necessary words. As if so much didn't need to be said, and so much was obvious. She was, he felt, pretentious and self-infatuated. Leaving was a fine idea. What he'd be missing was miss-able. In the stark light her face bore a coarseness he hadn't noticed, but supposed he would grow to dislike.

"Good choices don't make very good stories," she

said. "Have you noticed that?" The sun passed across her eyes, making her squint.

"I haven't," he said. "I thought they did."

"We'll see each other again, won't we?" she said. "We'll talk about that. Decide if it's true."

She kissed him on the cheek, then began making her way purposefully back down the narrow street.

Barbara had not come back to Ithaca. Though he'd heard things. That she had changed her name from Barbara to Alix and entered divinity school at Harvard. That she had been for a period an artist's model. That she had been ill—mysteriously. TB, possibly. That she had married a doctor and lived in New York City. They were all plausible futures for her. Nothing was mentioned about the sagas. He was starting law school in Chicago and meant after that to move home to practice. The foreignness he'd liked—conceivably, briefly loved—could take its place in the routine of memory. The place in his life she occupied—*Iceland,* he privately called it—had evolved to be a good story he told. A trip he'd once taken with a girl.

She was standing now, excusing herself to the table. She had given him another look—pursing her lips for his not having spoken, not making a to-do over her. But had she expected to find him simply because she was in New Orleans—after all this time? A small city's small accommodation. Still, so odd not to remember her sooner. Though no odder than that a woman he'd nonchalantly loved in college should turn up now and here. She was thinner, fitter. She didn't look fifty-four. He still saw himself as young. Youngest among the partners. There was no template for these things.

She was going, so it appeared, to the LADIES. The junior men had moved on to the "paradox of thrift." The "fallacy of composition." "Building a house from the top down." He had no part in any of that. His book was in admiralty. Enormous boats.

"Make way," the priest was now saying loudly. All the men were standing—to be gentlemen. "Miss Nail. Miss Nail is having a pee. Or are we wrong?" They were growing too used to her.

The sleeveless brown dress was simple but chic. Her legs and skinny ankles shone under the bar's chandeliers. Outside, the parade was still in partial swing. A ragged troop of clowns. The police bagpipers' unit.

"Well, you *could've* . . ." she said as she slipped past him, as if not expecting to be heard by anyone but him. She might've been about to laugh at him. Her dark eyes he now recognized.

"You *could've,*" one of the younger men had heard and repeated in a whisper. The LADIES was out of the bar across the hotel's golden lobby.

"I just didn't expect . . ." he tried to say, turning to her. She paused as if it was he who'd spoken first. She was much more attractive being older. No coarseness in her features now, just rich, unfailing skin. The men at her end of the table were discussing her, which she would know. That she'd drunk too much was visible in the changeableness of her expressions. As if she couldn't quite decide something. Her hands seemed uncertain, though her eyes were sparkling.

"Well. *Would* you, my dear?" she said dismissively.

"Of course . . ." he said. "I . . ."

"In the lobby. In whatever time it takes me to become presentable again?" She was moving toward the doorway to the lobby, beyond which the bellmen turned to notice her. Her shoes were slender, expensive, in pale blue. She had a sporting aspect and smelled of something tropical. She hadn't heard him say "Of course." Just looked around as she eased past. What would her name be now? Possibly Barbara again.

At the far end of the bar, on a riser, a drum kit sat, unused. A tall, older black man in a white shirt and dark trousers had begun to estimate the drums' positioning.

Soon there would be music, and the Carousel Bar would be full. People present for different reasons would become an audience. It was past five. The parade was finishing in the street. Some of his partners were standing, readying to leave, waiting to see if Miss Nail would return. The associates had begun talking to another firm's young lawyers at the next table. Hershberg–Linz. Oil and gas litigators from when it was all booming. Now they did commercial realty. Built buildings. Barely the law at all. The noise level was going up. "That Miss Nail," he heard someone say and laugh.

In the lobby, he waited by the vitrine where there were books and photographs of famous writers who'd stayed in the hotel. Tennessee. Faulkner. It was that sort of place—self-styled literary. Tourists who'd watched the parade were flooding into the lobby from outside—hot, weary, in need of what the hotel offered. The bellmen ignored them, smiling. The revolving door was permitting gusts of hot, mealy air to mingle with the inside cool. "Were those real?" he heard someone inquire. An Iowa farmer's accent. "They were *so* beautiful. The pink feathers. So many." People were pulling suitcases past the bellmen. It was long past time to check in.

"I was just thinking how nice it is to arrive someplace," she said, suddenly beside him. The tourists had momentarily captivated him. The priest was hurrying past, his white straw hat on, consulting his cell phone. "I was thinking about arriving to Paris, of course. Not here," she said. "It's too hot here. It's only March." There would be no words about long ago. But what then could they say? Make a list of things, but here they'd still be.

"Who's Miss Nail?" he said.

"She's Mr. Drown's unfunny fantasy."

"What became of him?" Sandy said. The client, no longer in attendance. "Did he skip out?"

"Well," she said. She looked fresher, her eyes less sparkly. A tiny pearl of water remained on her chin. She touched it and smiled. She smelled of a cigarette. "The king of wishful thinking is no doubt in his Gulfstream flying back to Dallas. We had a disagreement. A small one."

They were side by side, talking like any two strangers waiting at a coat check, soon to be elsewhere. She carried no purse.

"This *is* a grand old barn, isn't it?" she said, looking around. She still smelled good. "Bell boys, escritoires, a cigar stand." She liked it.

"My father used to do his hijinks here," he said. "In the fifties."

There was the sudden quick intake of breath. "Hi-jinks," she said. "There's a useful word." Her eyes passed him. "What did he do?" She seemed to have found a way to be for now.

He should leave, he thought. He had—*they* had—other plans. His wife. Clancy's with old friends from Chicago. He understood that any time you were with Barbara a re-appraisal of life might be coming. It had been that way before but hadn't changed anything. Still. Wouldn't any woman wish to inspire that?

"Did you think," he said, "if you came to New Orleans you would just conjure me?"

Her eyes passed him again, came back and stopped. Her mouth made a tiny pucker. "Yes, well. Didn't I?"

"I suppose so," he said.

From outside on Royal Street, there was a large crowd noise. A whooping. A bass drum pounding very fast. The parade after the parade was approaching. That was all they would say about the past.

"Lay on, McGuinness, you dog," someone shouted across the lobby through the crowd. Coyle. "You've stolen all our fun." He was departing, also wearing a hat.

"Sorry," he said.

"Do you have time for a walk?" she whispered.

"You said it's too hot."

"It *is* rather unnatural, though, isn't it?" She put a fingertip to her chin where the water pearl had been but was gone. A bruise darkened the bony back of her left hand. It betrayed her.

"How'd you hurt that?"

She looked at her hand as if at a wristwatch. "It wasn't very hard."

"Did someone do it?" Possibly she'd fallen.

"Of course," she said and rounded her eyes in mock surprise. The revolving door whooshed with warm air and street noise. "Are we taking a walk?"

"If that's what you want."

"I'm a paying guest here," she said, pertaining to the hotel. She looked around her again as if to admire everything. "I have a suite on a high floor. It's named for some writer I never heard of. I see the river."

He wondered—was he acting toward her now in a way he'd acted twenty-five years before? What would that way be? Awkward? Distant? Disapproving? Too infatuated? It hadn't been so satisfactory, then. Possibly there would be another way to act.

They exited out into Royal, where the second-line had passed. Here was the breathless wall of early spring heat, the rich aroma of afternoon, the dregs of the day. A single white-faced clown came strutting along in big red shoes, stopping traffic, toting a tiny metal drum he tapped with a spoon. Nothing ever surprised. Sandy was instantly hot in his suit coat and took it off. They could walk to the river she could see from her room. Not a great distance even in the heat. The wind would be cool there. They were surprisingly together here, but not a couple.

They passed antique emporiums, a Walgreens, a famous restaurant, the Word Is Your Oyster book stall. Two large policemen on motorcycles, blue lights flashing, sat watching. Someone was smoking pot in a door entry. Bums drank wine on a curb. It was the French Quarter.

For a period they walked, and she did not speak, as if her mind had traveled away and become delighted. There was still the damp breeze and the late-day sun slanting between buildings. Her brown dress blew against her thighs.

They turned through an alley—a shortcut to the cathedral and the handsome square with the statue of the dubious president upon his rearing steed. She had a small, delicate limp, he noticed. Something she'd acquired. Though it might be the blue shoes.

"It doesn't seem real here," she proposed, like a new thought.

"Real?" he said, pretending to mock her, which he thought she would realize. Possibly Drown, the client, was waiting for her in the high-up room while this was going on. "I was born here," he said. "It's real enough."

"Why would you ever build a city here, though?" she said. "You always talked about it. Why is it good? Do you have to stay because you're from here?"

"More," he said.

"Yes, of course."

"Where do *you* live?" he said. It seemed preposterous to ask such a question. *And where do* <u>you</u> *live?* As if he might go there.

"In D.C.," she said as they continued on. "Just barely. I have a husband." A cigar shop was in the alley, also selling masks and pralines. "Oh, do. Buy a cigar," she suddenly said. "You always liked cigars, didn't you?" The store was closed, darkened.

"Wrong *you,*" he said.

"Then buy me a wonderful mask, I adore masks." She laughed, forgetting about it. "Um-hmm." She was agreeing with something she was thinking. "I suppose there's a Mrs. Sandy."

His name spoken finally. He had not spoken hers. He was uncertain about it. "My wife," he said, not loud. "Priscilla."

She glanced at him. The brown dress had side pockets into which she put her hands as a gesture of acknowledgment. She had sweated little hemispheres beneath her arms, a shadow on the fabric. Not the right dress for now.

There was music in the park named for the spoiled president. Jackson. Street musicians were playing horns and pounding drums. People were dancing on the esplanade, sliding off to the side as the two of them passed. Others were having fortunes read under bright umbrellas in the late-day heat. The river was now very close, its smell up and all around, a fragrance like fair taffy. They would go all the way to it and see across to Algiers. The great turn south. What ought they to be talking about in this small time life allowed?

"There's a very nice clothing store in town," she remarked unguardedly. "It's run by some very nice Lebanese. I visited it today. I bought this dress. Your wife probably shops there."

He did not remark. He was wondering if he had thought about her "a lot" in thirty-five years. In some unrealized way, it could be argued he had thought about her every single day. Though he'd thought about many other things as often. To be thinking about something didn't mean what people said it meant.

"What sort of law do you do?" She looked at him as

if she sensed he might be suffering something. "*Do?* Do you say that? *Do* law?"

"Yes," he said. "Admiralty." He was sweating through his shirt. His tie was off and in his pocket. The breeze at the river would refresh everything. But not yet.

"Boats," she said to convey admiration.

"Supertankers," he said quickly. "Mostly insuring them, replacing them, selling them. Sometimes hauling them off the bottom."

"They all *want* a place to sink, don't they?"

"If I'm lucky," he said.

"Well, you *are*," she said. "You *are* lucky. Look at you."

They were climbing the concrete steps that concluded at a promenade and the river. Three grinning black boys sashayed up beside them, from nowhere. Not threatening anyone, just playful. Tricking. "I know right where you got them shoes," one of the boys said—gone mischievous and smiling. It was their old trick. Which pleased her. She looked at them, delighted to be near them.

"On her feet," Sandy said to shoo them.

"Aww. Fo' sho," the boy who'd spoken said. "Where ya'll be from?" Letting them go past.

"Boudreau Parish," Sandy said. Their old Yat joke.

"I been *there.* I been *everywhere,*" the boy said. They were talking and laughing as they sidled away to trick others.

They were at the great river now, where the air expanded and went outward, floated up and away in a limitless moment before returning to the vast, curving, mythical, lusterless flood. The tumultuous bridges up and to the right. The tiny ferry—a speck midway to the other side. To Algiers. Not the real Algiers. A steadfast baking sweetness swirled landward. And a sound—not one you could hear—more a force like time or something enduring.

"Oh, *my,*" she said, clasping her hands in front of her. Her bruise forgotten for now. From somewhere—from nowhere—he heard the riverboat calliope. *Grab your coat and get your hat, leave your worries on the doorstep.* He scarcely came here, but understood her. He thought of flying home from Iceland, across the snowy lobe of Greenland. He'd imagined then he'd be flying over many countries forever. But he hadn't. "It makes me want to cry," she said, wanting to seem—*to be*—rapt, transported, in awe. "It's so different than seeing it from my room. It has such volume." She smiled dreamily, let her gaze rise to the pale sky and south, where there were gulls, a pelican. Blackbirds. "Am I experiencing it correctly?" she asked. "I want to."

"It's all correct," he said, holding his hot coat over his arm.

"But there's a best right way." She again took the little abrupt breath in.

"I don't know," he said. "I've just always . . ."

"You've just always what?" Suddenly she was acute, as if he was mocking her again but in earnest. He wasn't.

"Always seen it," he said. "Seen it here. From when I was little."

She looked again at the brown, sliding surface as if she hungered for it. In the fractured, shadowless light, the diminished city behind them had ceased to be. She didn't look as pretty as in the hotel and seemed to sense that and not care what the cost would be. How many things did she not care a trifle about? When she was young it had been her great appeal—less than what she did care for. Now it made her seem rash. Again, he wondered—did *he* seem the same? "Oh," she said—just the next thing she thought. "It makes me want to kiss you. Sandy. May I kiss you now?" She turned, her eyes finding his face, as if he'd just arrived. Some other kind of not caring.

"Not here," holding his warm seersucker to his chest.

"So," she said, beginning immediately to walk, as if he had not disappointed her in the least. "What shall we do to take the place of kissing?" She would sober up now.

"We'll just walk along."

She nodded, "And so they continued to walk along."

They walked in the direction of Canal, against the river's stirring flow—west or possibly south—along the promenade named for the famous mayor. Moon. In the watery late-day breeze a moon *was* visible—as if waiting, sharing no light with the sky. Taller, newer buildings were ahead—the less gaudy, business parts—where his office was. More tourists were present here. Bums, drinking and taking seats on the riprap, fished with poles in the tilting shallows. A great dark freighter seemed then to *appear*—from under the bridges—drifting, yawing silently toward the great turn, attended by small boats. It mesmerized him even now. The incisiveness of navigation.

A tiny plane muttered overhead, not so high above the river's crown, trailing a banner, wishing all ashore *Happy St. Paddy's.* Some bar in the Quarter. Though it was days away, still.

"It must be nice to be Irish," she said, sounding disinclined—having not spoken in minutes as they walked. "Not to have to care about anything." A phone began ringing—more a humming, down in her dress pocket. She did not let on and presently it stopped. He felt relieved and wasn't sure why. Her limp had mostly disappeared.

"How do you make ends meet?" he said, a half step behind her in the warm, variable air, his voice hardly heard, conveying authority in that way.

"What are you asking me?" she said, casting smiling disapproval over her left shoulder, as if it pleased her to disapprove.

He'd asked but did not so much want to know. He'd been imagining if she'd kissed him, how it would've tasted. The anise. The tobacco. The lack of fervor. When she'd been young she'd been easily distracted. Slow to finish a meal. To dress herself. Slow to complete a sentence or to find her way to orgasm. He hadn't liked it. She only kept photographs of herself. One atop a dead giraffe she'd shot with her father in Africa. Another of her naked on a chenille bedspread—taken by a famous photographer whose name was lost.

"It was just idle," he said—regarding having asked what she did. Could she even have heard him with the hot-then-cool, metallic breeze blowing past and the thrust of the freighter completing the famous turn south? He might've asked about reading the sagas.

She'd altered her gait to be more carefree. The limp was gone altogether. "Do you ask all the girls if they're whores? And do they all deny it. Or just me?"

"They all do," he said, accepting the joke she was permitting them. This sweetness had always been available. Not to take each other so seriously when they were being frank.

"Let's say—as my non-answer," she said, almost gaily, "let's say . . . ummm . . . What I do is, I'm not very adept at making friends of old lovers. They stay lovers, or I don't like them." She was still walking ahead. "And I was just thinking about arriving someplace. How much better it is than leaving. I was thinking of someplace else, not this lovely place beside the father of waters. I already said that, I think. But it *is* romantic that you would ask me how I got on."

They passed along now, still not quite a pair, not quite apart—he in his seersucker trousers and blue shirt, jacket in hand; she in her smart dress, tanned legs, tanned arms, and blue shoes, which needed to be Italian. She was sweating at her hairline from drinking. He considered touching her shoulder, coming beside her. He imagined her shoulder would be cool in the heat.

The business buildings had now come very close, no longer unimportant—crowding in. He could see the very tall one wherein was his office. A streetcar went by. The freighter had slid far past, given its deep tuba noise in triumph and disappeared toward the Gulf. The moving air had taken on a petroleum sting. It had to be six, the beginning of the evening in New Orleans, when shadows cooled into darkness. A small flotilla of green-headed ducks bobbed at the river's margin in the relaxed wake of the freighter. People—tourists—on park benches watched the two of them walking. A handsome couple always attracted withholding stares. *Look. Aren't they just wrong? We've been there. We've been everywhere.*

"How's your father?" he said, coming close now, smelling her. There'd been talk, once, that the two of them would meet. The father and the new boyfriend-of-the-moment. Would the father even be alive? His own was long gone. Though not his mother, alone in the big house on Philip Street, not far from where they were.

"Oh, Jules is fine," she said, as if the thought amused her. Or his asking. She let the back of her right hand—not the bruised one—whisper against his trousers' leg. They could not walk so much farther. Hotels and malls and the convention center lay ahead. "They're *both* above ground—at least today," she said. "Fancy young boys take my mother ballroom dancing and steal her money. Jules lives in the Locarno with his

Peruvian wife, where he's writing a novel. Didn't you want to do that once? I remember you writing."

"Someone else again," he said.

"Did we not go to Hog Bay to visit him?"

"I don't remember," he said.

"Sure you do. *I* remember. He's built a school in Kenya. The Peruvian won't go near it." A pair of airedales took leave of their young owner and came toward them amiably to conduct an inspection. It was how things happened on the promenade. "Nice dogs," she said. "Sweet dogs." He had still not used her name. It made him feel as if some things were understood. Though she had used his. "Isn't it really hotter than it should be?" she said and fanned her hand.

"It's the tropics here," he said. "This is the way it is."

"It's never the way we want it, is it?" Words were missing again. He remembered how remote she could be just in an instant. The blunt turning away. It was something a cautious father would advocate. He had two daughters, himself. Seventeen and thirteen. Both had remoteness as an ally.

From away, from the narrow teeming streets of the old quarter, there was the sound of bagpipes again. The parade had made its way back down Chartres. They would miss it. Drums were pounding. Blue police lights flashing. "Ha. No bagpipes, please," she said. "It's far too late for that." It was another joke she knew.

"Are you still Barbara?" he said. Miss Nail. Alix. Who was she? He felt excluded for asking.

The airedales had followed them, their owner calling from behind. "Lulu and Gracie. Don't run away."

"*Oh,* yes," she said. "Barbara." She turned toward him in the midst of the now-more-crowded promenade. The river was a background photo. "Why?" She was radiant, as if she would quickly laugh. Her wonderful eyes.

"Just seems inevitable I should know." He remembered, or misremembered, that she'd been born in Kansas City. At least she'd said that years ago. It made as much sense as anything. Was *this* responding to her in a new way? "I remember you said, how good it was to be us."

"And you said I only meant how good it was to be *me.*"

"Correct." And just as quickly they were having a small "word." In public. In view of others.

"Sometimes," she said, "I think about you. Not very often. In New York last summer, I saw a *you* crossing a wide street. An avenue. I couldn't get to you. Of course it wasn't."

He went to New York. He had someone there he saw. Not often. "Probably not," he said.

"I thought . . ." she said, but paused. Two people—kids—a girl and a boy passed by, both beautiful, both speaking French. *Mais, quand même, quand même.* She looked at them as if she understood their conversation, then realized she'd lost what she was about to say. It could've been the thing he wanted to know. What she thought. "Maybe," she said, "it was *that* that brought me here now. Almost seeing you but not really." She brightly smiled. It may have been close to what she was about to declare. She seemed prepared to laugh again.

"I'm sure it was," he said.

"Would you go away with me?" she said. "I've never made anybody very happy. But I always thought I could make *you* happy—if I decided to. It'd be a challenge." Her smile was brilliant, no hint of sadness. "You look younger than I look."

"That's not true," he said.

"And I'd still like to kiss you." The dampened wind unsettled her hair. She gave her head a tiny shake that freshened her smile.

He stopped walking in order to take full enough notice of her. And to kiss her. Far beyond, in the city's cluster, the Monteleone sign sat atop its white rectangle.

From any window someone would see the two of them. Anonymous but interpretable. Farther down the promenade, he spied the priest, in a new bright yellow shirt and jeans, seated on a bench beside a younger man.

He stepped close, put his hand where he'd wanted to put it—on her bare shoulder, where she was indeed unaccountably cold. "Yes," he said and kissed her, leaning in to her as she rose in her blue shoes to meet being kissed. She smelled sweet—the anise, vaguely of a cigarette.

Later, as they walked back down into the old streets, she became talkative, as if something—more than their kiss—had freed a spirit in her, and they were together as they once had almost been. In Iceland. He'd begun thinking rather freely of his old law-school professor who'd died young. He'd been the adored and constant focus of everyone's attention, admiration, interest. Though in almost no time, people stopped talking about him. Professor Lesher. He'd had the terrible nervous tic. Was brilliant. Briefly, then, he'd thought of his father, who'd left the family and, if truth were told, never came back; lived his life in other cities, with other people. A great error. Though then the wound closes.

"What's happened to you, Sandy?" Barbara said.

"What would you say the outcome's been?" She'd forgotten about asking him to go away with her. They were on Iberville Street, nearing the corner where they'd begun. The storied old pile where she was a guest.

"I'm not that kind of lawyer," he said, knowing this wasn't her question nor the answer to any question. "We try to avoid outcomes if we can."

"My view is . . ." she said quickly, holding his arm. She'd stumbled on a broken paving, scuffed her knee, ruined her pretty shoe. He had his coat on again. Not his tie. "*You,* in particular, try very hard to be complicated. While *I* try very hard to be simple." She pressed close in against his arm, as if for protection. It was not easy now to walk in her shoes. Though you wouldn't walk barefoot in the French Quarter. When she'd regained her room (if there *was* a room), she'd put these shoes in the trash. "You have a bull's-eye tattooed on your heart," she said. "It's not complicated."

"I disagree," he said. It wasn't true.

"Would you like to make love to me," she said altogether casually. There was the calliope starting once more, behind them at the river. Some Beatles' song he couldn't remember the name of.

"Of course," he said.

"All those things I taught you. They get practiced

on someone else, I suppose." She was just going on. She again made her quick little gasp of breath.

They had come to the revolving door, where they'd stepped out into the heat an hour ago or less. The big, blue-uniformed doorman, with gold braid and epaulettes, stepped forward, smiling, pushing the doors along. "All right, all right." A rush of cold air escaped. Inside, the lobby was crowded still, and bright with people milling and loudly singing. All the things she'd taught him was a far too dense subject to commence now, though she had never made him happy or tried to. For him, the same. He had merely, briefly, almost loved her quite a long time ago.

He stood out of her way, touched her shoulder again as she left his arm. He had said her name once but did not say it again. "Some other time," she said, somewhat unsteadily, the glass doors turning. She had meant possibly something else. Though anything she said now would do.

"Yes," he said, as she went in through the circling doors, and he turned for his walk—not so far—up Canal.

On the drive uptown, where he was meeting his wife and others—he would be late—he entertained another thought regarding his father. He'd last visited him in the handsome house his father had purchased on Lakeview, on the near north side of Chicago—there, with his new wife Irma. His father had fancied one of the old stepped brownstones. A bay window and an oriel with stained glass. It was October. The lindens and beeches were in their array across the park. His father was by then representing an Irish firm that made kitchen ceramics. He'd had enough of lawyering. He would live two more years and die climbing steps into an airplane. Completely happy.

"I couldn't live in that city one more minute," his father had said, meaning New Orleans. "It wasn't your mother's fault. There was no Irma then. We just had nothing more to say to each other, hadn't in years. Yes, I know. So what? But. I just became . . . what's the word . . . *de-fascinated.* It won't make sense to you. I hope it never does."

He had flown up to see his father on family business. The estate. The changed will. How his mother, the spurned wife, was being looked after. His father had maintained a diligence, but now wished unexpectedly for a hearing. He was tall and bright-eyed and smooth-faced. Spirited and utterly deceptive. He had been a judge, a king of Comus. Was a grandee. "There's entirely too much self-congratulation in the world now, just for doing what you're supposed to do," his father had said and stepped to the curving bay window, the leaded panes separating red from green from yellow from blue. He stood looking down into the leafy street as if something in it interested him. "I no longer experience self-congratulation," he said. "Nothing's worth being proud of. You *must* guard against it. It's not the worst human flaw, but it *is* the most self-deluding and painful."

"Yes," Sandy said. "I will. I understand." He thought he did.

Which was the last subject they'd talked about. His father was a man of large pronouncements and hard lessons boisterously learned. This was all the hearing he wished for. Later, he'd realized his father was only thinking about seeing after his abandoned wife, for which he wanted no particular recognition. It was all quite irrelevant. Though for an instant, when he'd thought he understood, it had seemed his father had been talking about some question or act of great consequence. It hadn't been true.

He'd recall this conversation at the most unexpected moments, as now, when he might've expected to entertain other, onward thoughts—the dinner he was soon to have. His wife, with whom he would have it. The anticipated, colorful, meticulously rehearsed affairs of her day. This last hour—this barely-achieved time with

Barbara—would *not* be rehearsed. There had been little or no consequence or outcomes to think about. Nothing had been harmed, no one disappointed. He would simply not see her again. Which by itself conferred a small—what was it? Possibly like a trust, but not quite. As his father had said, we have little to pride ourselves in. Which argued for nothing in particular, yet would allow a seamless carrying forward into the evening now, and the countless evenings that remained.

Happy

Happy Kamper called on Friday to tell them Mick Riordan had died, and she was driving west, but could she come up tonight and drink a toast or two or three to the old warrior's memory, maybe cry a bit on Tommy Thompson's shoulder.

The Thompsons were entertaining the Jacobson-Parrs for dinner and a stay-over, and Tommy had gone up to Camden for big lamb chops and summer corn and beefsteaks, and had a case of Montrachet already in. All were looking forward to a beach fire. It was their *annual,* the sacrament of closing down summer in Maine. Sam and Esther, who were in Cape Neddick, would be flying to Islamorada before Columbus Day.

Tommy, of course, had immediately said, "Yes. Absolutely. This is terrible," without looking at Janice.

They'd all six been a *gang* in the '90s, when Tommy and Esther Parr were having the most of it as novelists, and Janice and Sam were keeping things afloat running the gallery to mammoth success, which was why the Thompsons had a year-round house in Maine and a flat in rue Froidevaux. No one really worked anymore—except Esther Parr. Tommy Thompson had had his couple of good-if-modest runs with novels, but never liked working that much.

Mick Riordan had been their editor—Esther's and Tommy's—for the best of their palmy years. An Irishman, whose father had been a famous Dublin imagist of the Twenties, Mick had set forth from Trinity, published one comic novel, written for the literary pages, worked in the radio, had begun to establish his own stylish signature, was about to get married to a Roscommon girl he'd studied with, but then just decided New York was the future. He was big, fleshy, softly handsome, with a head of unruly hair—like his father—and pale blue eyes. He brought a witty-jokey, confiding, non-confrontational brio to his relations with higher-ups, and liked to drink, liked women. He boasted that he *almost* shared a name with the famous O'Riordan communist. Eventually he took a job with his father's connections at Berensen & Webb and intended—as many did—to work only until his second novel launched him toward celebrity and the vaunted American writing life that was so much larger than little Dublin's.

Which never came close to occurring. There wouldn't be a second novel or a pretense even at a smattering of stories. Editing was dumb easy, he realized. So much easier to bring along talent than wield it. Plus, he took enthusiastically to the publishing life—the clubs, the newest restaurants, the drinks parties, the late dinners with the fancy writer pals. It wasn't the Duke and weekend shoots and ocean swims and the Abbey and suppers at someone's country place, lasting past dawn. But New York was where everything that mattered began. Ireland was where it ended. Americans were intellectually constipated, couldn't maintain a decent conversation—forget about a tune—didn't drink enough, took everything too literally, and rarely, genuinely laughed. But it was authentic and accepting. A friendly, quick-witted, good-looking paddy stood out and could achieve tolerable placement, even if the placement were only semi-literary from the standpoint of achievement. In a short time, he'd married someone else, produced two quick children, moved to Bronxville, bought a house on Broad Ave. And that was it. Life could conceivably go on this way forever—take the train in late and come home later, reading on the weekends, take the girls wherever they needed taking until they got older, and accompany Marilyn to the Adirondacks in the summers, where her family had a compound on a lake. There was, admittedly, a mild sensation of being a bystander to life. But it was America. Everybody was a bystander. Nobody, he felt, was much full-on about anything.

By 1970, he was forty, his kids were old teenagers, he'd gotten divorced—having met Bobbi Kamper (Happy) at a weekend art party in Vermont (she was a sculptor). He'd taken a flyer with her to Cabo San Lucas. And that was it for marriage. He now lived on the Upper West Side. Bobbi lived in the Village, where her husband had died at a young age. Mick was now burnishing a colorful reputation for turning so-so literary novels into causes célèbres. He relished the company of writers old and young, liked smoking Camels, liked drinking at the Grammy and the White Horse, Raoul's and the Oak Bar. Liked jazz, liked the Hamptons and the North Shore, had bought himself a small lobsterman's house by the ocean in Beck's Harbor, Maine, where he retreated for a month each August, "to read." "I feel as if I've come a long ways," Mick Riordan said, then "yet not to have journeyed so very far." It was a complete and self-chosen life, far from the tall, shadowy brick mansion in Ballsbridge, where his father had held forth (both his parents were decades gone). It was almost, Mick often said, that he was only half-Irish, had come away with the best bits and none of the old crap-de-loo.

He and Bobbi kept separate accommodations. She owned lurchers, which he didn't like and made no secret about. She had achieved, in the '80s and '90s, a reputation for large, kinetic, solar-powered, outdoor metal and glass "installations" that mimicked the wheeling of the constellations and "troped" different directions in different seasons. Many people in Bucks County and Connecticut and Taos owned a Happy Kamper. Her work re-framed the natural world, especially the ocean, in mysterious and revealing ways. People felt they were "changed" just being around them. Sam Jacobson represented her in the gallery, and for a spell she was on everyone's lips and magazine covers, sat for profiles in *Interview, Vanity Fair,* and *Der Spiegel.* Was seen photographed with her lurchers on the Morrissey estate and in Paris and Moscow. She adopted a uniform—large, blue-tinted aviators (for a congenital eyelid condition she didn't have), Birkenstocks, and bright-colored skinny jeans (yellow, pink, green). She weighed slightly more than a hundred and was tiny and fragile and dour, which contributed an interesting dimension to her name—Happy. Her father, a beloved cantor in a Reform congregation in Riverdale, had given her her name as a child even though, as he said, "she was usually anything but." She had gone to Sarah Lawrence, "with all the other neurotics," Mick Riordan frequently said deep in his cups. His and Happy's union, he said—upon getting older—was a *mariage de convenance* without the marriage and with little of the *convenance.* They fought. They made up. They took long driving trips. They drank to extremes. They were famous for un-pretty rows in expensive dining rooms, which everyone, including Tommy and Janice and the Jacobson-Parrs, had been onlookers for and regretted. Happy began going away to Taos to sculpt, leaving Mick to fend (she was fifteen years younger). Mick, as time passed, went to half-time at Berensen & Webb. He sold the Maine house when his daughters no longer visited, and bought a smaller stone cottage in Watch Hill, from near which he could get the train. He began to spend more time "in the country," amusing himself painting miniature Jack Yeats-ish oils and playing canasta with the older writers who lived in the neighborhood, and going into the city only when he had to—staying with friends who had extra beds. He took on "three stone" and began, by his own admission, to resemble Brendan Behan in late life, if he'd made late life. There were rumors of some lung troubles he was ignoring.

Life—and it *seemed* very suddenly—was *this* now.

And little more. Plans were smaller plans, or not plans. Trips were envisioned, then put off. Friends were invited to Watch Hill, but somehow postponed. Happy drove up to see Mick in her vintage Willys—sometimes on his birthday—always without the dogs, never for long, staying with sculptor friends in Mystic. Mick had simply but noticeably gotten old—was the general take—although he remained attractive company and liked guests, though there was no room in his cottage. He played speed Scrabble with anybody and was good at all games, drank martinis and watched the BBC on telly. And though he didn't enjoy driving anymore, he liked to be taken on rides through the little seasonal seaside towns up and down the coast. Weekapaug. Quonochontaug. Charleston Beach. More like England than Ireland. The publisher was keeping him emblematically on at a reduced retainer—"My valedictory" Mick called it. It was understood his poet father had left him fixed enough to get out of life with dignity and money left. He remained "pleasingly, at least partly, viable," in his words, was still half-handsome with the extra weight that worked a hardship on his knees. His hair stayed. People who were close to him—Tommy and Jan less than Esther and Sam—felt he was all right (though they also felt Happy might look in on him a bit more than she did). Other people not so close knew *of* Mick Riordan, thought perhaps he was deceased, or returned to Ireland—which was never in the plan. He'd long before become a citizen and cherished it. "Ireland," Mick said, "was a feature of the prior millennium, having lost all sense of historical moment—which the U.S. had never bothered with in the first place."

And then he'd died. A week ago he'd had a "small stroke" that had left one side of him "tingly" but still workable. He was able to call Happy in New York and impart this news. No extra doctoring seemed required. Mick was not keen on doctors. Happy couldn't get away on the day he called, but three days later did—driving up with the dogs in the Willys. It was early September. Mick was on the front porch when she drove in—up and gimping with a cane and a bloody mary. He'd made "real" pimento cheese—a great favorite. (People shopped for him.) The lurchers were put into the fenced back yard where they restrained themselves to merely digging. Mick seemed not exactly fine but also not quite right. "He tilted when he walked and didn't have his usual hue," Happy told the Thompsons and the Jacobson-Parrs. She announced to Mick she'd be taking him up to RIH, the next morning, to which Mick temporized. Her cantor father had died of stroke, and she knew these typically arrived in twos and threes. No saying how many Mick had experienced already. She'd called people at Brown. It was arranged for him to check in.

Happy went to the farmers' market in Westerly to shop for dinner, brought back swordfish, his favorite butter lettuce, and haricots verts. Mick would make vinaigrette. At six they had their "real drinks"—martinis—and talked about a novel he'd been sent for his mature opinion—which pleased him. He helped dry the lettuce, sitting at the kitchen table with his second drink. He grew quiet, as if engaged by his chores. Happy paid no extra attention; things didn't seem that dire. "I've begun to make a plan for . . ." Mick said, then fell silent. She glanced at him from the sink. It was eight. Dazzling light still burnished the ocean. She could hear the dogs' collars jingling as they inspected the hollyhocks. Mick, she said, seemed to be sleeping sitting up. He'd always nodded off with a couple of pops. She could let him doze in his chair and wake him when the fish was poached. She turned on some music, felt the cool evening sift in through the windows. Chet Baker. Johnny Hartman. Mick's preferences. "My one and only love . . ." For some reason she said his name, though the fish wasn't quite ready. She told Tommy she suddenly knew perfectly well he was dead, his hand on top of the lettuce. And dead he was. "Peacefully," Happy said. As if the plan he'd begun to make were to die. Just seventy-three years old. Everyone thought he was older. She said she didn't cry right away. Mostly just called the daughters to come.

Tommy Thompson went back into town and bought two more lamb chops and more tomatoes and ears of corn to shave off the way Janice liked it. He bought a bottle of gin for Happy's arrival and some olives. He and Janice had backed off spirits time ago, and Sam and Esther were already teetotalers. "Like the Fitzgerald story," Esther had said. The one in Paris with the little daughter the main character's never going to get back because of drink and the mean sister. No one could remember its title, though everyone loved it. Esther even remembered a line. "He wasn't young anymore, with lots of nice thoughts and dreams to have by himself." "Served him right," Esther added, though she admired Fitzgerald, even if he was a complete crumb and nobody read him now, and women hated him. Sam said he'd thought the line was Hemingway's.

Happy had called to announce her ETA for eight. She was just going past Kittery. Two hours away without terrible traffic. Tommy heard in Happy's voice the telltale throatiness, the resonance and meticulous enunciation that suggested she'd already had a drink. Her "sovereign's" voice, Mick had called it, ". . .

perfect for issuing proclamations." They could all get to bed early, Tommy thought. Talk of Mick—what there needed to be of it—could happen at breakfast on the deck. Happy could take the "little" bedroom in the guesthouse at the other end from Sam and Esther. The dogs, assuming she had them, could sleep in the car. It was cool enough at night.

By 7:30, the tide had sagged away from the near rocks, enough to lay in the fire pit. Tommy and Sam walked down with shovels and kindling in a paper sack. Tommy'd set driftwood to dry on the seawall for the fire. He and Jan often came down for sunset with a bottle of wine. There were few mosquitoes due to the steady crossing breeze on the point.

He and Sam both dug for a while, then Sam sat on the steps to the beach and smoked a cigarette, something he enjoyed. It was not hard work making a sand pit—which would be pleasingly filled by morning. A loon sat low on the glass sea and called to another loon you would never see but was answering. Voices teetered across the bay from other houses and people's evenings. Someone was pounding on wood with a hammer. A lobster boat sat motionless a half mile out, its captain tinkering in the engine. Jan and Esther were up in the house cooking, getting ready.

Sam said that Happy had called him in the past

month about Mick's little paintings in the Jack Yeats style. Mick's father had known all the Yeatses. "They *all* knew each other in Dublin. All the greats. It's a tiny island. Only one real city."

"What did she want you to do?" Tommy asked, assessing the size of the pit.

"Well. Appraise them. For sale. What else? He's leaving them to her. He knew he'd be picking up the *Trib.* I'll get around to it one of these days. They're quite a few of them." Sam breathed smoke into the dark air. "I'm having a little procedure on Thursday," he said. Sam was tall and famously handsome—clever—but had been almost completely idle since college. He'd taken over the business from his father and didn't much like working. Wished he could sail more. He loved being Esther Parr's husband. It was all he needed. They both came from wealth.

"Are we sharing the details?" Tommy asked, looking out to sea at the lobsterman, bestilled. A lovely, simple life.

"Just that it involves my ass," Sam said, smoking.

"Okay. Let's see," Tommy said, starting to groom the sides of the pit with the flat of the spade, the sand damp and cakey. "Let's see. A brain tumor. Something cognitive."

"You missed your calling. You're wasted writing

your shitty books." Sam flipped his smoke out where the sand was wet.

"Are Mick's paintings any good?"

"Mick was a capital guy," Sam said. "But only as good at anything as he had to be. Life wasn't all that hard for old Mick."

"In a word," Tommy said and stood the spade in the sand and admired the pit. "Or in a *few* words."

"Or a few words," Sam said. "Sums us all up. Happy, happy, happy life. Period."

They began to walk back to the house.

Happy arrived in the Willys a bit beyond eight. Everyone knew she'd arrived because two great dogs were seen through all the windows careering around the yard off their leashes, smashing the daylilies, knocking aside lawn furniture, then stopping suddenly to dig the grass, throwing up great clods where they'd detected prey to be, and pissing and shitting great clods all their own, before disappearing. Pity the creatures unlucky enough caught unawares.

"Happy's arrived apparently," Janice said at the kitchen window, a glass of wine in hand. "Her hounds do declare her." They all preferred calling her Bobbi; Esther had known her at Pratt when she *was* Bobbi; pretty, too-thin and insular Roberta Kamper of

Fieldston—previously *Rachel* Kamper of Fieldston. But "Happy" now—to honor the fact that Mick Riordan had just died three days ago and *he* had called her Happy—not without irony.

"Good-ee," Sam said, who'd never taken to "Happy Kamper," though he'd made her rich.

"Just—please," Esther said. "You'll be dead someday, my darling. And no one will want to see me."

"I'd want to," Janice said. "I'd always want to see you."

Tommy was going to the door, looking back. "I invited her," he said. "Or I would've."

Outside, where everyone parked on the grass, Happy was alighting. She'd set the dogs loose by letting them pile out over her and rushing off. "Sorry," she said, reaching in to collect her big straw purse. Blue-tinted aviators, new black skinny "mourning" jeans, a white silk cowgirl shirt with silver furnishings. A silver band holding back her black hair. "I couldn't think of a house gift. You're currently out of dogs, aren't you, Tommy? What was that sweet girl collie's name. She was wonderful."

"Jasper," Tommy answered. "He."

"Didn't he die?

"Five years ago." He took her straw purse just to hold.

"Has it been? Since Mick and I were last here?" She gazed up at him and smiled.

"Longer," Tommy said and stepped up and kissed her cheek. "I'm really sorry." He spoke not very loud.

"Yep," Bobbi said, letting him kiss her without moving. "Behold the whatever. Is there a word for what I am, Tommy? Surviving paramour. Ex-significant-something or other." Her voice was the sovereign voice. Gin was apparent. Probably in the big purse, violating all the laws of Maine. The dogs were barking at something at the beach, where he and Sam had put in the pit. She and Mick had liked driving drunk, had been avid about it, competitive spilling off many roads, into several shallow ponds, but somehow always missing jail and death. Now, though, was the end of summer. Local cops were feasting on out-of-staters, giving no quarter. Happy's plates said New York. She'd *have* to stay the night, or they'd be buying her out of jail at 3 A.M., when no one wanted to be doing that.

"We'll worry about what to call you later," Tommy said. "What about the dogs?"

"My children of the night," Bobbi said. "They'll be good." She was moving toward the house.

"They won't run away?"

"I feed them. They're not stupid," Bobbi said. "Would you run away from Janice?" She kept going. "Mick's dead. Did you hear?"

"We all did, sweetheart," Tommy said. "Sam and Esther are here. We're all stunned."

"I see," she said. "Me, too. I'm in total shock."

Cocktails went wonderfully. Janice made a fuss over Bobbi, who seemed happy to be Bobbi, not Happy, as if everything tonight represented a reversion (specifically for her, not anyone else) to some way of being that pre-dated everything life had sadly become. Janice's goal, without announcing a goal, was to spin an aura in which Bobbi had just dropped by, and no one had really died, and there were lots and lots and *lots* of subjects to be gone over—after much too long an absence. Certainly Bobbi needed to tell the four of them about her new projects and where she planned to be through the fall and winter ("Taos, obviously") and about the famous museum in L.A. *finally* getting off its ass and pulling the trigger on the acquisition they'd been holding off on for six years, and how she'd just been queried about becoming artist-in-residence at some big state college in Alabama that had recently bought their way into being a world-class art department (people stolen from Yale and Santa Cruz). They wanted her—

Bobbi—to be their anchor. What a complete and total hoot *that* would be, Bobbi said, for a little *tsatzheleh* from Palisade Avenue to live wherever it was. "Do they even have Jews in Alabama?" she asked. She was drinking the gin, had on her blue shades and new gold sandals, had her sovereign voice up and popping.

"They do," Sam said. "They'll make you pick cotton on Saturdays." He'd been in charge of the music and gone for Dave McKenna, "Dancing in the Dark," a choice Mick would've approved.

"Fuck that," Bobbi said over the music. "Jews don't pick cotton."

"Depends," Sam said, "if the price per pound is up or down."

There was nothing you seemingly could do. Tommy understood he was getting drunk on an empty stomach. It was light out still. The tide was almost ebb. The evening water shone black and yellow with the remnants of the sun. Occasionally the big dogs could be spied bounding past the windows. Once, one seemed to have something struggling in its jaws.

Dinner was served at precisely a quarter to ten. Everything perfect. The lamb roasted to pink, with the tangy ginger marinade Janice had found in the *Times*. Esther had made a vinegar and mustard dressing for the tomatoes and had shaved the corn. Plus, "Bobbi's

Brussel sprouts," which she'd been assigned to dice but gotten tired of and handed off to Tommy. Some current of tension had at first circulated brightly, then subsided with the food and everyone eating. Sam had later put on lively Brazilian music, and everyone had "come down" from something without realizing they'd been wound up. Wound up about Mick dying. Wound up about something among the four of them—reluctance—that had changed when Bobbi arrived. Wound up about Bobbi deciding to avail herself of sympathy no one had quite known they possessed and could offer, but in fact had realized they could. And would. It was very good, Tommy thought. To think that at their age they had reserves they would draw on and allocate. He hadn't been certain of that.

But he wanted them to go down to the beach very soon. There, would be a thin stratum of last low-horizon light. Blue and orange fading to greenish dark, conferring a sense of peace and complicity. He and Janice too often neglected it. He would bring down some Cristal and all drink a toast to Mick Riordan, then head off to bed.

Quietly, patiently over an after-dinner Jameson, Bobbi told them of Mick's last moments in the kitchen of the cottage at Watch Hill, while she prepared dinner and he sat at the table, beginning to discuss a plan he was hatching; she couldn't remember if he'd said what it was, possibly something he would write—she couldn't be sure. His speech, she now said, might've been a little wiggly from one of his strokes. She believed Mick never for a minute intended to go up to Providence the next day and had elected (if that was the word) to die precisely as he did, seated at the dinner table with most of a martini in front of him, as if that was the most logical "next step" in what he might've calculated his life to be. He just was waiting, she felt, until she—Bobbi—could get there and everything fall into place. "It wasn't really sad," she said, still wearing her blue glasses, seated at the after-the-meal table with Sam and Esther, up from Cape Neddick. "Isn't that strange?" Bobbi said, peering at her whiskey as if she were talking to it or about it. "The whole four days after, when I was just there, communicating with his silly daughters, and seeing about the cremation, and finding someone to stay in the house, calling Donleavy in New York, and the lawyers. It was as if Mick was *there*, and we were doing these things together." Bobbi nodded at her estimation of what it had all been like, and also of the weight of death versus life. All four of them agreed, though in different terms, that it was probably good. Not good that Mick had died. Certainly not. But good that Bobbi felt okay about it happening the way it did. Relieved (if that was the word, which it probably was).

Esther Parr started to speak on the subject of having been in the room in Brooklyn Heights when her grandmother—another Esther—had died, and the sensation she'd experienced of something, some weight, being lifted, and of she and her mother and her sister Rachel looking at each other and almost laughing. She decided, however, she would not go into that.

"Let's visit the beach," Tommy said (he felt) valiantly, but also reverently (why, he wasn't sure).

"I'm dead. I'm totally dead," Bobbi said in declining. "I have to feed the creatures." Her dogs, whom she'd paid no attention to in the last two hours. Occasionally one of them had pawed the door and barked or whimpered, but Bobbi had passed them off. "'We're fine,' they say. They amuse themselves. They're never bored. They were bred to hunt lions, so everything seems fun to them."

"The tide's in too far now," Sam said. Janice began picking up plates and silverware. Rustling about. Esther rose to help.

"Where do I sleep?" Bobbi said. She took her glasses off, still seated, wiping her eyes not of a tear but of the dross of fatigue. Her face was naked and frail, her eyes deep in their sockets. She didn't look the way you expected her face behind the glasses to look. Tommy knew how old she was. Sixty, almost. What was it she was experiencing? Possibly there *wasn't* a good word. You wouldn't devalue it, but not quite grief. Less.

"In the cottage," Tommy said. "The little room's all made up." She'd slept there once—when Mick had been drunk and awful and couldn't be put up with in the big bedroom, so she'd moved. It was years ago. Other dogs ago, who'd left fleas and broken a screen and chewed through things. Nothing that couldn't be fixed—though Mick and Bobbi hadn't bothered. It had been how they did many things. Not looking back so much.

"Remember the last time?" Bobbi said and smirked, fitting her aviators back on, masking herself. One of the dogs barked softly outside, and then the other one. Sam had gotten up and stepped out into the yard to smoke and admire the last lighted clouds. Or possibly he'd sensed something. He knew Bobbi from forever; knew what generally followed what in her patterned behavior, how easily she worked round to resentment.

"I remember," Tommy said.

"We remember," Janice said from the kitchen where she was rinsing dishes with Esther.

"You two were such complete shits," Bobbi said, adjusting her glasses behind her ears then giving her head a shake as if she was waking up.

"Were we?" Janice said, invisible but acute. Sam could be heard outside speaking to the dogs. "'A little neglect breeds mischief,'" he was saying. "'For want of a horse . . .'" The rest was lost.

"Oh yes, you *certainly* were," Bobbi said, still at the table. "You were both perfectly disgusting. Your poor little screen and some cheap Afghan pillow, was it?" Her martini glass, a third full, sat in front of her. She dipped a finger in and licked it.

Nothing of that need be mentioned, Tommy preferred. It *had,* though, been a kind of turning point. Bobbi had forgotten, or allowed herself not to remember. He was electing to put it behind them because old Mick had died. It hadn't been a large matter, though they had not come back, it was true.

Janice said nothing more, went on with Esther rinsing and filling the dishwasher.

"Well, Mick said." Bobbi wouldn't be stopped now. "And you know Mick. He said when your hosts act like you two acted—like complete shits—in Ireland you crap in the bed and leave it as a message. Ha! At least we didn't do *that.* We were too nice. We were *good* guests."

"Thanks for that," Janice said. In the kitchen, she and Esther were being amused and annoyed by Bobbi. Tommy, though, was simply being present, and quiet—in the dining room, where the candles had worked down, and empty glasses were left, but the overheads were up bright, signaling an evening was over. He felt what seemed to be the hollow of obligation. Which would be to what? An obligation (false) to a time that was now gone, of which Bobbi Kamper was the unwished-for vestige? Or better, obligation to a core of—it must be—modesty? Something that may even have been near his insufficiency as a writer and would outlive him. He'd need to ask Janice once again when they were in bed and the lights off.

"Maybe we all should go to bed," Tommy said, and put a smile on as a corrective—against something going off the rails. No one wanted that.

"I'll drink to that," Janice said in the kitchen. "Esther's asleep on her feet in here, while she's supposed to be helping me."

"Ho-hum," Esther Parr said. She could be heard exiting the back door that opened down the hill through the woods to the guesthouse. Sam was still fiddling with the dogs, having a second smoke. The door to the hall clicked closed—Janice slipping off to bed without good night. She deferred to her own private etiquettes.

It was her house. Everything could be gone over after Bobbi was gone.

Tommy heard Sam in the yard, quoting more poetry. "'A dog starved at his master's gate predicts the ruin of the state.' You dogs should memorize more things. You'd be better companions." Sam had most of Blake by heart. And more.

"You're such a husband," Bobbi said meanly. "How d'you do it? I could never learn the trick." She'd realized Janice had gone. She could say whatever came to her head. It was how she was experiencing loss—as a freeing up, a setting loose from what few likable qualities she possessed. It was not a question he wished to answer. It was not a question. "Do you remember when you tried to fuck me?"

"I really *don't* remember that," Tommy said. "When would that've been? I remember most of the women I've tried to fuck—especially the ones where I failed."

"Oh, and you *failed,*" Bobbi said. "You certainly *did.* Cravenly. Abjectly. It was at the Dupuis'—those awful people from New Orleans who took the gigantic summer castle in Westport, and we were all there and had to stay the night. Janice was there. You weren't such a good husband *that* night. You were extremely drunk. I didn't make an issue of it. Though I told Mick, later.

He thought it was funny. And also pathetic. Though he didn't much care."

"Odd the things that slip your mind," Tommy said. Perhaps she believed it. Mick always said Bobbi drank gin and began inventing—scenarios, lives, affronts, loves, misdeeds—all of which he then had to live with.

"Mick thought you were only moderately talented," Bobbi said. "Esther was much more gifted."

"I always thought that," Tommy said.

"We know, don't we?" Bobbi said. "About ourselves."

"Sometimes we do." It seemed to appease her for him to share even an unimportant acknowledgment. She may have had few such agreements in these later years.

"What's the theme of our book, tonight, Tommy?" Bobbi said in the diminishing candlelight, Sam still out delighting the dogs, everyone else in bed.

"Maybe there isn't one."

"No?" Bobbi said. "Isn't that scary? For there not to be a—what? What would you say? A *larger consequence* to all this?" She leaned back as if to get clear of her own words.

"I wouldn't say so," Tommy said.

"I have Mick's ashes in the car. I've no idea what to do with them."

"You'll figure it out," Tommy said.

"Couldn't I just leave them with you here? I'm not really an ashes kinda girl."

"No," Tommy said. "That wouldn't be good."

"Ah!" Bobbi said. "So. There *is* a theme. 'And in the end the poor grieving girl wasn't allowed to leave the old man's ashes because it wasn't *good.*' I give that to you for free, Thomas. You can write it."

"Time for bed," Tommy said for what might've been the fourth time.

Bobbi Kamper was rising not so steadily. Sam would be asked to accompany her down. "Where will the dogs sleep?"

"In the room with you," Tommy said.

"Are you not going to commit suicide this time?" She put both her hands on the table for support.

"In memory of Mick," he said. "It's *my* free one."

"Give us a kiss, ole sweety," she said. "Make Happy happy." She took her blue glasses off again. Her face was small and precise, made smaller by time. Not unpretty. He would kiss her. He had always liked kissing her, had over the years kissed her many times. Innocently. Meaninglessly. This would be another such kiss. It would conclude things as well as they could be concluded. He leaned to kiss her.

He stood in the yard where Sam had been with the dogs. Down the hill, in the guest cottage, where lights were burning, he heard voices—Sam's and Bobbi's—then some laughter. Then Esther. "As if we all didn't realize . . ." he heard her say. They'd known one another much longer. It was different among the three of them. There seemed to be nothing that connected anything important to anything else here. In the end (which was now) events just stopped. He had a crazy notion—to go to her car, find whatever simple cinerary Old Mick's ashes were collected in, carry them to the beach and pour them in the pit—if it was still there, where the tide would find them. Return them to the flood, as he did often with cold ashes from the stove in the little fisherman's shack by the beach where he once wrote books. It would be a better outcome for the old fooler than his mortal remains being left back someplace, overlooked, mistaken for something else, forgotten. Bobbi was not an ashes kind of girl. It was why she'd come. Such an odd thing. And he *could* always just take them. Only you wouldn't. His sense of obligation to that core of modesty—its better aspect—forbid that absolutely.

Though he thought, as he stepped inside the house,

switching off lights, turning toward bed, that she'd been very wrong—Bobbi—about his and Jan's incivility when the dogs had wrecked things, and Bobbi and Mick had laughed it off, laughed at them, no doubt. He and Janice had only mentioned what anyone would've and had not ever brought it up again. It was a small matter. And hadn't they tonight admitted Bobbi to their life, afforded her comfort and some small release from her moment of sorrow when she was alone and had only them—not exactly friends, no, but not enemies? Had they not, all of them, done their very best? For Bobbi? And for Mick? For all of them? Which was only, of course, his view, and was possibly self-serving and might just as well be forgotten in light of all—in light of Mick and the moment itself, and in light of how they would all want to conduct themselves tomorrow, when a new day would dawn, and there would be much they would still wish to say.

Displaced

When your father dies and you are only sixteen, many things change. School life changes. You are now the boy whose father is missing. People feel sorry for you, but they also devalue you, even resent you—for what, you're not sure. The air around you is different. Once, that air contained you fully. But now an opening's cut, which feels frightening, yet not so frightening.

And there is your mother and her loss to fill—at least to step into—while you manage those very sensations. Fear. And others. Opportunity. And always there is the fact of your father, whom you love or loved, and whose life has quickly become only about its end—much of the rest quickly fading. So. You are alone in a way that is so many-sided there is not a word for it. Attempts to find the word leave you confused—since that confusion is not altogether unwanted or unliked.

Try to find the word.

It is not necessary to talk *much* about my parents. My father was a country boy from near Galena, Kansas. Large and handsome and good-natured. My mother was a skeptical, ambitious town girl from Kankakee. They'd met in the club car of a Rock Island passenger train between St. Louis and Kansas City, where my father was headed to take a job. It was 1943. Neither of them could've said if they had a care in the world, or anything they weren't willing to lose. That they were far from perfect for each other and would never have married if my mother hadn't gotten pregnant—I don't blame them for that. But if he had merely lived longer, she could've divorced him. I could've gone to military school—which was my wish. Things would've turned out other than they did. No matter how patented life's course seems when you are leading it day to day, everything could always have been much different.

Across the street from our house in Jackson—we had not yet moved into the duplex which lack of money would soon make necessary—an older residence had been converted into a rooming house, in front of which was a wooden sign with a phone number. DIAL 33377. Nothing more. My mother—in her strange, incomplete grief—disapproved of this house, disapproved of even the sign. "The *DIAL house*," she called it with a kind of disgust. People who lived there were transients, she said. "Transient" was a designation that meant *undesirable* to her. It meant weakness, a failing that could corrupt you. And corruption was the force in nature she now feared. My father had protected her from that—even feeling about him as she did. But being alone now in this small southern capital—a place where he'd brought us and where we knew no one yet couldn't for the moment find a way to leave—subjected us, she felt, to every sort of pitfall and danger that could ruin us and make our chances at restoring life vanish before they could be grasped.

As I said, after my father died, the students in my school had begun to subject me to strange ambivalence, which on some days made me feel that his dying had transformed me into a "special person," deserving sympathy and respect and even affection-like admiration. As if loss was an improvement granted to few but desired by all. Yet at the same time, these same people—boys and girls alike—seemed to look on me with the profoundest reluctance, as they would on a person from an alien race whom they were working out a reason not to like. I, of course, did not understand this. But the effect was that I became submissive to all of it, believing in it when it was fortifying and believing in it when it left me feeling abandoned, without a thought for my future except a bad one.

In the DIAL house there was always activity. I took an interest because whether I was being revered or disliked in school, my presence as a stranger guaranteed me no friends once my school day ended and time would be on my hands. It was also true, then, that my mother came to believe she needed to take a job. My father's position had provided only for his burial—money that was now used up. My mother's job, which she did not keep long—only until she met her first boyfriend—was as night cashier at a local hotel. Which meant she left for work when I was getting home, and came back after I was asleep, or should've been.

It was an older neighborhood there—large, once-stately homes inhabited by elderly widows of long residence who rarely ventured out, and who offered nothing to a sixteen-year-old. The DIAL house, which had once been one of these grand houses, was a blight to the eyes of these elderly people, since unexplained behaviors were often going on there, sometimes noisily late into the night, which was not the sort of life people were accustomed to on Grand View Avenue. I, however, understood that though my mother and I didn't use the word about ourselves, her and my existence bore a resemblance to the life in the DIAL house, much more than to life in the shuttered, shrubberied mansions along Grand View. *We* were transients. We were sheltered and stubborn in our view of life. But had we been able to stand outside of our circumstances we'd have known who we were and had become. Such changes are not easy to evaluate when they're occurring.

All sorts of people came in and out of the DIAL house. There were several rooms—at least twelve. It was three-storied and in need of paint, with many windows. It had been owned once by a well-known judge, who'd had children and grandchildren—one of whom, it was said, still occupied the top floor and suffered shell shock from the war, which wasn't long over. I would sometimes gaze up at what I fantasized was his window, and believe I saw him looking out, obscured by a thin curtain. I never saw him outside, though I would not have recognized him if he walked up to me and said my name.

Secretaries lived in the DIAL house. Waitresses. Married couples, young and old. Commercial travelers passing through town. Musicians who played the local honky-tonks, and whose loud cars would be parked in front but then disappear in the early hours.

My mother, as I said, believed unsavory things went on there and required me to stay away. Two men lived together there, I knew—younger men who were window dressers downtown. They would sometimes come and go holding hands.

There was also an entire family living in the DIAL house. The father drove a cab he owned and parked in front. They were Irish—something I knew because my mother spoke to the wife on occasions and had learned about them. She felt these people—the MacDermotts—were exceptions to her severe views about the other residents. She respected the MacDermotts because they were Catholics, which she'd been raised up to be in Illinois, and because they were a family holding together far from where they belonged. She saw them as brave.

These Irish, the MacDermotts, had a son and a daughter, and possibly because they had not been in town long, these two did not go to school. The boy, Niall, was a year older than I was. The girl, Kitty, was younger and stayed indoors most of the time. But Niall was outgoing and friendly and sometimes would drive the cab when his father was sick—which was often. My mother was very clear that I was not to have anything to do with anyone in the DIAL house. The buxom, winking secretaries, the cheap musicians, and the two queer boys—I should be wary of all of them, as if they carried an illness.

But she made an exception when it came to Niall MacDermott, who was tall, sandy-haired, blue-eyed and polite, and spoke in his happy musical way she liked hearing. It seemed to bring her out of her worries and woes. Some quality of being Irish, she believed, allowed the world not to bother him too much. It allowed a widow, such as she was, to accede to a brighter view.

Sometimes Niall MacDermott would come across the street and perch on our porch steps and tell me about how life was in Ireland. He had gone to Catholic school in a town called Strathfoyle. His family had left there, he said, and come here for better chances. He didn't think, however, that for his father to be driving a cab instead of working on the docks was much of an improvement. Plus, living where they were, in a rooming house, crammed into small bad-smelling spaces when they'd once had a whole house paid for where they'd come from—it made no sense to him.

I, of course, had nothing to tell Niall that was as interesting as the things he had already done in almost the same amount of life. I knew only the one other place we'd lived—near where my father was born, in Kansas. And I knew that my parents had never gotten along too well, and that I wanted to go to military school but now couldn't. And I knew that my father had died—not long before the MacDermotts moved to the DIAL house. Niall asked me what it was like to have my father be dead—in particular, whether I'd had to *see* him dead—which was how such things happened in Ireland. He'd had to see his grandfather in his coffin, ghastly-looking and wearing a light gray suit. He would never forget it, he told me. He asked me if my mother was thinking of finding a boyfriend, which he said would not happen in Ireland. Widows stayed widows there, or left town—which was unfair. He asked if I'd talked to the "two fellas," the window dressers. They were nice, he said. Nothing was wrong with them. He asked if I thought his sister Kitty was pretty (I didn't) and said that they were "Irish twins"—nine months apart, to the hour.

To all these questions—seated where we were on the brick porch steps—I gave, I know, unsatisfactory answers. I *had* seen my father in his coffin, but it hadn't shocked me. I wanted my mother to have a boyfriend, so she would not pay so much attention to me. I much preferred to hear about the life in Strathfoyle, which was mysterious and inviting, a place where, when I went out to my own life, I would go, even though Niall assured me I would likely not be welcome. People wouldn't be nice to me, he said. There were too many unfriendly English running things. Though if Strathfoyle was a part of Ireland, I could not see what English people, who lived in a whole other country, had to do with anything.

What I did understand, though, was that I didn't know much and possibly never would; while Niall MacDermott knew a world of things that mattered to him and would play a part in his future, rather than what he knew being just an accident of who he was and where he was born.

As my school year went on Niall's father—whose name was Gerry—was more and more "under the weather," which was how Niall put it. My mother, in the meantime, seemed to grow less agreeable about the MacDermotts. She said that Mrs. MacDermott—Hazel—had hinted that Gerry had a drink problem; and on another occasion, that he had a "lung condition" from smoking, and that being in Mississippi, where it was damp, made it worse. Arizona would be better.

My mother said that Gerry's problems were a "burden of the genes," and I should stay away from him. Though Niall, to my surprise, she maintained a regard for, describing him to me as ambitious and attractive and smart, which I believed to be true. And because my classmates treated me the way they did, having Niall willing to act toward me as his "younger friend"—not his equal but nearly—seemed a good opportunity. A chance to model myself on someone with a future.

Harry was what Niall called me. As in "Ain't that just right, Harry?" "You're taking the piss now, Harry," or "Go on with ya, Harry." I didn't entirely understand these expressions, but liked it when he said them. My name, in fact, wasn't Harry, but Henry Harding, after my father, who, my mother said, had been named by his uppity relatives after a famous painter. When I asked Niall why he called me Harry, he just laughed and said, "Oh, it's just that calling you Henry Harding is a bit of a mash-up, a fat word sandwich." No one in Ireland would ever use it. Niall, he said, was the commonest name in all of Ireland. It signified passion. And owning it made people enjoy him and everything work out smoother. Being Irish, I believed, carried lessons worth learning. It did not occur to me—or it occurred to me only indistinctly—that I was of course not Irish and would never be.

After a while—though my father's death and its complexities hung over life inside our house—in my dealings with Niall MacDermott my father did not come up so much. I knew Niall's willingness to befriend me had begun with nothing more than an act of kindness.

Yet I also thought that he liked my mother, who was more than twice his age but looked younger and liked *him.* More than once I featured a reckless scene of my mother and me and Niall on a train bound for Chicago or New York or someplace far away from Mississippi, where people would know nothing about us and would not see us as the mismatched parts we were.

My father had died in July. But by October, my mother had become accustomed to working at the hotel, and to an extent had stopped considering the world, including the people in the DIAL house, as the sworn enemies of all things dear to her. It may also have been that she'd met Larry Scott by then, who was, of all things, a college professor and was divorced, and whom my mother had met—where I never knew. He did not take much interest in me nor I in him.

School had not gotten better for me, and I disliked it, though my grades were satisfactory. I'd begun to think again about a military school I'd heard of in Florida, considering whether I should run away and simply show up there and plead to be taken in, which I felt would cause my mother to relent and give her permission. How this could work out was not part of my thinking. We had almost no money. My military school fantasy, I already understood, would eventually come apart like paper in water.

Niall MacDermott had now begun to drive his father's taxi more, and often at night, when his father stayed in. Out our front window I would see the cab sitting at the curb in front of the DIAL house, its yellow roof light lit up and the motor running. "Irish Cab" plus a phone number was stenciled on the door. The figure of Niall would be in the driver's seat, reading a paperback book in the dim inside luminance. Niall smoked cigarettes—like his father—and occasionally he'd flick a butt or an ash out the side window. The cab was a four-door Mercury of a late-40s model and had a ball-cap visor to block the sunshine when the cab was operated during the day. It was not as nice a car as my mother's Ford.

On Friday before Halloween, which was to be on Saturday, I came home from school, and Niall was again sitting in the cab in front of his house. If a customer called, the phone rang in the house, and Niall's mother or his plump sister would come out and down the walk and tell Niall where he was supposed to go, and away he'd drive. Niall had told me his father had made the decision to accept blacks as customers, as long as they were picked up at a house and transported to another house. He would not pick them up from the street, Niall said. This was not how things were done in Mississippi.

Blacks had their own cab companies, the way they had their own everything else. Niall told me his father was expecting trouble—from whites *and* blacks—but was not afraid. Ireland sported its own troubles, he said, and you got no place running from them. There were too many blacks who needed to be taken places to ignore them. He would pick up someone who was English. How bad could it be to pick up a black man.

When I saw Niall in the cab in the afternoon, he waved as if he'd been waiting for me. I hadn't seen him in several days and believed he'd been working at night. He climbed out and came across in front of our house. And right away I noticed something different about him. He looked sharper. His hair was shorter and neater so you saw more of his handsome, smiling face, which looked scrubbed since he did not shave yet. He was wearing what I came to know as an argyle sweater and a snappy pair of brown corduroy trousers and polished black shoes. I had the feeling that he was leaving—possibly back to Ireland—and was waiting to say good-bye. There was a fragrance about him, like lemons—similar to the tonic you got at the barber, where I went for my haircuts when my father was alive and there'd been a life I fitted into. My mother cut my hair now and didn't do a respectable job.

"I picked up a whore in the cab last night." Niall just started off talking, as if we'd been having a conversation already. Which we hadn't. For some reason he was looking straight at me—intense—in a way he'd never done, as if he was trying to make an impression. He seemed charged up but also to be keeping something back. He said "whore" so as to sound like "hure." I don't know how I even knew this word, but I did. I also knew what *hures* supposedly did, without knowing the particulars. "She wanted me to drive her down to New Orleans. Which of course, I couldn't. So she told me interesting things about the higher-up gasbags in this town," Niall said. "Hilarious things."

"What are they?" I said. Again, Niall seemed changed. He seemed to me to be over twenty, and to want me to be over twenty also. Only I wasn't. I was just a boy whose mother cut his hair and who missed his father and woke up at night, realizing he'd been talking without knowing who he'd been talking to.

"Oh. I'll have to tell yez," Niall said. "You'll bleed with laughin' 'n be ragin' for something new every time. Which I might just can supply. She also says there's a whole big part of New Orleans jammed up with Irish. I have a feeling I'll be seeing her again, if you get what I mean."

I guessed he meant he would take this woman in his

father's cab again, and maybe she would tell him more hilarious stories about officials in town—whoever they were—and maybe drive to New Orleans.

"I was just after speaking to your mam," Niall said, still with the effect of keeping something hidden. This had all come out of nowhere. Plus, Niall had been talking to my mother by himself, which meant something. I guessed this was how growing up happened. One fine day you're not who you'd been. "She says you like the pictures. Is that an actual fact?"

"Yes," I said. "I do." And I did. On Saturdays, when my father was there, he would take me downtown to the Prestige, where we'd sit through a whole afternoon slate, taking in horse operas (he called them), comedies with the Stooges, a jungle show, cartoons and newsreels from World War Two and Korea. After which we'd walk sore-eyed out into the sun, and I'd feel weak, and also as if I'd somehow done something wrong. I didn't know what. Which all ceased when my father died. I hadn't been to a movie since then, and my mother didn't have time to take me and wouldn't let me go alone.

"Look, then," Niall said. I could see his pack of "smokes" under the argyle, in his shirt pocket. "How 'bout we steal the cab tonight and go out to the Holiday. Under sixteen goes in free. You're well under sixteen, if I'm not mistaken. You've been old gloomy pants long enough. Your mam thinks it'll do ya' up, and I'm sure it will. I'll regale you at length about the higher-ups and their perverted shenanigans."

I was already sixteen—by several months. But I looked young for it, which didn't make me happy. I knew Niall meant I could lie and sneak in. "It's a Bob Hope gasser," Niall said. "We'll have a ball." Immediately I wondered if he intended to take the *hure* with us and what would happen then. I'd never been to the 51-Holiday, which was on the outskirts and was a drive-in. Once, at night, my father had driven us past when a show was playing. "There's the old passion pit," he said. "You'll be snugged in there someday." On the big screen, a chariot race was in progress—with wild horses and men in gold armor waving swords and shouting—all in complete silence. From the back seat where I could see, these events on the screen seemed to be really happening—not in a movie, but out in the night, as if there was another existence that I could see but not go into. I liked it.

"I'll go," I said, whether a *hure* would be coming or not. I was surprised my mother had said I could go and trusted Niall to look after me. This was possibly another way growing up happened. You were unexpectedly freer. She, of course, would've known nothing about the *hure*.

"We'll depart half seven," Niall said and seemed keen about it. He put his hand on my shoulder and gave me a shove back—something he'd never done. "Tidy up a bit," he said. "You're headed for a hot date with old Niall tonight." He had the big smile going.

"Is anyone else coming?" I looked down our street. One of the old ladies from the residences yet to be converted to a rooming house was outside in her pink housedress, sweeping chinaberries off her front walk. She stopped and frowned at Niall and me, then waved her broom brush in our direction, as if she was angry. I had no idea why. "You nasty boys. Shoo. Go away," she shouted at us. "You don't belong here. Shoo on. Shoo on."

Niall sneered at her and gave her back the double thumbs-down. "Listen to her shite," he said. "We're rubbish. But we'll show her *she's* rubbish."

I'd never seen Niall sneer before. It was strange to see his face turn to that so fast—as if he had it ready. Though I'd seen my mother sneer before—at my father—more than once.

"So. It's put on your laughin' boots, ole Harry," Niall said, turning away and shoving into me again. He was starting back across the street to the DIAL house, where I'd never even been inside. He seemed suddenly to be in high spirits, as if what the old lady had said to us had made him happy.

At seven thirty Niall was waiting in the cab, in front of his house. It was almost dark. The little yellow roof light showed in the twilight. He was smoking. Lights were blazing in the DIAL house windows. Hillbilly music was being played on a radio, and I could see somebody—a woman—walk past a window without looking out. The air was warm and summery though it was late October.

"I'm pondering joining the U.S. Navy," Niall said as soon as I got in, as if he'd been waiting to tell me.

"Why?" I said, though I knew it wasn't the right question. But my father hadn't served in the war due to his heart problem. I didn't know why Niall should serve if he was Irish.

We were driving out through the old neighborhoods toward the north side and the outskirts where the 51-Holiday was.

"The old man conjectures if I join up, I'll get handed a skilled trade, then they'll make me a citizen same as you when I get out. There ain't no war going on to get me blown to Jesus. The old *da,* of course, joined with the British forces—dead against his will. Awful business. I'm not on for that. I prefer an ocean cruise and hula girls." Niall punched my knee and flashed his smile across the dark front seat. "How's about you, young Harry? You go for hula girls? I bet you do."

"Yes," I said. "I do."

"I *guess* you do." Niall was still in high spirits and wanted me to be. My mother had said to me that afternoon, "Your friends are being kind to you because you lost your dad. I like him. Niall's personable. You and he can have a fine time. Just try."

"I will," I said. And it was true. No one else had been kind to me. At school, they treated me like a sick person they didn't like—when they weren't ignoring me. I didn't say this to my mother. It would only have discouraged her about her own life.

The 51-Holiday was out the highway where there were just dark drive-in bars and falling-down shacks and jukes with cars crowded in on Friday night. A string of cars with headlights shining was extended back from the 51 ticket booth. The screen was already showing advertisements for businesses in town—a used-car dealer, a flooring company, a camera store, the hotel where my mother was working at that minute. Even a funeral home. There was still a crease of orange daylight in the low sky to the west, rendering the big square screen washed out and dimmer than it would be when it was full dark.

"We need to inch in as close to the front as we can," Niall said, navigating us past the little wooden hut where a girl sold tickets out through a window.

"Two?" the girl said.

"Just the one," Niall said brazenly. "The infant here's not even fourteen." I stared forward acknowledging nothing, as if I couldn't hear well.

The girl peered in at me. "He don't look that young."

"How do *I* look to you?" Niall said, smiling.

"About half-smart," the girl said. "Where're you from, Louisiana?"

"There, see? There's your answer," Niall said, ignoring the question about where he was from and handing out a dollar bill. "You can't tell just by lookin'. I'm Alfred Einstein."

"Fooled me, Alfred," the girl said, pushing red-paper tickets back through the opening. "You look pretty much like an idiot."

"Well, thank you very much," Niall said. "I'll be 'round to your house tomorrow for my kiss."

"I'll be waitin'," the girl said. "With my pistol."

"They all love me," Niall said, as we moved past into the big fenced enclosure, where other cars were finding places and getting situated, their headlights shining up at the screen and washing out the advertisements.

I admired the way Niall went about things—in a

smooth way. Driving with his elbow out the window, using the steering wheel knob, his cigarette tilted out. I liked that he didn't mind driving the taxi to the movie, and that he'd arranged it with my mother, and made an impression that might alter how she thought about me. I liked that I felt detached from my own difficulties—school, and my misery about my father and not knowing how to overcome all the bad feelings. Niall took life in his stride and seemed purposeful—whether it was being forced to leave home when he didn't want to, or about encountering *hures* in the middle of the night, or lying his way into the drive-in. He had a natural understanding of whatever stood in front of him. It was a better way to approach the world than always having to be right and somebody be wrong—which was how my mother saw life and how I'd been raised to see it.

Niall drove us around to the far side of the movie lot, where there were fewer cars to block the view. I assumed he'd been here before. This would be a place someone would come to be with a girl in the dark. The old passion pit.

Niall maneuvered the cab close up beside a post where a metal speaker was attached by an electrical cord. He lowered his window and brought the speaker right inside with us and hung it on the window glass, then shut the engine off. "Perfect," he said. "We're grand. Get ready to laugh your arse off." It was a word he used. It was Irish, I assumed.

But right away it was strange to be sitting side by side in a taxicab, the nose aimed at the giant screen eighty yards away, just as if we were driving down the highway. But it also was exciting. Life ahead was promising new things in rich supply. "When does it start?" I said.

"Comics go first," Niall said, "then the eternal eejit Bob Hope comes on. '*A whole ocean of laughs,*' the advert says. Paris is in for the setting. You'll need to go there, yourself. Live it up." He bopped me on the shoulder one more time. "I don't suppose you'd want one of me ciggies? I find 'em calming."

"No," I said. Though I did want one. My mother had told me never to start. She smoked since my father had died, and our house smelled of it. She smoked in bed at night. I would only ever do it, I thought, if I was alone. I didn't understand why Niall needed to be calm.

"How 'bout Monsignor Sneak E. Pete?" Niall said with his big grin still on. From under the seat he produced a brown-paper sack out of which a short bottle neck was exposed. He un-screwed the cap, took a swig, and expelled a gasp. "Ow-ow-ow-ow-ow" was the noise he made. And inside the car immediately smelled like my father's breath when he and my mother had had their "cordials." Which he called it, he said, because drinking them made my mother cordial—though it never lasted long. "Shall I tempt you?" Niall said. "Just to file down the edge." He held the sack forward. And I took it. And even though my lips would be on the bottle where his had been, I did what I'd witnessed him do—took a drink, without knowing anything of what it contained or what would happen.

The liquor was very warm from being under the seat, and it instantly caused my throat to close, and my breathing almost to stop. I wanted to shout from the pain and also to gag and cough in one eruption. Only I couldn't allow that in front of Niall. I'd be counted as a fool forever. Instead, I got still and did not breathe at all. I let what I'd drunk drain burning out of my chest and start burning in my stomach—which wasn't as bad. My eyes were full of tears. My face was on fire. I didn't know how I was going to make any of this stop.

"In the grip, are we?" Niall said, smiling in an appraising way, registering that I was unable to speak and possibly not move. "Take yourself a wee breathy," he said. "You're likely not dying. You didn't need to gulp it. Leaving some for the room is customary. You've preserved your amateur standing. That's assured."

"What is it?" I croaked with the breath I was instructed to take.

"The queen's reserve," Niall said. "Pap keeps it in the hack, then forgets I'm susceptible. Possibly more so."

My belly and throat all the way down were scorched. And though I didn't feel tipsy—as my father had always said—I knew I'd shamed myself and assumed Niall thought belittling things about me.

"Give us wee bumpety," Niall said and took the sack and turned up a second big swig, then screwed the cap back. He was constantly smiling, no matter what he thought. "You're on brig rations now," he said. "You need to learn the proper etiquette." He forced the sack back under the seat.

I decided from the smell that what I'd drunk was gin—which was what my parents had drunk as their cordial. And I determined I'd never touch it again. I felt like my neck was swollen and my throat half its normal size, at the same time as my stomach felt emptied. My mother had made a pot roast for dinner, and I'd eaten a good bit. But I felt vacant down inside and had almost instantly developed a small, needling headache, which made me want to go home.

The drink had had an effect on Niall, as well. He'd suddenly lost his good humor and had pushed over against his car door, as if something he didn't like had happened. I'd loused up the business of the liquor by being an amateur, which I supposed he hadn't appreciated. Though I didn't see what I could do.

The comic feature, when it started, was one I'd seen at the Prestige and didn't think was funny. I tried to laugh, but Niall didn't laugh at all. The Stooges were doctors wearing white coats and worked in a hospital and kept getting in everybody's way and punching one another and falling down. "Would you look at 'em," Niall said from against his door. "It's pathetic. Get away. The ole man says they're all midget cretins. It's typical. Why do we watch 'em?"

When the Stooges were over there was an intermission, and everyone was invited on the screen to visit the refreshment stand. "Whadda yez want?" Niall said, not being at all friendly. He'd opened his door so the light went on. People from other cars were streaming toward the low concrete building in the middle of the big lot where there were lights on, and where the projector seemed to be located. "I told your mam I'd coddle you," Niall said. "What does baby want?"

"Nothing," I said. "Thank you." Seated under the dim inside light, I felt a long way from anywhere I knew. Niall had somehow become someone I might not have recognized. He wasn't smiling anymore.

"Says 'nothin,' gets nothin,'" Niall said down into

the interior, as if he was sorry I was there. He closed the door and walked off into the shadows toward the refreshments.

I did not know what to do then. I briefly revisited being at the Prestige with my father and the good time we'd had. But those thoughts always ended with my father having a heart attack in the house in the middle of the night and being carted out on a stretcher, already dead. That could easily make me cry, which I didn't want to do now and here. I did think, though, that Niall and I were just two boys—even if he could drive and drink and smoke and knew *hures* and was aware of things I wasn't. Becoming stony and silent and being crabby about everything had, in fact, made him seem not older than me but even less grown-up than I was. As if his actual person was now being disclosed.

When Niall got back, he'd brought a paper sack of popcorn, which smelled good, but he didn't offer any to me. He looked over as though he expected me to say something. But I didn't intend to speak what I'd been thinking. It would've made him madder. Though I'd decided mad was not what he truly felt. There probably wasn't a right word for how Niall truly felt. We were alike in that way, when all was said and done.

The feature had now begun out on the screen—the

light cone shining over the car roofs, halfway illuminating them. People were hurrying back to their cars, laughing and talking. Beer cans were being opened and car doors slamming. A man said, very loud, "What the hell are you two doin' back there? Don't make me have to call the police." A woman started laughing. "We're married. It doesn't matter anymore."

"Eejits one 'n' all," Niall said and wound his window up so the speaker clanked against the glass. "Roll yours," he said. "I don't want to hear 'em start beltin' away. The da's bad enough every night."

I did what he said, and the cool night air was immediately blocked, and I knew before very long we'd get hot. My head still ached, and I feared being hot would make me sick after the gin.

Paris Holiday was the title of the show. It was in bright, smudgy color and began on an ocean liner, with people dressed up and just walking around talking to one another. Some were speaking in a language that wasn't English, which I guessed was supposed to be funny. A man with a large nose, wearing a fancy sport coat and a felt hat came in and just stood in the middle of the room, which was like a hotel lobby, and talked to all the people while trying not to smile. This was all that went on and wasn't hilarious at all. I'd never seen Bob Hope, but understood this man with the big nose was him. His voice sounded like the voice I'd heard on the radio, when I'd listened with my parents. I hadn't thought he was funny then either.

Niall, though, *did* think he was funny. He laughed loudly at things Bob Hope said, and at things one of the characters who spoke in the other language said. "Man, oh man, would you look at that," Niall said about a pretty blond woman who came on the scene wearing a gray fur coat. "I'd be forced to give her a good swiving, I'd say. I guess the baby wouldn't, of course." He'd taken another drink out of his paper bag and hadn't offered me any. I didn't want it.

"I don't know," I said.

"So you're not entirely sure, is that right?" Niall said this as if I'd made him irate. I should've said I *would,* but I hadn't thought of it. Perhaps I was a little tipsy.

"I would," I said.

"Ya feeb. Course ya would," Niall said. "That's Anita Christ-a-mighty Ekberg. She's Swedish. They fuck everybody."

I looked at the blond woman, bigger on the screen than anything imaginable. The woman who was Anita Ekberg—a name I didn't know—didn't seem real. I didn't understand how to think about fucking her. I'd only heard this word from boys in school, who told jokes about it. "If Anita Ekberg was sitting where I'm sitting and leaned over and said, 'Hey, Harry, give us a wee poke,' doubtless you wouldn't know where to start. Would you?"

"I would," I said.

"Ah, you wouldn't. That's plain as the egg." Niall smiled at me in a scornful way. More things were happening on the screen. Bob Hope's big misshapen face filled the picture, his eyes shifting this way and that, his nasty lip curling not in a real smile. Anita Ekberg could be seen walking down a long hallway, her high heels in her hand, carrying her fur coat. She *was* good-looking. Anybody would see that. Fucking her might not have been that hard, even if I didn't know what I was doing.

And then for a while we both just watched. Niall appeared to have berated me enough—calling me a feeb and telling me I had no etiquette. He himself laughed at all kinds of things on the screen—goings-on I couldn't really get the sense of, though I laughed as if I did. "He's speakin' fuckin' Frenchy," Niall said about one of the players, a small fellow with a face like a horse who was looking mystified, though Bob Hope seemed to understand whatever he said. "French is fuckin' lame," Niall said. "Though it's hilarious once you pin it down." He had the sack out again. "Have a boost," he said and reached it across. My head still ached, and I didn't want a boost. The women in the car beside us were laughing to beat the band, and the men were whooping at the little horse-face character who was pretending to throw up on two old ladies in deck chairs. I took the sack and held it to my lips and let just the tiniest trickle get in. A clammy paper shred stuck to my tongue, plus a piece of popcorn. "Must be prudent," Niall said. He no longer seemed angry. "We want you home upright." The sip I did swallow didn't burn or make my breathing stop. It was actually halfway sweet.

"Okay," I said. I was happy he'd come back to his better self.

"I'm guessin' you miss your ole dad an awful lot," Niall said, his voice grown softer. He turned down the movie noise that was banging out of the speaker. People were laughing in the next car and in other cars. It had gotten warmer in the closed-up car, the way I knew it would. "Helluva thing," he said and nodded at me. We'd never spoken about my father as a living person. Being friends with Niall had seemed good because that hadn't been necessary. My father, dead or alive, was everywhere I turned. But not between Niall and me. Taking me to the movies and paying attention to me was a kind of secret sympathy. He could have taken the whore with him and gotten drunk and done whatever he wanted. He didn't have to put up with me, who didn't know anything and was always sad. A feeb.

"I do sometimes," I said, on the subject of missing my dad. I could hear my voice under the movie sound. It was as if somebody else was using my words, saying my thoughts. Only, I didn't want to be talking about these things. My heart right then began to race—at the possibility of saying something that would make me start blubbering. It had happened before.

"You know what I'd welcome the chance to do," Niall said and reached across the warm, empty space between us and put his hand against my cheek—which startled me. It was nothing like him hitting me on the shoulder. It was more like what my mother had done many times in the past months.

"No," I said, though there were not many choices of things two people could do. Two boys.

"Give you a wee kiss," Niall said and let his rough hand roam back through my crew cut the way my mother did. Popcorn smell was on his fingers, and the gin and his lemony fragrance. I looked right at Niall's thick, dark eyebrows. They were dense and wiry, like a man's. "It might set things straight a bit," he said, leaning closer.

"I don't know," I said, my heart still hammering. It had not had time to slow down.

"Just give us a try," Niall said. He put his hand on my knee, put his weight on it, and with his other hand turned my cheek and my mouth toward him and brought his face up to mine. And he kissed me. On the lips. Just like I'd seen two movie stars kiss up on a screen, or the way my mother would kiss my father when she loved him.

I can't say I wasn't shocked. And I can't tell you what I did while Niall MacDermott was kissing me, which was only for a moment. I know I didn't move my arms or my hands, didn't move my face away or toward him. I didn't take a breath or let a breath out. My heart *did* suddenly slow down, and the rigidness from when Niall was mad at me began to seep out. I can't explain it, but I felt myself relax—not as if someone was kissing me, but as if someone had taken me aside and said something kind—which only my mother had done up to then.

Niall made a low noise in his throat just at the moment he was kissing me. An *mmmm* sound, which seemed unnatural, but was something he wanted to do. I did not make a noise that I know of and was glad when he pulled away. He licked his lips as he sat back and stared straight at me, right into my eyes. He seemed to be asking me something—to say words or to do something. Maybe kiss him. But I had no intention of doing that. For two boys to kiss wasn't the worst thing. It really wasn't so different from kissing my mother, though it wasn't *really* like movie stars kissing when they were supposed to be in love. I hadn't enjoyed it. He had kissed me. I hadn't kissed him.

"So how was *that*?" Niall said. His wiry eyebrows rose, as if he expected to hear back something he liked. And I would've said something to make him happy, only I had nothing to say. It had been a great surprise, since I'd never kissed a boy or even a girl. But I had no intention of doing it again. Though it didn't really matter that we'd done it. Or that he had.

"Did you hear me what I said?" Niall had pulled back against his door again. He'd taken his hand off my knee, though he was smiling. "I said something," he said. "I said, 'How *was* that?'"

"It was all right," I said.

"It was *all right*," Niall said. "A bit of *all right*? Take it or leave it?"

"Yes," I said. I didn't know what else to say, except "leave it," which I knew he wouldn't like.

Niall turned toward the steering wheel, put his two clenched fists on each side of the circle and tapped them. On the screen, far into the night, Anita Ekberg was in the fur coat, looking beautiful on the deck of the ocean liner.

"Jesus," Niall said—not to me I didn't think, but to himself—as if I wasn't there. "You're a fuckin' waste, aren't you? A fuckin' little waste."

"I thought . . ." I started to say. Who knows what I intended. I trusted the right words would come, and they did not.

"You *thought* . . ." Niall looked over at me where I'd moved against my own door, as if I might be ready to jump out. His smile was the sneer I'd seen before. "You thought . . . what? You thought I liked you? You thought I thought you were cute? You thought—I don't know what?" He seemed not to be angry, just disappointed at what he'd hoped to accomplish by kissing me not having worked out. I was sorry it hadn't, either.

"I thought you were sorry about my father being dead," I said. It was now very, very hot in the car, and the movie's sound, even softer, filled the space.

"I *am*," Niall said. "Didn't I say that? Don't be tellin' your mam about this. Is that a deal? Between us? She wouldn't take to it. She'd have me sent off. Not being an entitled citizen."

"I won't," I said. Getting Niall sent off was the last thing I'd ever want to do. He was the only friend I had. If I lost him I might as well give up on life. If we went to the movies again, I thought, I'd kiss him, since all in all it really didn't matter so much to me.

On the way home, Niall drove the way I admired—one-handed, window down, elbow cocked out, the cool night flooding in, brightening his cigarette end between his fingers. I had my own window down, and the night came spinning in around me. My head had quit aching. We hadn't stayed for the whole movie. Niall had lost interest, though I'd liked parts where the characters went to Paris, a place I'd done a *World Book* report on and wanted to see—though Niall said the Paris streets on the screen were all in California.

Niall did not speak for a long time. He seemed to be thinking. I wondered if possibly kissing me had been just a normal act of consideration, and if you were Irish you knew that, and no one got confused. A kiss could mean different things. I felt better for having gone to the drive-in with him, no matter what had gone on between the two of us.

"Tell me something," Niall said, not taking his eyes off the road. We were back onto the old town streets. To the world outside, we were a taxi, not two boys in a car coming back from the picture show. I felt secret and protected.

"What?" I said.

"What's the very worst thing you ever did do?" He took a deep drag off his Pall Mall and blew smoke into the night out the side of his mouth.

For a long moment I didn't say anything. And I can't say I was trying to think of an answer. I was intending not to answer at all.

"I can unquestionably tell you mine," Niall said. "Or at least the top three. Possibly, of course, they're only the ones I'm willing to admit to, with the worse remaining in the cupboard. Maybe start with the *best* thing you ever did, which should be easy since you're such a pattern of perfection. Tell us the prizewinner. Your secret's safe with me." He smiled as if he was pleased with himself.

"I haven't done many good things," I said, and in fact couldn't think of one good thing I'd ever done. Though I'd never tried.

"We'll forgive that," Niall said. "You have it in common with others."

"What did you do good?" I said.

"Failed to fuck me sister when she asked me to. My crowning moment so far. Which didn't last long. I eventually let my guard down shamefully. You mustn't tell your mam that either."

"I won't," I said. It didn't truly seem like the worst thing a boy could do. Though I didn't have a sister.

"So now *you,*" Niall said. "I have to hold something over you. So you don't rat me out. Come on."

"I lied to my mother," I said. We were on our street, coasting down the hill past the old residences and the brick school named after the Civil War hero.

"I don't care a monkey's fat arse about that," Niall said. "There has to be worse. Brave up. This is what friends do. Reveal their awfullest."

I didn't want to reveal my awfullest, but I said it then because I wanted Niall to be my friend more than I wanted to protect myself.

"When my father died," I said, "I wasn't as sad as I should've been. I felt terrible, but it didn't seem like enough."

"Aw, come on," Niall said. "Do you feel worse about yourself than you do about *him* dyin' off?"

"Yes," I said. "I do."

"Well then, *te absolvo,*" Niall said, stopping in front of the DIAL house, where there were lights in most of the windows and one had a jack-o'-lantern with a candle. Our house was dark. My mother was still at work.

We sat for a moment then, the engine ticking, the fragrance of sycamores in the air around us. With his hand holding his cigarette, Niall made a gesture in the darkness between us.

"What's that mean?" I said.

"It means all's forgiven. It's what the pansy priests say at you through the grate when you spill it. It's a way of sayin' 'Who gives a shite. You'll do worse. You'll kill and steal and break people's hearts and fuck your sister and burn down houses.' I've often *wished* me own pap was dead. Top that one. I wasn't going to bleat it. But there we are. We've pled our troth. Whatever. *Te absolvo.*"

Having said that, he popped open his door. "Come along," he said. "It's time for innocent little Harrys to be in their beds. We've done our best and our worst, and we don't even know the difference."

Which was how that night ended—with the difference between good and bad blending together in the darkness. As if this was all that life had so far taught us.

Niall MacDermott didn't stay much longer in the DIAL house. For maybe a month, he was around our house. My mother continued to take an interest in him, despite her age. It seemed unusual, but that's the worst you would say about it. In any case, I saw Niall more and was happier and began for a while to get along better in school.

One day when I got home, my mother said, "Niall's

joined up. There's been some scrape with the taxi and the blacks." A judge, she said, had given Niall a choice of fates, and Niall had taken the easy one and had gotten on the Trailways to Louisiana the very afternoon. He'd said good-bye to my mother but not to me, which I took hard, given that we were friends.

In not too much time, Niall's family left out of the DIAL house. The cab disappeared. Their windows were dark. My mother didn't know where they'd gone, though after a while Niall wrote and said they'd gone to New York, but could soon be back in Strathfoyle. He told us he'd thought the service would solve his problems, but realized he wasn't cut out for the military life, had no stomach for fighting. He'd "picked up a blue ticket," he said and would take a freighter back, himself. Things would be happier now.

When I read the letter, I wondered what kind of boy would I say Niall MacDermott was. We go through life with notions that we know what a person is all about. He's this way—or at least he's more this way than that. Or, he's some other way, and we know how to treat him and to what ends he'll go. With Niall you couldn't completely know what kind of boy he was. He was good, I believed, at heart. Or mainly. He was kind, or could *be* kind. He knew things. But I was certain I knew things he didn't and could see how he could be led wrong and be wrong that way all his life. "Niall will come to no good end," my mother said a day after his letter came. Something had disappointed her. Something transient or displaced in Niall. Something had been attractive to her about him in her fragile state, and been attractive to me, in my own fragile state. But you just wouldn't *bank* on what Niall was, which was the word my poor father used. That was what you looked for, he thought, in people you wanted closest to you. People you can bank on. It sounds easy enough. But if only—and I have thought it a thousand times since those days, when my mother and I were alone together—if only life would turn out to be that simple.

Crossing

They were three ladies. Together, he gathered. Taking the ferry over from Holyhead. Americans—as he was. Though the one might've been Canadian, the silver-haired, shorter, laughing one who seemed to be having a better time. Something . . . oot, aboot, the hoose . . . made him think that. They were all high-spirited. Going across to some concert in Dublin. Some place on the docklands, he'd overheard. Some others on the ferry were going as well. From where, were these women?

At one moment they all three sang together—loudly. "Once, twice, three times a lady," then laughed in a silly way. Whoever'd recorded that song was who they were traveling over to see—possibly that night—then be on the boat back tomorrow. What was it about them?

Americans traveling to Ireland from Wales. Ladies of a certain age, his mother might've said. Why did he think they might be music teachers? From the Midwest. Three classmates. Taking the grand tour.

Most others in the wide, echoing lounge were more subdued. Typical for the ferry. Things on their minds, duties of the day, troubles out ahead. The boat trip not a novelty for them. Even the children were quiet, nibbling their sour, tinned-meat sandwiches and warm dills, staring sleepily out at the gray, tilting sea. All of inside smelled of burnt coffee and disinfectant and crisps and something treacly. Rubbish. "Once, twice, three times . . ." They re-tried the line with less brio. No one seemed to notice.

He himself was coming over to settle with his solicitors. The dull and lengthy formalities. Documents needing signatures. Rights to assign. An oath. Nothing that included Patsy—who'd departed now, was tucked away with the older girl in the far North. He might've flown from Bristol. But the train and the boat, he'd thought, might make a dismal day less so. There was little hurry.

A young woman sitting across on the hard green bench reminded him of her, although Patsy was handsome, and this woman not. The Irish look. Chin slightly incomplete. The rounded, palely flawless cheeks. Two plump hands. The placid blue-eyed gaze of profound un-interest. It could make for great appeal, depth, even beauty. Or it could not. Here was not beauty *or* appeal. Only forbidding depth. Heaviness. The waist an equator, the legs large in a too-tight brown skirt that rode up revealingly. The tribal features.

Something about this woman, for a moment, reminded him of college, in Ohio, of a quality in himself that had often led to ill. An autumn, like now. A party in a rented house in the countryside. Late at night. Drinking. He'd offered to take a similarly large, unattractive girl back to town. Just a ride in. He didn't know her, but thought he experienced a vagrant appeal. At a certain point they'd pulled off to "look at the stars" above the river. It had seemed the moment to kiss—to which she'd acquiesced without conviction. Then she'd said, "No more of that." "Why?" he'd asked. "Why ruin this?" she'd said. He hadn't thought there was a *this* to be ruined. There was only now. He hadn't known what to say, but wanted *this*—whatever it was—to turn out better than ruin. He'd asked her *when* precisely in the night's ribbon of events she'd realized she would not do more with him than kiss. What had he done to make that be all—if it was. He was wheedling and ignominious. But he wanted (he thought) for there to be something they would *say,* some connection, if there was going to be nothing else. "There *wasn't* a moment," she said, looking indifferently into the still spring night and the river. She was from across in Pennsylvania. A mill town. Not far. He was a scholarship student from Louisiana, far, far from there. Though he sat very close to her now, felt confident about girls from the North. "I'm not attracted to you," she said. "Plus, I have my period. Can't we go?"

Later, he heard she'd married some loutish boy from home. It was understood the boy drank too much. From time to time he would see them at school and wonder if she'd told the tosspot husband about his pitiful attempt, about quizzing her—which in his mind was the worst of it. The quizzing after failure. When she saw him, he thought to speak, offer her a word. Possibly apologize. But she stared at him spitefully, as if he'd played some part—some mean part—in how things had turned out for her. A shitty chain of events. Though he knew—as stupid as he'd been—that this could not be true.

Though that impulse—to want to "understand," to interrogate; it was just the wish to have his way. It was what Patsy had thrown at him when things grew no longer bearable for her, would not forgive him for, took their daughters, moved out of reach, disappeared forever—or so it seemed.

Last night, having gone to sleep thinking of the

journey today, he'd had the ridiculous sensation—not quite a dream—that the entire passage of life, years and years, is only actually lived in the last seconds before death slams the door. All life's experience just a faulty perception. A lie, if you like. Not actual. At the end, though, to feel this way was freeing. It was his habit to imagine many things as freeing.

The American women had moved on to Michael Jackson. They all started their sentences, he noticed, with "okay," then answered back in a rushed way. "Okay. Listen, listen. This is how it goes." They had seen a documentary in which Michael Jackson had been portrayed as a childlike genius who everybody loved, instead of as a leering, predatory molester. The short woman—not a Canadian, he now thought—said she'd seen it many times and always cried at the end when "Michael" died of drugs. She couldn't believe he was really dead. "Yep. Yep. Yep. Gone as gone can be," one of the others said. It did not damp their spirits.

The night things had come all unraveled, he and Patsy were in Dawson Street. Raining and cold. November. Buses rattled round the sharp turn into Nassau Street across from Trinity, down from Stephen's Green. Always the buses came too fast, especially on a shining wet, lightless night with traffic teeming. They'd been walking to a lecture in College, had stopped at the light. A boy had been standing beside them, toes to the curb. Just when the big bus rumbled past—too close—someone pushed this boy from behind. A tire—they all saw it—went onto his head. Dead instantly in front of everyone. Silence set in for one great and terrible moment, then everyone began calling. *Stop! Stop!*

The accident hadn't been caused by much—a small misunderstanding between two friends. Nothing intended to end in death. But Patsy suddenly couldn't bear it. A moment can come from nowhere and life is re-framed. Stupid. But we all know that it can.

To try to recover, she took a trip. Gathered up the girls. Traveled to Greenland to walk in the great healing cold and ice. He went back to work. But nothing was the way it had been. Though nothing had been the way it had been for some time. Her family had the big house in Inishowen. She had grown up at the sea. It was suddenly all about his false, lawyerly need to "understand." To interrogate. Which was not really understanding. So American, she'd said. So dishonest. Americans think they can master anything. "I was always that way," he'd said. "It seemed a strength." "I know," she'd said. "I didn't know you well enough, did I? One's *your* great flaw. One's mine." To make it easier, he gave up the house in Ranelagh, permitted himself to re-locate to Bristol, where the firm had offices. It was still close to the girls, who came to visit when she allowed.

The young, impassive Irish woman rose, offered a dismissive look, and walked to the canteen queue and took a place. Possibly it was his business attire and the nice Gladstone, and reading the *FT.* Perhaps he'd been "looking up" where her skirt had hiked. He hadn't been aware. The gray sea slid below the spray-damp window, chilly as always inside the ferry. The three women were looking at him across the vestibule. You could see Ireland now—the stack, the Nose of Howth, the Wicklow Mountains on the port side. A great silver jet just settling in. It would not be a good, or an especially bad day. Perhaps he could stay, sleep at the Merrion, eat at Pep's, take a good breakfast in the morning. It would be Saturday. The horse chestnuts in Stephen's Green would be radiant in mid-autumn. Not a bad city. It could fortify you.

The "Jeremys and the Simons," Patsy called the English, whom she despised as only—he felt—a Donegal Catholic could. He was thinking of that and her, as the ferry back to Holyhead passed, off a quarter mile, its wake high and surging against a coming sea. Why was this in his mind? The failure of trying to understand. It wasn't relevant now.

A man with a small brown-and-white terrier moved into the Irish woman's empty seat—nearer the exit, for the arrival. A houndstooth hacker with the trilby. A silver bracelet and bright red socks. English. You couldn't hide them. The air of uneasy, undeserved isolation. The two of them caught each other's eye, acknowledged nothing. The dog, which had a matching silver collar, lay upon the man's small foot. Possibly he'd seen this man and not realized, which was why "the Jeremys and the Simons" had come to mind.

One of the American women suddenly said—again, much too loud, "Oh. Hel-*looo*! How're yeewwww!" They were making fun of someone who wasn't there. Some disliked colleague they felt free to talk about far from home. They all three looked at him across the shabby lounge and pretended they were embarrassed. Then all three laughed. American fun. "We're sooo bad!" They weren't.

One of the women was staring at him, smiling, making plain she intended to come and speak. She whispered something to her friends, then stood, squared her shoulders, thrust her chin in a stagey way, and came forward. He was fifty. She was sixty. He wasn't dozing or sitting with someone. He was therefore able to be bothered. Or at least approached. They were riding over through the returning ferry's wake, and her passage across the floor became tilt-y and made her pretend to stagger, but not really.

"Okay. We're just having a silly contest," the woman began, now straight in front of him. She wasn't the one who'd said Hel-*looo*! But just in six words, there was the unmistakable gravel-vowels of Chicago. The three jolly music teachers from Chicago. On a flyer. "Once, twice, three times . . ."

"What's your contest?" he said, wanting to be agreeable. Even welcoming. They were countrymen together, here. The accent told. The woman was wearing tan slacks, a pink jumper over a white blouse, and very, very practical shoes to walk in—also in tan. They were all three plump and dressed nearly alike. Happy voyagers.

"We try to guess who's American. And if we're right, we find out why they're here. Later we have a toast."

"*Here,* being on a boat to Ireland?"

"Okay!" she said and produced an intensely big, wide-eyed smile, which contained in it a we're-no-fools warning should he elect for sarcasm, and making a joke about her being a middle westerner. He wouldn't.

"I'm from south Louisiana," he said. "Nothing more than that." She hadn't asked where he was from.

"Well, *that's good*," she said. "We're from Joliet. Not the prison. It's closed."

"O-*kay*," he said, the way they did. "I'd have to turn you in, I guess."

"You don't sound like Louisiana," the woman said.

"I've lived away a long time."

"Is that the Irish Channel out there?" she asked, glancing past him out the thick spray-blown window toward the water and Britain.

"The Irish Sea," he said. "The Irish Channel's something else."

"I'm Sheri." She smiled more brightly. "They're Phil and Trudy. The three wild girls from west Joliet." Not Canada. Not even quite Chicago. The ferry heaved and pitched. "I could get seasick," Sheri said happily.

"We're nearly there," he said. "Mine's Tom."

"Tom," Sheri said as if such a name was surprising. She had a rather large nose, but was otherwise attractively age-appropriate. For someone. "Are you a college professor? That's Phil's guess. She's usually right."

"Lawyer."

"A *lawyer*!"

"They have those here," he said.

"Well," she said. "None of us guessed *that*."

"I guess I'm doing something right," he said.

"Well, we're all divorced, so we know about lawyers," Sheri said. The big heavy-legged Irish girl who'd sat across and was nearing the head of the canteen queue, regarded the two of them disapprovingly. Noisy Americans. Blabbing their business. Owning the world. "What're you doing here, Tom? Do you have a big case, or whatever. On vacation? We have to know."

"A small case," he said. "Mostly over now. I'm finalizing my divorce. Today." Surprisingly, he was telling it. Not that he oughtn't. He simply hadn't much—to anyone.

"*No,*" Sheri said. "Get away. You're not." She leaned in a bit, toward his face.

"I am," he said. Then said *yes,* and realized he could possibly cry—at the thought—but certainly wouldn't. Idiotic. Though a small un-observed seam behind which were small tears, had been pierced, momentarily. "Diamonds from Ireland" was the old lament Patsy always remembered. From their turbulent times. Though, still, if this frowzy woman—this Sheri—saw tears it wouldn't matter. She'd cried her own.

"So." Sheri stood up a bit stiffly, but still leaned toward him. "Isn't it a shit-show now back where *we* live, Tom. This imbecile president and all. Who do we blame but ourselves?"

"Ourselves," he said. A tear had inched free. Touching his nose, he pinched it almost dry.

"We're *all* crying now, aren't we?"

"We are," he said and smiled cheerily.

"Can you even vote?"

"I can," he said. "I didn't."

"Well. What's the use. We're dead ducks."

"I hope we're not," he said. The other two were saying Sheri's name and peering down together at a mobile phone. "She's getting his number" could be heard and giggling.

"Would you like to come with us, tonight, Tom," Sheri said. "We've turned out to have an extra ticket through an exuberance of Phil's. You'd love it. I know you would. Do you know his music?"

"No. But that's very kind. I've got someone I'm meeting."

"Just so you're not alone on your hard day," Sheri said. "We'd make it interesting."

"I'm sure," he said.

"Change your mind . . . We're at Buswells. Wherever Buswells is. Cocktails at six. On us. We have to toast you."

"That's kind," he said again.

"Come on, come on, *come on*! Sher-i! Leave the poor man *be*." She was holding them back. The ferry gave a big horn blast, nearing its berth, the big engines gathering. They were there. It was just noon.

He had his documents in his Gladstone. He was a bit hungry. In town, he could have a walk, stop at O'Neill's for the carvery (less the pint), go by the offices and see old Fallon, who'd been stand-up, but now was retiring. At sixty—moving to America where his kids were. Atlanta or Houston.

The three women were off and down the gangway, laughing. Soon they'd be singing. "Once, twice, three times a lady." He was letting the lounge clear out, taking his time. Voices were echoing. Cars underneath were banging over the iron planks. His hour at the solicitor's wasn't until four. The Englishman with the dog watched him, wishing to go last.

He was not one to cry, of course, not even in the worst shit of it. Not that it was a weakness. Times were, it would've been good to cry—the opposite of a weakness. Most occasions—standing up now, commencing a little uneasily toward the WAY OUT sign—most occasions, when you cried, you should've cried earlier. Still. To leak out a tear in the presence of some busybody from Joliet, inviting him to have cocktails, and for things to become "interesting." What was *that*? Was he pathetic now? Most tears, in any case, were theatrical. Actors produced them on cue. And what if he'd gone to pieces, hugging his chest, rocking up and back, howling—as he'd once seen a convicted man do on hearing a terrible sentence pronounced? How would that've been? Shedding just this little diamond, at a most unexpected moment had been permissible. A dour gesture of self-perceiving. Nothing to be blamed or red-faced about. It had, in fact, left him feeling a measure better than expected, given all, given the days behind him and all that lay beyond.

The Run of Yourself

The second summer after Peter Boyce's wife died, he decided he'd rent the little house near the end of Cod Cove Road. Not the house he and Mae had rented for years, but the older, smaller, grayed-clapboard farm place they'd sometimes walked past in evenings, and talked about buying. Previous Augusts, they'd rented the red Cape nearer the head of the road. There, Mae'd fancied the stone pergola and the screened gazebo, the polished woodwork and the spinet, plus the hilarious red appliances. And the ocean view—though it had lacked a beach. The red house, which was owned by gay doctors in D.C., had peonies and daylilies and bleeding hearts that Mae could potter with, a burning bush that turned early, and warm breezes that pushed away the bugs. The absence of a beach had been a drawback; but the house was bright and clean and roomy, and easily defeated the scratchy impermanence of other Maine houses their friends had rented. Their daughter Polly had invited her classmates up from Tulane, and later brought her husband Terry, and later on their daughter Phoebe. New Orleans' neighbors stopped on their way to Dark Harbor and Stonington, and there were boozy late nights when Mae played the piano and sang, and everyone felt well looked after for having "a Maine place" they didn't have to worry over the rest of the year. Peter Boyce would always have been as happy to remain in the city, even in the torrid time. Estate practice—his special field—slowed in summer. He liked the patient ease 'n' ebb of the vacated town, of staying back when others had left. There'd be a chance to start a book and finish it. See a matinée at the Prytania. Eat a quiet meal where it wasn't crowded. He never complained, however—for the pleasure the red house rendered to Mae, who was from County Kerry and for whom New Orleans had never been the perfect fit in thirty years.

On summer evenings, when walking past the "little house," they'd stepped into the yard to peek in through the wobbly panes, assessing the ancient, empty kitchen with the hand pump that probably still worked; the boarded-up hearth in the parlor—the great gouges in the ceiling where some fixture had hung. "It's an outright haggard," Mae had said. "A decent *coop* for chickens, one of which I'm not. At least yet." Here there *was*, however, a beach with a path the caretaker kept mowed through the rosa rugosas and bayberries. The owners occasionally mentioned selling, Fenderson said, but were true Mainers. Scotch Irish. "They die clutching their first penny. And they don't sell *en-uh-thin*." He knew Mae was from the west and said it for her benefit.

In any case, the little house was deemed rude and too small. And neither wanted the carrying charges for only a month a year, and couldn't imagine renters like themselves. "You'd end up torchin' it just to get free," Mae'd said, as they walked back up the road. "Which you could say about most places." "Lawyers never buy unless there's no other choice," Boyce had said. By the day after Labor Day, they'd upped stakes and gone back, never coming round to the subject through the long winter following.

Deciding, then, to take the little house for August was, Peter Boyce knew, only chronic restivenesses brought on by Mae's death. Grief, he realized, had evolved into jittery, inner, barely governable clamor—a sensation he didn't recognize in himself but did in others. He was never impatient about anything. Impatience, he believed, was a form of laziness. And he'd certainly have never come to Maine without Mae's "felt need" for a respite from "the pinks"—her term for his set of old New Orleans friends, who were all in the pink. But restiveness about what? Of course about Mae, that she must soon come back and all of life to carry on—even the Maine part. Or otherwise do what? Follow her greedy example? There was no thought for that. He'd read the line of Trollope's many times over, the first winter alone in the house on Sixth Street. "There is an unhappiness so great that the very fear of it is an alloy to happiness." Did it mean, he wondered, that happiness would never again be within his grasp? Or, with grief as its alloy, happiness would come back fiercer? Alloy. It was two-minded. This would be the challenge of loss—to learn about this.

He'd decided against coming back the first summer. Mae had taken her life a week past the middle of August, and he'd brought her home and buried her—fully conscious that for a girl born in Catholic Tralee to be buried in suburban Metairie, Louisiana, an alien place (and improperly in Catholic ground) was at the least inglorious and incongruous. Though she'd never gone home to Ireland—not once—even when her parents died, and had left no instructions about her "obsequious details." There didn't seem to be a wrong thing to do. Here, he could visit her, if he wanted to. Which so far he hadn't.

But after Thanksgiving the first year, a winterish fatigue had set in and lasted past Carnival. Nothing surprising. Walter Hobbes, a partner in another firm, invited him for a fishing excursion with other men. To Duck Key. But he'd declined. He liked being in his house—even alone, only blocks from where he'd grown up on Coliseum Street. Reading late into the night was a luxury. Finishing the Trollope. Then commencing the Forster and the Woolf—this generation he liked for its spirited lack of certainty. With grief and thoughts of Mae crashing about, he read to replenish time, not for pleasure or a hunger to learn. He was, he knew, bookishly practical. He tended to see most occurrences as happening the way they should—which required sealing many things away. Mae's death.

Though being bookish meant that whatever you read, the mind went to the places it needed to go. An unwilled reaching. In spring, only to quit thinking, he bought a bicycle, rode it on the levee and around the park. Somehow, a year and a half managed to escape un-observed.

When the second spring came, he found himself

thinking of the red house. Next door were the year-round, scotch-drinking Parkers—an Episcopal "prelate, retired" (Mae's words) from Connecticut. Parker's wife Patty had been caught by Mae geezing her from their upstairs bathroom, as Mae sunned on a towel in the grass. "And whut then? The old muff sniffer?" Mae'd said. "As if I'd put the whole product line out on the street." But in the red house, Boyce knew, he'd only have paced the rooms, rehearsing what'd been said and seen in this one and that, dinners eaten, wines drunk, who'd imitated who more uproariously, Mae playing Debussy and Satie. Polly had already declared she'd never again set foot in the red house. Now divorced, she'd paid a visit home in April, sat on the back gallery and opined that her father needed to find a new place wherein to re-invent himself. Maine was corrupted now, and emptied out by death. She seemed unusually certain about his grief. Twenty-eight and already an unhappy lawyer in Chicago, she'd thrust herself into the cultural life, subscribed to the opera, enrolled Phoebe in ballet and Chinese, was entertaining thoughts of a new career in arts administration. In New Zealand, possibly. This was her way, Boyce supposed, to manipulate and disapprove of him by example. They'd never gotten on well. Even for Mae she'd been a task. A pretty, clear-skinned, long-limbed "Irish" girl of fifteen, who adored school and had friends (Mae had named her Niambh, for bright and radiant), she'd matured unhappily. Put on weight. Become caustic in her views. She had a cruel mouth—a Dublin shopgirl's mouth, Mae said—and an outlook in keeping. "There's just so much you can do," Mae said. Polly had changed her name after college ". . . to something civilized. Niambh. What's Niambh?"

On the phone in March, Boyce had contacted Fenderson—this time, about the "little house," the older farm place at the end of Cove Road. The Birney house, it was called. He hadn't thought he would, and then he simply did think it. It seemed necessary. Fenderson's wife was the town clerk. She could arrange the fixing up, give the house a scrubbing, take the sooty curtains down, fashion a patch for the ceiling, see the sinks worked, find lamps, a reading lamp for the bed—was there a bed (there was). There'd always been decent window light and the same, fond breezes off the water. No mosquitoes. No Parkers. The distant owners agreed. Boyce could bring up extra things in the car, buy what else he needed. He had no better plans.

Mae had died in the red house. In early '06, she'd suffered "a bout of the breast-type cancer"—which seemed to go away. A small surgery, no chemo. They made their plans for August. Then very fast there was a new *site* in the spring, which brought down the onslaught—sickening poisons, enfeebling radiation, hair vanished. But no more surgery. Mae sat in bed on Sixth Street through the early summer, watched the Iraq war on TV, ate yogurt (what she could keep down), didn't play the piano, didn't offer her lessons, didn't go out, became mottle-skinned, lost weight, rigorously demanded Boyce massage her back—which all of a sudden felt like cardboard with nothing behind it. She determined with complete certitude she was going to die, though Boyce assured her she very well might not, that the local New Orleans doctors were up on cancer. Slowly her hair grew back gray, though she kept it short now, where before it had been heavy and long and brown and luxuriant.

Mae's English father, Jack Purcell, had been a poet and a church organist—a relative of the *great* Purcell. In London, he'd prepared for a career in pharmacy, but had met a West Kerry girl, who would not stay in England *or* go to America. If he loved her, there would be a move required. He could set up as a chemist in Ballybunion, play the organ in church, write his ditties—which he happily did. Mae, though—his prize—he sent away to relatives in Boston. She'd soon come to study music at Princeton, where she'd met slender, rather delicate Peter Boyce from New Orleans. Soon, the mother left the father and fell back in with her old footballer, Owen. "It was the way things worked in such backward places," Mae said. She'd never taken to her mother. Never thought being Irish was anything. In America, she'd changed her name from Maeve to Mae, the way Polly had changed hers. She'd early on told Peter Boyce that her face—the standard, piano teacher's plum pudding face—was too round when it should've been sculptured; the eyes "too apart," an all-too-unkind mingle of her father's muted English features and her mother's brute, rural ones. Being Irish, she said, was "an underlying condition. A common and dismal accident of origin that foretold a mediocre end." He had never agreed, thought she was handsome and earthy and beautiful in her way.

Though the minute she was sick, to Peter Boyce's surprise, she embraced it all again—the Irish. "You come back for it," she said, whether you ever wanted it before, or it wanted you. It seemed to please her for a little while.

After the new siege in June, Mae became sullen. She began to curse broadly—whereas before she hadn't. She said withering things about, and sometimes to, the parents of her piano students, who complained about the lessons ceasing. She uttered terrible things about New

Orleans, about Peter's law partners and their wives, and all their friends. The pinks. She began staying in bed, listening to Rush Limbaugh, denounced her previous moderate politics as crap, supported the war, said she'd be voting for Bush, and might divorce Boyce if he didn't shape up. "I've invented you, anyway. I've needed to," she said—which he thought might be true. "I can, very well, un-invent you." Her drugs were setting loose a depression, her oncologist Dr. Milly said (though Mae didn't seem depressed). A husband needn't take offense. Just go along with whatever. Drive to Maine. Things would improve. They'd see.

Early summer nights, though, Mae roamed their big house, flipping on lights, turning up the TV too loud—would sometimes be naked—making sounds (groans) he couldn't interpret. She spoke to people who weren't there. "Could you very kindly just *not* do *that*!" he heard her shout out from all the way upstairs, so he wondered was someone there. "Take the one at the top. The feckin' *top*!" She went on. Another time, "And *why* is it, again? Just tell me. I'm not battling anything. Nor am I brave. Just tell me, you cunt. Because you're desperate. That's why. You've lost the feckin' run of yourself."

Still, old Milly told Boyce, her chances of surviving

were well north of fair. Something else was besetting her. The drugs possibly.

What Boyce came to find out, too late, was that Mae had stockpiled her pain pills—which had always made her slightly loony. She'd discreetly requested more and stronger as they were making plans for Maine. Later he understood, though not very well, that Mae had worked herself into a space all her own, and for reasons all her own—past bleakness and cancer. A place of controlling her fate. She'd actually never been in pain much. Milly simply hadn't paid attention.

She'd all at once, then, become completely fervent about leaving for Maine. The cool would be tonic compared to New Orleans (which did no one a bit of good). She'd become prettier, he noticed. "Rather like the 'Girl With a Tinsel Scarf,' don't you think?" she said, referring to the old print her mother had kept pinned up in the house in Ballybunion. "It's simple," she said. "I just need to die to regain me youthful blush." She told Peter she'd now display the full product line for Patty Parker, once arrived. For him as well.

In July, she ceased letting Milly come and was restless to be off, felt exhilarated. She now neglected to flush toilets, became hostile toward Boyce, and toward

Polly, who came to visit but left shaken. Once, in the living room, standing naked alongside the baby grand she no longer played, looking starkly pretty and thin and self-possessed in her bobbed hair, she said to Peter Boyce, "You see, I simply haven't lived enough in history. Didn't capitalize properly on my music talent. It's your fault, sweetheart. You're a layered, privacy person. A man with measures and reserves. You think you'll get to experience life over again. Whereas, I—I live as though I never lived it even once." Neither was true, he believed.

They made the drive up in three days. Virginia. Connecticut. Across the pretty bridge, leaving New Hampshire. She pointed out where the Bushes lived—"in everyday splendor and are probably there, now, being decent." The red house was cleaned and readied for them. Fenderson's wife had stocked the fridge, bought wine, polished the windows. Old Parker came politely over to say they'd be inviting them soon. He made no mention of Mae's bobbed hair. They had their kids coming. And guests. It'd be a while. Just settle in. The month would fly by.

"I'm definitely feeling something lift off," Mae said in the very first hour, seated at the back window, facing the lawn and the sea. "Some burden. So strange. Isn't it, Pietro?" She sometimes called him that now, as she had when they were young. "Nothing's quite fitted together for me for months. But just in this moment. It's grand." She was wearing loose-fitting, green cotton trousers. A coarse, brown homespun shirt. She was less large now—like a boy, he thought. "Chimera," Mae said brightly. "We think it means something terrible and scary. But it really just means when things don't fit right. Possibly that's the worst there can be." She smiled to him across the living room. He'd been bringing in suitcases.

"It's how they taught us in law school," Boyce said, happy for a close-to-normal exchange. "Logic, reason, rationality—it's not discovered, it's made up." He smiled back at her. "You *make* things fit."

"That wasn't at all what I was on about," Mae said, the smile gone off her features. She was already elsewhere, only seeming to address him. "You understand everything the way you understand them, my darling. It's fine."

In the early days of August, Mae became much of her old self. *Robust* was her word, as if she'd gained back weight and stamina, which she had not. But cracking jokes, moving around the red house with spirit, humming in the bathroom, going to the village in the car, shopping, sitting in the gazebo, dialing Polly in Chicago, buying the Boston papers, going down to the Parkers' little beach and gathering sea glass—she was as if restored. She slept more—though was still up all hours. She told Boyce she noticed in the village that people talked *so much.* In the market, they bleated and bleated on. It was epidemic. She sat at the old Kimball on the sun porch and played and sang along to the romantic Irish airs her father had written to woo her mother. "A complete bollix, it should be pointed out." Irish was her outlook now. Much more than when she was a girl. She'd changed completely once, and now would change again.

She wished also to make love—and often—which made him happy but also disoriented him and seemed a sign of something, since she was never much enthused before. He still massaged her feet and back where she hurt, put cream on her shoulders and arms as if she'd become young. They took walks down the road, past the little house, but didn't venture close now. Boyce felt he wasn't really performing anything helpful—just being conducive. Whatever was fostering her life, she was driving it.

On August twentieth, one of the foggy days when water on the bay was featureless and flat, and mosquitoes were about in the saturated air—the sort of day no one liked—Mae was expressing a craving for sweet white melons, found only at the farm stand in Warren. They could make it "a nice adventure," she said. Later they could buy oysters at the monger and be home before dark. She'd sat in bed being pensive. She'd rarely talked about being ill since they'd arrived. "You wouldn't deny an emaciated and sickly Spouse Mouse her wish, would you," she said. "You couldn't. A sallow, pretty girl like me."

Boyce was tired from having had a walk. There was food already in the house, melons in the village. Later, he wondered if he might even have understood. Without knowing.

He'd backed their car out the red garage while Mae got herself dressed. Though when she came to the side door, wearing pink flamingo slippers and her striped housecoat, her face was blotchy, as if something was exciting her. She'd put on lipstick. "I won't be much fun, today, Pietro," she said. "I'm a little blue, and I might turn on you. Set you quaking. I do crave a sweet melon, though. Could be the difference between life and a cruel, slow death for me. Bring us back supper, too. And hurry on. Sorry for the false alarm." She wanted him to be in the car and driving away. Not turning back. She was mirthful—not blue—her fluffy foot on the stone step of the side door, her housecoat gapped, revealing a bit of white under-cloth and her pale thighs. She waved, shook her head when he waved back, easing their car into the road as she disappeared inside, hurrying through the rooms of the red house. Spouse Mouse.

From the beginning, when he brought things from the car into the Birney house, opening cabinets and closets, trying the cellar door, running the taps, airing the rooms—from the beginning Mae's sudden absence had been bludgeoning; shocking for her to be missing, even from a house where she'd never set a foot down. Though for an instant, then, it became almost a relief, her absence a comfort, a presence. And then the abject gallows-drop of clear fact.

In the first days he simply walked the sparse rooms he and Mae had peeked in through the wobbly windows. The rooms seemed larger. He spoke words, his heart sometimes racketing. "Yes,"—to something. And "It turned out he liked it after all, though it wasn't big." And, "She had of course never been inside." Addressing who? Afterward, he sat out on the granite step, calmer, smoking—indulgent, musing, self-conscious. He did not want to live something over again. She'd been in error there. Which didn't mean it was all so simple.

On rich autumn college days, they'd embarked from Old Nassau on their "Driving America Tours." Across the Delaware into the Pennsylvania countryside, mile on mile. Small villages, large ones, river hamlets, fields, farms, dams, factory husks—ruminating life like cartographers, the country foreign to them both. More than once they'd spied a house at the back end of some dusty cornfield—marooned, paint peeling, roof going, windows out. The family departed. They'd exit the car, walk the road, just to step inside over broken glass, beams opened where ceilings had fallen, floors rotted to open earth, laths shining through plaster. Then up the dangling stairs to bedrooms—ruined couches, cribs, stacked picture frames, piles of magazines, fixtures sawed off, a window, a view to the field, a small hill, a distant town with a water tower bumping the sky, vultures swaying, deer staring back.

They were much alike. They were evidence. To Peter Boyce, these houses solemnized possibility. Life to reclaim. In his young and loss-fretful way, he believed people could come back, their places waiting for them. "To abandon it all," he said once to Mae Purcell, age nineteen. "A house must mean *something*." He'd worked a triangle of window glass out of its dry glazing and spun it out into the air, down among the corn tassels. They wished to conduct serious talks. This was their purpose.

Mae rolled her eyes. She was short of graceful. Sturdy. A pianist with strong hands that could do an octave-two. Already smarter than he would become. "It's utterly common in Ireland," she said. *Or-land,* her way of saying it. "*You* see the world in terms of always having another whack, don't you?" She turned away. "My mam's great-gran got chucked out by a Welsh cattle drover. Pushed into the sea. Means *something*? Means *nothing* to me. You'd make a very good . . ."

". . . I'd make a good what?" Peter Boyce said, eager to know what he'd someday make in her eyes. "What would I make a very good?" He loved her already, believed she loved him.

"I could say a priest. Or an old, conserving Englishman. I hate priests, though, and have mixed views of the English, due to me pap. Say a *husband,* then. All right? For somebody reckless and stupid enough." This satisfied her. "You'd be rubbish as a farmer, for sure. You never know when you're banjaxed." It had been their way even at the beginning. The Birney house carried a memory of those afternoons. He hadn't planned for it.

After a week in the house, Boyce began sleeping poorly, and when he did sleep, he dreamed Mae was alive, and woke up sweating. After which lying awake induced unkind interrogations. What had he done wrong? Why, very much indeed, did she do this? Suicide was a clear choosing-to-go—not only an aggressive act of selfish spite. More an act of independence and disobedience. Mae had always helped order his thoughts. But they were disordered now. Things not fitting properly. A chimera.

He therefore began a routine—going to bed early, taking a glass of Stoli from the freezer, leaving a light in the stairwell, listening to the Red Sox and the CBC, reading 'til sleep found him. He'd brought only *Mrs. Dalloway*. A choice made at the last minute for length. He'd read it in college, remembered almost nothing. A party and some foppish man from India no one liked, except Mrs. Dalloway. Or was that the one set in Cornwall? Not much headway made, in any case—though she was scarcely an interesting woman to put in the middle of a novel. Conceivably, that had been the point.

Sometimes in his pajamas, he'd walk barefoot down and out into the yard and stand in the cold grass at two A.M. and listen, breathe in the sulfurous reek of ocean, the night humming. Something often crashed in the underbrush, emitting a gasp. Bird wings fluttered in the privets. Cars sped past on the state road. Staccato voices drifted up from the beach, then laughter. Wooden oars clattering. A foghorn. He was, he felt, entirely who and how someone would expect him to be in these moments. Alert. No need to invent himself. He recognized who he was here.

Arriving to the red house each August, he and she had at once adopted—and treasured—the formalities of instant residence. Suitcases popped open, windows thrown back to air the bug-spray tang out of closed-up rooms. Then putting beds in order, hanging their own towels, unboxing kitchen utensils. The eager, precise routines, followed by a calm-but-bracing exhale to the spirit of belonging-for-now. Then the first bottle of Pouilly from the cooler, the first-day sun going below the trees and the bay. The chime of church bells from the village. All of it very, very full. Some people are born full—which was how everyone at home thought of Mae. *Too* full, the Parkers would've thought and said privately. Noisy. Playing Vivaldi too loud. Handing out looks. Taking the piss. Now this was missing. The note she'd written for him, left on the dining room table—found when he returned with the melons (she must've laughed when he'd gone, and she was left busy with herself). "Better, you know, to die in a house you don't own than one you do." A joke to excuse everything. Which it did not.

In the second week, someone went into his car at night, forced the glove box, took nothing, even loose change, but inscribed, "Go way" on the trunk surface using a sharp edge. He rang the sheriff, who came but said it might've been there on the drive up. Another day when he came from mailing off probate documents, he thought someone had been in the kitchen, but couldn't be certain. A different smell in the air. Sweat. Then one early morning before light, he'd heard a car door close and someone walking in the grass under his window. A metal "*tink, tink, tink*" that made his heart pound. He came down the lighted stairs in pj's and pulled open the front door. Suddenly. He would never have done it in New Orleans—stood empty-handed to face an intruder. You got killed that way.

A man was in the rectangle of light cast onto the grass. A man he'd maybe seen in the village. He only knew shopkeepers, the postmistress, Giles at the Gulf. They never admitted knowing him. The figure in the yard wore a wet suit, carried diving gear—a metal tank (*tink, tink, tink*). A spear gun, flippers, and a mask.

"Goin' fishin'. Okay with you?" The man spoke

in their singsongy way—as if the two of them knew each other and now was the result of that. The man squinted in the light, smiling or scowling. “Wife useta live in your house,” he said, then paused as if Boyce had begun to say something. “Rentin’ here, are ya?” The silver spear gun had its spear loaded in.

“I used to rent the red house up the road,” Boyce said. “But yes.” The man was bowlegged, short, crudely muscled under his rubber suit. He was out of place here.

“*Your* wife died, didn’t she?” He wasn’t seeking permission for something.

Boyce’s eyes stung from sleep. “Yes. Two summers ago. She did.”

“Don’t mean to be particular,” the man said. His posture had changed. He’d relaxed. Causing someone discomfort made him feel more himself.

Boyce had put on the terry-cloth robe he’d found behind the bathroom door. A woman’s.

“I’ll leave you a tautog, if you’d eat it.”

“What’s that? A tautog,” Boyce said.

“A blackfish,” the man said and grinned in an unfriendly way. They never told you their names. “A rare Maine maritime delicacy,” he said. “Not really.” His teeth weren’t as bad as some.

“I’ll eat one,” Boyce said, feeling stunned.

“Oh. Okay. So will I.” The man kept grinning, then

started across the yard as if something had been determined, leaving his tracks in the dew, heading toward the beach path. *Tink, tink, tink, tink.*

"And thank you, by the way," Boyce said.

"Hm-hm," the man might've said, but nothing else.

Polly came at the end of the second week. She had lawyer business in Boston and drove up in a rental. There was a new "friend" now, in Boston. She was thinking of moving there. Terry had decently given his permission to take Phoebe with her, out of Chicago. Things in her life appeared to be brightening. There was no mention of New Zealand and of arts administration.

Polly, however, was instantly disagreeable. She didn't like the little house, though she'd insisted he abandon the red house. The fact that her mother had never visited or even been inside the little house made her for some reason resentful—as if Boyce were having an easy time coping with her mother's absence, was luxuriating in giving up on Mae's memory, re-inventing himself already, which she'd advised that he do. No one grieved the same, he thought. Which was good. But everyone grieved. He felt tolerant toward her. Though, in fact, he *didn't* feel lonely—not in any way he comprehended lonely to be. He felt only underused.

Polly *did* like the little beach when they walked to it at dusk. Boyce wore old green cords, a denim shirt, and sneakers to make himself less like her father than a friend. Polly's mother was dead. He was the surviving parent. Possibly his life was unknowable to her now. Which he didn't wish.

Polly smoked a cigarette—which was new—and toed the sand for sea glass while Boyce sat on a rock and watched. It was chilly, and the beach stank. Millions of tiny bugs thrived in the caked seaweed. There was a milk carton, bits of charred wood, a green-striped lobster buoy broken in two. The ocean was full of crap. When he came down to read and have his morning coffee, he always expected to find a body washed up.

Polly'd added more weight. She wore very tight blue jeans that weren't helping. She'd sprayed a streak of metallic red into her hair, which was pulled severely back. Across the water somewhere, a nail gun popped, then the whine of a power saw. A new house going up out of sight. A Coast Guard buoy-tender sat at anchor a mile out. The two of them waited and looked at the horizon and the open, still-bright ocean. The water was already too cold to swim—which Polly wouldn't have done, though once she'd swum and loved it.

On the walk back, Peter picked a capful of blackberries for dessert and showed Polly the old stone wall in the undergrowth and the lost road that led to the concrete pillbox from when U-boats had surfaced on moonless nights and put spies ashore to disappear into America. The pillbox interior was cold and piss-smelling when they stepped in, and had been used for sex. Polly turned away in the low door opening and drew a breath. "Why would you show me this?" she said and was angry.

"I expected it to be different," Boyce said. "I'm sorry." He'd meant to come and look inside before he brought her but had forgotten.

He served them dinner at the metal table, under the dim kitchen globe—steaks, squash, tomatoes off the truck. He had Sancerre, which he thought she liked. He was trying to display for Polly his adaptability, which would argue for his presence here. That he was not unknowable—only a layered, privacy person as her mother had said. What was wrong with it? Grief needn't be any more natural for him than for her. Did everything have to occur on the visible surface?

Polly sat with her elbows fixed on her chair arms, turning occasionally to look out the window through which light shone on the lawn and the rose thickets. She pulled at strands of her brown and red hair, drank the Sancerre. She'd pulled her hair as a little girl. Mae had judged this unattractive, like standing with your mouth agape or going in your nose. "You'll soon go bald as an apple," she'd said.

He was prepared for Polly to voice displeasure—over something—yet went on eating his steak. Polly spoke guardedly about her new boyfriend, Hugh, whom she'd met through opera acquaintances. He was forty-eight, lived in Truro, played clarinet in a Dixieland band, kept a boat in Eastham. She talked warmly about Terry, whose parents lived in Winnetka, were retired Navy with time on their hands. They had seen more of Phoebe than he and Mae had, which Polly resented. He and Mae were not good grandparents. Phoebe was sweet and smart, looked like Boyce's mother as a child. He said he wished Polly would bring her up. Next year, possibly.

Boyce looked at Polly across the table—charitably, he hoped. Pauses had become ringing. Polly was acting as if her point of view were being ignored—which it wasn't. She drank too much, that was clear, which added pounds. So odd, he thought, to have raised an unhappy child, when he and Mae had been happy throughout. What could you say? "If you aren't careful, being disappointed will become your whole character." Mae might've said that—like pulling her hair. He wished she'd stayed married to Terry, whom he liked.

Eventually, Polly put her wineglass down on the table a little too hard. She could be what she wanted. But he'd liked her best as a pretty, chatty college sophomore in a sorority.

"So, what interests you, Peter?" she said—meanly he felt. He didn't wish to think about his *interests,* which were finding a way to live that didn't seem stupid or implausible or heartbreaking. Though why talk about it? "I'm reading *Mrs. Dalloway,*" he said. "And I'm pleased being in this house because there's so little to do that's difficult." He had an urge to laugh, but laughing would've accused Polly. Which he also didn't wish to do.

Her eyes snapped at him. "Doesn't it seem strange that my mother, your wife, killed herself right down the road, and you're here all by yourself, renting this shitty little house like some old queer bachelor? What's wrong with you, Peter?" She'd never called him Peter. But for so long she'd never called him any name.

"Why does it make you angry how I am?" he said.

"I'm just curious." She was angry at everything.

Then the words did find a way to his lips, like speaking in Mae's voice. Everyone contained the voice of their spouse. Spouse Mouse. "I'm just learning how to get along, darling. Like you are. It's only been two years. There aren't any books to tell you specifically about two years. Maybe *Mrs. Dalloway.*" He didn't know why he said that. He heard Mae say it. Like an instruction.

The muscles in Polly's jaw rose and subsided, then rose. Why would she drive up here to punish him? "What does *that* mean?" she said stiffly.

"I don't know," he said. "Your mother and I were married such a long time. We loved each other very much. You mustn't feel excluded." Polly stood abruptly, picked up her plate and his, carried them to the porcelain sink, and again made too much racket setting things down. "What would you *like* me to do?" he said. He wanted this to be over. Death cast a too-long shadow.

"Be normal. Does that seem strange?"

"This *is* normal. I'm just not doing what you're doing. Just not your way. That's all. I'm not angry."

She ran the sink water to hot. "I'm sorry I asked you anything." There was the cruel mouth her mother lamented. The shopgirl.

"Don't be sorry," he said. Then he almost said, "I'm your father." Or possibly, "I'm *still* your father." But didn't, though at some prior moment, he supposed he should've.

"I *am* sorry," Polly said, her back to him.

And that *was* the end of it. They didn't eat the berries he'd picked. He wondered, later, as he climbed into a cold bed, if every single thing between them would always be about Mae, who'd left life because she wished to stay no longer—having things her way. They weren't betraying her by living—a thought that *did* fit. Polly, who'd brought nothing to give him, had brought a small bit of clarity.

In the middle of the night, he lay listening to sounds out of doors. Polly was moving around the downstairs. The front door opened, the hiss of her feet in the grass the way he'd heard the tautog man. Polly was phoning—the musical little beeps ceasing at ten. He smelled her cigarette. She spoke in a tired, sad, defenseless voice: "Hi. It's me." A pause. Then, "Of course. No." Pause again. "I just needed to hear you." Pause. "You know that. I do. Go to sleep. He is. Yes. Typical." Then a beep, followed by her feet moving in the grass again, pushing back into the house—a different woman from the one he'd had dinner with.

In the morning, Polly said little. Just some details about Phoebe's school. A word about her work with insurance clients. He cooked breakfast. Then, the moment she was finished, she left back to Boston. He wondered if he could've done something to please her. Possibly not.

Summer, he noticed, was departing. August was the beginning of autumn in Maine. Afternoon light bent through the spruces from changed angles and warmed the scrubbed wood floors. Clouds grew large, the euonymus redder. The hydrangea tree bloomed suddenly, and the last of the daylilies dried on their stems. He liked it. So different from the south, though of course it had happened every year they'd been here. The breeze was already cooler—a vein of cold to come. When, he wondered, would it be winter? Things he hadn't noticed.

The caretaker-agent, Fenderson, came to mow the grass and put plastic geraniums in the window boxes. He was tall and gaunt and wrinkled, with dense white hair and reckless teeth. Some impenetrable deceptiveness was in him—same as the lobstermen, the hardware clerks, the librarian. One thing had made them all. He'd been a coach, gone to Dartmouth on the GI Bill, was a selectman in the village.

They talked a moment in the yard, then without asking, Fenderson walked straight into the house, brought out a red-lettered FOR SALE sign from the cellar and, sparing more comment, hammered it in the ground at the driveway turn-in. The owner, he allowed, had been married a number of times in her life. He smiled about this. Sometimes, for reasons to do with her unconventional life, she experienced the need to sell. This, at least, was his belief. Having a renter had possibly encouraged the urge. Though in a while the sign would come down. You'd need to raze the place and start over on bare ground, Fenderson said, climbing back in his old Ford. A tiny white poodle took up its place in Fenderson's lap. For some reason, Fenderson said then that his family had immigrated from County Cavan. Ballyhaise. "Scotch Irish," he said through the window and leered as if something was uncouth. "They die clutchin' their first penny." Fenderson had forgotten he'd said that to Mae when she was alive.

It rained for three days around the eighteenth, and when it stopped and turned humid and warm, Boyce decided that the house now being for sale was perhaps a communiqué—of a sort. Another piece of evidence. He hadn't asked the price—though nothing went cheap by the ocean. If you elected *not* to bull-doze the house, much would be required. Floors. Drywall over the rotted laths. Windows needing replacing. Footings restored. All the ceilings had brown continent-shaped stains from the leak-through. The roof would need to go. The inside had smelled of cats when it rained.

Down in the corner of the half-dirt cellar, among old FOR SALE signs, he found an ancient Wehrle beside a riddled oil-burner disconnected from the registers, plus a scuttle box holding coal. There were dusty bicycles, assorted moldy luggage, telephones of all vintages, two doorless refrigerators, abundant signs of animal activity, boxes of canning jars, oily tools in a metal cabinet, a bassinet, several boat oars, plastic Christmas trees, a stack of tattered American flags once flown from the metal pole in the yard. There was also a padlocked closet, the hasp of which was loose so the screws slid out. Inside it was an old bolt-action .22, and a stack of Joan Baez songbooks. He thought, standing in the gloom, it would all go. The house had carried distinction, was acceptable (merely) to a much-married woman's family—the Birneys—but not enough for them to stay. Unlike his great, columned house on Sixth, the meaning of this little house had been exhausted. To think of caring for it was only a spasm, a displacement for something ineffable. Means something, means nothing.

Boyce called the Parkers to ask them for supper. The tautog man had left a second slab of fish on the step—there, when he'd waked up, its gills still pulsing.

Parker's wife was formal on the phone, as if his having married a suicide—who'd performed her odious, unchristian savagery right next door—was a badge of degradation. They still "had" her family—until after Labor Day, she said—when, she supposed, he'd be turning back to "where was it? One of the 'M' states." Boyce said—without meaning it—that he was weighing buying the Birney house. "Oh, you *should,* definitely," Patty Parker said brightly. Then, abruptly, she asked how he was *doing*—as if he'd been ill. When the ambulance arrived to take Mae, she and old Amory had stood beside their mailbox watching, looking pinched. They'd never said a word to console him. New Englanders. He had no idea why he'd have dinner with them. Mae had said they were ghouls. "High-drawer Anglicans. Worse even than Catholics for not *being* Catholics."

Patty informed him that the people who'd taken the red house were from Maryland. They were also black. "Well-spoken. Polite." ". . . some strange Scottish name." McDowell. They seemed happy to be left alone, she said. "Well . . ." with finality, ". . . it's just all strange, isn't it, Peter? Life. It goes on. 'The nearest friends go with anyone to death comes so far short,' doesn't it? It's Frost. I love him. Don't you?"

"Yes," Boyce said and did not know that poem. She was being self-justifying.

"Didn't you go to Princeton?"

"I did," Boyce said. "Class of seventy-two."

"I thought," she said. She imagined she was smiling, he knew, but wasn't. Patty Parker had been an English teacher in Darien or some such monied sanctum. Had gone to Storrs. He didn't need to talk to her again. They managed good-bye.

On the twentieth—the second anniversary of Mae's death—Peter Boyce went down to the beach with his coffee, intending to read deeply into *Mrs. Dalloway* before the morning tide. He didn't find Clarissa Dalloway intriguing, if he was supposed to. Petty and not particularly smart—even if not completely uninteresting to read about. He liked the once-handsome suitor, Peter Walsh better (not surprisingly), although he seemed to be a great narcissist. Clouds were lifting off the bay where there'd been grainy August fog before. A breeze had materialized. A single-hand lobsterman sat a quarter mile out in his skiff, his wife in the stern reading her own book. And farther—fourteen miles—Monhegan, its western cliffs white in the sun.

They'd all gone jollily there, once, with Mississippi friends—the Clubbs—who got seasick both ways. Madeline Clubb found a deer tick on her inner thigh on the way back and demanded to go to the hospital.

They'd never gone again. "Art colonies on islands," Mae said, "were always rubbish." Non-hegan, she'd called it. Boyce thought islands were mostly inconvenient. The mainland almost always better.

He took out a Toscano and lit it so its smoke mingled with the fog clinging to the beach, where tide had carpeted the sand with vegetation and chunks of wood from a storm at sea. He thought, then, of just odd things—nothing anchored to coherence. You really needn't think about things always head-on, Boyce believed, and put his book on a rock, almost finished with his coffee. Mae's dark-day anniversary required *some* observing. Give sorrow words, etc. But it was one other lasting lesson of the law that one shouldn't *search* for answers. The needle was never in the haystack; the needle *was* the haystack. Old Timmerman had written that on the board in torts. Eliminate everything something's *not,* and there the solution will be—death being the sovereign *knot.* That's what he felt he was doing being here. Eliminating what Mae (and Mae's death) was not. It's what Polly wouldn't see.

His mind ran on . . . Mae had been a poor housekeeper. Over time she'd let herself get fat—her *winteridge.* She'd been the one who shouted "Woo-hoo" at poetry readings and recitals, which always embarrassed him. She was never confident he—"Lawyer Boyce"—

was living life fully enough. (Which she clearly also thought about herself.) Though he felt he was and always had. His firm was the top one. The learnéd firm. White shoe. Just five of them, to keep things sleek; each with a strong book. All good schools. Any one of them could've been something extraordinary—a classicist, a concert musician, a war correspondent, a famous architect—but had chosen the law, with its great subversive allure. He himself wrote the occasional bittersweet Cheeveresque short story, which he only showed to a few. He loved New Orleans. Either you did or you didn't. Which had never been simple for Mae, who'd never connected. "A simple Irish girl amongst the pinks," she'd said. Being *married* to her had also never been simple. Though they'd made the most—she, teaching piano spiritedly, raising a daughter less well. Being his interesting, unexpectable, out-of-the-ordinary Irish wife. All in all they'd made a life that sheltered them. What else was there?

Why think of *that* now, though? Things happen that seem life-altering, then everything grinds down to being bearable—sometimes slightly better. Which could be a formula for doing anything you fuck-all wanted; or that nothing ever meant much—which he did *not* accept for an instant. Estates, real property, wills—they meant things, were the deep heart of the law. Still. Who ran their own brain? Your brain ran you. He should've told Polly *that*. It would've relieved her. It's what "normal" was. Perhaps he *had* said it.

Down the beach—far down where rocks formed a prominence, close to where the red house sat just above—someone (a man and a boy) were fishing in the slack tide. The man, tall, in yellow Bermudas, was showing the boy how to fling the bait, demonstrating it clumsily, then letting the boy take the rod—who did it with more grace and success, the bait arcing through the misty air and plopping down. The man stood back and watched as the boy reeled in, then cast again with the same ease. A large woman in a big white hat sat beside a little girl on the rocks behind them. She was pointing and talking with approval. These were the black people who'd rented the red house and wished to be happy alone. Reasonably enough. Doubtless they knew nothing of the prior tenant's wife's taking a hundred Vicodins in the same bed where their children were sleeping. Patty Parker could always inform them as they were departing to assure they wouldn't return. He would've paid them a call, walk down, attempt a rapport. But it wouldn't be fair. The story would have to come up.

He thought for a while then about his dad. Their epic fishing trips to Michigan. The old man, a business type—large, laughing, frequently drunk—half-nuts on a good day, his mother said before divorcing him. On the Au Sable in his ancient Hodgman's, carrying his custom Paul Young and a mahogany net—his father would clamber out of their canoe, the painter rope knotted round his waist, and let the canoe pull him downstream, feet skittering across the sandy bottom, while he fished and fished. "I'm getting right down where the big fish are, son," he'd shout, delighted, his big grin, flailing away left and right. If he'd stepped in a hole or stumbled on a rock or missed his footing—that would've been that, in full view of his only son. Though alone in the canoe, reserved little Petey Boyce had been thrilled, laughing and waving at his father, who was always pretending to fall, shouting out "Man overboard." "Save yourselves. Women and children go to hell." He dreamed of it even now, twenty years after they were both gone—his parents. His father, headlong, closer and closer to death. What had he been doing? It was the same one could ask of Mae—with the answer surely different. He was fishing, but he was doing more than fishing. Some great private exhilaration he'd discovered. You'd never find out, even if you'd asked them.

He heard a siren's whoop at an indeterminate distance. A fire in an empty cottage, he thought. Not his. Nothing was left on. He looked above the bank of bushes and rose tangles for a feather of smoke, but saw nothing. The siren came closer, louder. It sounded like on the road, then passed the house. In a moment it whooped a last whoop and stopped.

Boyce took his cup and *Mrs. Dalloway* and reached the house as the sheriff's brown-and-white SUV passed the driveway, headed toward the dead end where a path wound down to the nude beach at Nicholl's Cove—Nipples Cove was the local wit. At night there were parties and music there, which he'd heard from bed.

He left cup and book on the back step and walked to see where the sheriff had gone. People and cars were collected down at the turnaround where kids parked at night—idling back past the house after midnight. Condoms and Kleenex clumps were always scattered about, flattened by car tires. It was a nice, old-fashioned place, Mae'd observed. Kids still did such things—like Ireland. He began to walk down.

An ambulance was there, strobes flashing, rear doors opened. Two technicians were bringing a gurney up from the beach, a blond girl strapped on with a white sheet to her chin. A deputy was assisting. An orange-striped Coast Guard copter was audible, then suddenly visible over the trees.

Citizens had gathered beside the ambulance and

were watching. The bowlegged man who'd left the tautog was there, dressed now in civilian clothes, holding hands with a skinny woman in sunglasses, an old German shepherd beside them. Two small shirtless Asian boys—Hmongs—stood by, arms folded, whispering to each other. And others. Townies. Tatters of fog hung in the vine tangles that sealed the road from the beach. Air was cedar-y and ocean-y, a faint skunk aroma woven through. This was the life of things, Boyce thought, approaching. If you were part of it, this is what you did, talked about, heard, remembered. The day such 'n' such happened on the beach.

The two EMS attendants got on with loading the blond girl into their truck. They were both big and unhealthy-looking, a man and a woman in black shorts and white shirts with red patches and belts full of gear. The girl on the stretcher had a round, surprised face. Her eyes were open, and she was smiling and talking. The ambulance said BELFAST. Another, older deputy was waving his arms, saying "Okay. Stay back, stay back," though nobody was crowding up. The female medic got in the lighted back with the girl, following which the male climbed in the driver's seat. The deputy closed the doors and stood back.

The Hmongs immediately began walking toward the beach trail as if they were no longer interested.

They had fishing rods. The ambulance whooped once, bumped backward to the edge of the undergrowth, clanked down forward, then swayed back up Cod Cove Road, not sounding the siren, lights blinking. It was the same attendants who'd come to take Mae. From Belfast. An uncomforting coincidence for the anniversary. Possibly, of course, he'd misremembered.

"Getting a charge out of our small-town amusements?" the tautog man called out. The deputy was climbing back in his SUV. The other deputy was already inside. The tautog man was shouting as if Boyce didn't hear well. "If them Mungs hadn't seen her, the tide woulda carted her off to Labrador. Drunk, drugs, and whatever." He said it singsongy. A quarter mile away, the ambulance emitted one wild whoop as it found the highway.

The tautog man fixed Boyce in the gaze he'd fixed on him in their early-morning yard encounter. He didn't seem any longer like the muscleman who'd relaxed at the mention of Mae's death. He wore an Hawaiian shirt and cutoffs and was barefoot. His head was buzz-cut like a soldier, and his mouth bore a jagged scar at the side where something had gone extremely wrong quite a while ago. This had been invisible in the darkness. His looks were the kind Mae liked—Neville Brand playing a stevedore. "'Bout time you're headed home, ain't it?" The man offered the same heartless smile. "Down south somewhere? Idn't that it?" He'd been drinking in the morning. His eyes were rheumy and slowed.

"New Orleans," Boyce tried, meaning to be cheerful.

"We know that girl," the skinny sunglasses woman broke in. "Stover." The woman was too skinny, wearing a dirty T-shirt and also cutoffs. She'd had too much time in the sun and other things. Her shirt said PRAISE on the front. Her pointed nose made her features intense and suspicious. Though her brown eyes sparkled. Together, they looked like a pair you'd see having a fight in the street in the French Quarter.

"Could've been like that dead girl down there in Costa Rica or wherever," the skinny woman said. "Him and me were going on a beach walk. We didn't even see her. Them Mungs did."

Mae would run from these two, have her exit line all ready. "*Desolé.* Quiche in the cooker. Better scoot." Later, when they were drinking wine in the gazebo, they would all come up for re-appraisal. "Our personal rustics. The larger community writ small," she'd say. He would be more tactful, would stand now and wait. Though for what to say? The fish? He'd eaten it. It'd been wonderful. In fact, it had gone bad. He'd thrown it away. He'd never been a practiced liar. Lying took effort, then got you in trouble. The elderly dog began wagging its tail as if someone had spoken to it.

"So, are you buying the Birney house, then?" The tautog man weaved a few degrees, toes gripping the road dirt, a pair of busted-out Nikes under his arm. His gaze lacked discipline. He still didn't know the man's name. "Sean," possibly. They were all named Sean.

"No," Peter Boyce said, "just a wild hair."

"And *then* . . . here's *winter*! *Hel*-lo?" The man leered derisively.

"I useta live in that house," the woman said. She let her mouth fall slightly ajar. It was the way she expressed surprise and many other emotions. More words were waiting, but lacked impetus.

"Did you eat that black bass?" the man said. His mouth gaped like the woman's. The terrible scar's effect.

"Yes," Boyce lied. "It was great."

"I bet you didn't. I told *her*." His damp eyes moved up, then down. He knew a lie. It made him feel superior.

"Us two used to be married." The woman had decided what she wanted to say.

"Now we're back dating," the tautog man said, looking cruel.

"Once the fireworks get over, then life begins, I guess," the woman said.

"He knows that. *His* wife died." The man's voice was full of booze. She looked at Peter Boyce and seemed perplexed.

"My husband died," she said. "My *other* one. I'm sorry for your loss."

"Thank you," Boyce said. "I am, too."

A phone began ringing. It made an old-fashioned telephone noise. The dog began gimping toward a green Pinto parked by the path to the beach. The tautog man and the woman shared a look. "We both know who *that'll* be," she said.

"I *certainly* do." The man grinned garishly.

The phone continued louder each time until the woman went off to the car to answer it. She had a wobbly, bent-knee gait from a demanding life. The man, wrecked shoes under his arm, stood in the road, not watching her.

"I hope I see you again," Boyce said. "Thanks for my fish."

"Oh, yeah, you'll see me again," the drunk man said. "Good luck on you, preacherman." He'd confused him with old Parker. It would've made Mae hoot with delight.

Later in the afternoon, as he sat on the doorstep, thinking about his father, he decided now was the right time to leave—on Mae's anniversary. No one else was coming. Twenty hours' drive, and he could wake up in his own bed. Whatever all this he was doing—erecting and defending a redoubt—it wasn't natural; any more than would've been true for his father, the crazy fisherman. It wasn't as if he was young now, or wanting to become something different. Small, graduated adjustments were all he needed. That was why there were attorneys for the world—to assign the best consequences to life's small adjustments. Not that Mae, here or gone, was a small matter. She was now his great subject. But why she'd done what she awfully did was, at this day's end, not business she'd wanted to share. And not business he could do anything about. There was nothing further to learn or imagine or re-invent around here. Love now meant only to take in and agree.

He'd gone to New York the first winter. A client had arranged a stay at a fancy club, where there was a great, gilded library and a heated pool where men swam naked and diplomats were members. In the city, he'd attended several movies and an unmemorable play in the round. The club sponsored trips for the members. To India. Treks across the Pyrenees. St. Petersburg in the spring. Famous retired professors went along and gave lectures. On such trips you met people—women of a suitable age and temper, who weren't merely full of longing. He thought of joining the club to try it out. Though women didn't seem the element missing in life. He knew in advance he'd feel crowded, imposed on, and would quickly slip away without a word. After three days he'd gone home and never thought of joining the club again.

Then last fall in New Orleans, he'd met a woman named Sarah Gaines. A cousin of a partner's wife. They'd had dinner twice at Clancy's, gotten a little tipsy. She worked in FM radio and had the consummate voice. She also knew a great deal about the history of home furnishings and intended to write a book about Scandinavian bric-a-brac. She was regal, rather than pretty. She was fifty but too large in a way he couldn't quit thinking about when he was with her and that made him feel small. A dimple in her pillowy chin continually appeared and disappeared when she spoke. She'd never married, she said. Things had just happened in the wrong sequence. Her dogged unwillingness to move away from where she was born in eastern Ohio. Her devotion to her mother through a long siege of dementia eventuating in death. The unexpected return of her father after twenty years' absence, and then *his* decline. She respected marriage, had desired it, was a lapsed Catholic who liked children. She "adored" New Orleans, she assured him. There was a lot to tell.

However, she seemed to have no interest in him that he could see. She never asked questions. Never mentioned his work or Mae or Polly or Phoebe. She talked, instead, about Ohio and where she'd been to college in Athens, talked about the pressures of her job at the radio station and how it was dog eat dog there, even though it seemed congenial and easygoing. Women, she said, were the hardest to work with, the least trustworthy. Then on their third dinner, at Café Degas, she asked if Boyce would like to come home with her. He thought about it, knowing full well that to think about it was insulting. But he said no. Possibly when he knew her better. Which seemed sensible. Though in the car, she'd begun crying. Was it because he'd said no, he wondered, or because he'd mentioned knowing her better—which plainly he was never going to do, and certainly not once she'd begun crying for some unspecified reason. In the car he experienced a swirling sensation that Sarah Gaines might be going crazy or *had always been* crazy, and that tonight was a scenario repeated throughout her life. He began to find it difficult to breathe in his own car. When he'd walked her to the door of her little condo on Magazine, he'd hugged her awkwardly, then shaken her hand, said good-bye, and drove the short distance to Sixth, feeling exhausted but also contrite, as if he'd been mean and uncaring and unfairly dismissive. When he called the next day to see if she was fine, she was at first unforthcoming and spoke very softly in her radio voice. She said she had taken herself for granted—a too-typical failing—and in all likelihood had taken him for granted, too, for which she was sorry. He thought of her dimple. Possibly, she said, if he would call her again they could attempt a "do-over." She'd pay this time. Mae, he believed, would've liked Sarah Gaines, would've admired her independence, though would've thought she needed to complain less; would've counselled him in tolerance and chastised him for being dull and prudish when poor Sarah Gaines had only tried to be open. He wasn't, however, contrite or forbearing enough to re-embark on Sarah Gaines. Or on some other Sarah. He did not see her again. A woman, he already knew, would disrupt and confuse his life, wouldn't fit, though he wasn't sure precisely why, or what *would* fit. He simply realized that being a widower was not, in spite of what others thought, the same as being single.

Later in the afternoon of the day he'd thought he might leave—he decided abruptly that he wouldn't. That it was defeatist. That small adjustments were within reach. Alone in the yard beside the empty flagpole, staring at his car with "Go way" scratched into its paint, he decided to take a kitchen bowl, again, down the path to the blackberry patch, fill it, and make a pie, or something close. It was perfectly out of his character to make a pie—he wasn't sure he could. Mae had made many blackberry pies in the red house, pies they ate too hot and burned their tongues on, and which had always been funny. Someone, he noticed, when he arrived down the path, had been in the patch already. Footprints dented the bushes. Though enough were left. Maine always comprised an aura of things happening just beyond where you saw them. Secrecy, but not really mystery. Like the girl at the beach today. Things you just didn't know about. It was almost likable. Though it wouldn't persist if you were here for long. Everything would be divulged—like dents in the blackberry patch. Marriage had been the only true mystery. What had he read back in the winter? It kept the conversation going. Now the conversation was over.

From the path, he couldn't make out the beach for the dense growth, though he could hear people—kayakers most likely, gliding the mirror surface of the bay, voices floating lightly up. Paddles bumping gunwales. They—possibly two of them—were having a private conversation on the open water, presuming no one to be listening. "Yes," the woman said. "But. You're only seeing that from one point of view." "I often do that," the other said—the man. Then laughter. An inexact science—how you maintained things. You could only try. You made a pie. You failed to make one. You didn't leave too soon. He'd collected enough, he thought, and started back.

When he arrived to the house, Fenderson was standing in the yard, hands in his paint-spattered overall pockets, watching the crows return to the timber across the road. High up, the fading contrail of a jet lowered to Boston. Crows were the businessmen of the avian world, Mae said. They went for work, then came home and argued about things all evening.

"I knew you'd had to be around hee-yah, law-yah Boyce. Your caaah was in the yaaaad." Fenderson enjoyed mocking the locals. He'd been born in New Jersey. "Mr. Boyce" signified some program. Something planned. "Stealin' some ma berries, then, are ya?"

"It's in the lease," Boyce said, metal bowl in hand.

"Livin' off the land. Whadda ya know?"

Fenderson walked off in the direction of the front door where he'd put the plastic geraniums under the front window, days before. His truck was idling in the road by the FOR SALE sign—the tiny poodle staring out. Boyce noticed a bumper sticker. *A Drunk Driver Killed My Daughter.* This didn't match Fenderson. The sticker no doubt came with the truck when he bought it. Fenderson seemed intending to go inside the house, but stopped and turned. "Wonder you'd mind can I show yer house." He surveyed the yard and the old concrete cistern cap so as not to meet eyes with Peter Boyce. Fenderson knew showing the house was *not* in the agreement. "People down the road—they're black people—came in the office today. They're rentin' your old place. Saw the sign, I guess. Money burning holes in they-yah paw-kets. Can't really say no. If I don't show 'em the house they get touchy. You're the lawyer."

"When do you have in mind?" He enjoyed free and unfettered use of the little house. No conditions. Fenderson would be expecting him to decline. Assign the blame on him, being from New Orleans. A southerner. The old ways.

Fenderson looked at the crows, taking up their evening perches in the cedar scrub across the road—flapping and fidgeting. "'Course they want to do evahthing yes-tuh-day. They wanta see the sun set. I guess, it won't set tomorrow." Fenderson peered down at his paint-specked canvas shoes, waiting. Fenderson had also flown combat sorties in Vietnam, owned medals for valor. But he was an old faker. Nothing bothered him.

Boyce looked at his bowl of berries. "Maybe they'll want some blackberry pie." It was okay—to relent. Now he *would* meet them—the McDowells—at least in a way.

"May *be*." Fenderson broke into his broad smile, his big, raucous teeth on display. He didn't like Fenderson. Something was cold and sinister about him. Though it didn't matter. "I'll sure ask 'em," he said, then he made a "whew" sound and started back toward his truck, happy with his victory and for it to be easily accomplished.

He'd organized a pie by five. The lattice crust, rolled with a vodka bottle, wasn't sweet enough, so he'd sprinkled sugar on. He had too many berries, so that he had to bring up the bigger, scorched Pyrex from the basement. Naturally, he lacked gelatin, which meant the pie would be runny, which was acceptable if it was sweet enough, which it would be. He'd leave it on the stove top. A pie would pronounce the house as welcoming, denote residence. If it hadn't sold by Labor Day (ten days off) maybe he'd consider a low-ball—have another whack, Mae would say. Change his mind. He didn't have firmer plans. Though he still hadn't asked the price.

But then what to do now, while the house showed? He and Mae had never visited the bars in the village.

She'd lacked the "requisite desperation for the American pub," she'd said, preferred her glass of Pouilly in the gazebo, watching swallows hit through the evening light, hearing bells across the bay chiming hymns. "Softly and tenderly . . ." Sometimes she'd sing.

Locals called the little bayside village Gilesburg from ancient charts. Though newer maps had it as Amity, a joke, since lobstermen ran down the kayakers, sliced one another's lines, smuggled in weed, and gave the finger when they snatched your parking place at the hardware. "No lights, no running water, shit in a hole, and schtup your sis is how they prefer it," Mae had said. "Very much like life in the North of Ireland—not that I was ever that fortunate."

He drove in to the village along Shore Road, rounding the long bight of the bay as the sunset occurred in all gold. (The McDowells would be viewing it now.) First, the girls' camp gate, then the dump, then the quarry, the Dollar General, the strip of failing retail, a bulk farm, a wrecked-car pasture, moccasin outlets, plus the staple of uniform Maine settlement—ruined boats on blocks, traps-and-buoy piles, wood splitters and canvas Quonsets—every single person with a rusted truck, a broken plow blade, a dirt bike and a dog. Out of sight of water, Maine was Michigan with no sense of humor. And then after Columbus Day, the Mainers reclaimed it all. Businesses went dark, restaurants were shuttered, locals ignored you if you went in the ditch, and summer cottages not burglar-proofed turned up re-purposed as meth labs or torched or both. The sheriff took time off. He couldn't survive here, Boyce understood.

Tiny Main Street sloped straight to the public dock and the dry storage berths where the sports wintered their yachts. The old town bars were for boatyard crews, nail-pounders, and fights—somebody's wife pairing up with the wrong house painter or the wrong house-painter's wife. Grudges were savored; everyone was armed. It was all recorded in the little four-sheet *Amity Argonaut* Mae used for starting fires. He didn't visit except for the Post Office.

The Launch Pad, however, was new to the street. A new red BAR sign hung below a new red neon lobster. Clean windows, attractive light within. Just one drink, Boyce decided, then drive to the house. A hand-lettered placard at the Launch Pad door announced "Canadian money always welcome. Canadians almost never." Inside was fresh pine paneling, a long, lacquered bar with Christmas lights on the back-bar mirror. A small, empty dining area was in the rear with netted globes and candles and silverware laid. The air smelled of sawed wood and something cooking. Somebody, Boyce supposed, believed they saw a future here.

Only, it didn't seem open. Though in a moment, a tall, slump-shouldered teenage boy stepped through the swinging kitchen doorway, talking on a phone, and motioned Boyce to sit at the bar, then stepped back out of sight. Male voices in the back became audible over the sound of a dishwasher. Someone would know how things with the girl turned out that afternoon. She'd seemed very happy on her gurney.

An enormous man came gliding through the swinging kitchen doors, wiping hands on an apron. "S'okay!" the man said, going behind the bar and picking up a towel to finish. "Wha-canna-getchya?" He seemed very pleased with himself

"Stoli, rocks. A double," Boyce said, wanting to seem pleased, too.

"Playing *two*!" the bartender said. He had round, packed arms inside a T-shirt, a weight-lifter's dense chest, a tiny waist and a large head with oiled, dark curls. His head swayed as he talked and poured. His looks were too big for him to be truly handsome. His T-shirt said GO SEAHAWKS. "Vacation-land, are we?" the bartender said, holding the glass up, pretending to measure.

"I'm renting the month out on Cod Cove," Boyce said and smiled.

"Wow. Ok-*ay*." The bartender set the drink down.

He reached and clicked on the big TV above the back bar. With the remote, he ran through channels until he found Fox. "Keep you company," he said. "Sound, no sound, it's the same price."

"No sound's good." He felt not significant here but unexpectedly good, while strangers combed through his rental house. At the end of the bar, a young woman had emerged from the Ladies—the toilet noise still going. "Do you know anything about the girl they found down at Nicholl's Cove?" Boyce addressed the bartender.

"Do we know anything about the girl they found down at Nipples Cove?" The bartender smiled, addressing the young woman seating herself several stools down in front of an empty glass. "This spellbinding creature is her first cousin," the bartender said. "We're all cousins here. Our ears don't exactly match. Did you notice?" Both his earlobes held tiny diamonds.

"*Nothin'* about you *actually* matches," the young woman said. She looked toward Boyce. "She's fine," she said about the girl on the gurney from the morning. "She drinks too much. Surprise, surprise. I may do the very same thing tonight." She nudged her glass forward with her little finger. "That was *so* good, I'll just have one more." She smirked. "After which your sorry services will no longer be needed."

"*My* sorry services?" the bartender said, enjoying himself.

"I know far too much about them," the woman said.

The bartender set down a drink on a napkin in front of her. "No one's complained about my services so far."

She touched her fingertip to an ice cube and submerged it, then looked at the TV, showing American soldiers in desert gear with automatic weapons, breaking into a house made of mud. They were smashing in a metal door with a battering ram, then crowding through the opened space.

The bartender was departing to the kitchen. "Scream out if you two need me. This nice man's offered to pay for you, sweetheart. He's a sport." He went gliding off, light on his feet.

"No, he didn't," the young woman said and turned her head to the side with a small smile that said she wanted to be recognized as a nice person. "I'm Jenna." She had on camo-cargo pants and a long-sleeved T-shirt she'd been wearing for a while. When she smiled, her eyes crinkled, and her face brightened and showed well-cared-for teeth. "Who're you?"

"Peter," he said and smiled. The Christmas lights on the back bar winked every two seconds. Sinatra was singing "South of the Border, Down Mexico Way." It was very good to be here. He relaxed and breathed deeply for the first time all day. The Stoli made his brain go plush. He might easily have been driving down a dark highway, headed south, but he was here.

"What do *you* do?" the girl said.

He smiled again. "Lawyer."

"Where at, in Maine?"

"New Orleans."

"Woo-hoo. Bourbon Street." She directed her gaze back to the TV. "Never been *there.* Want to." A reporter was talking to the camera before a night sky that contained an immense spotlit mosque. "Do you have some children?"

"One," Peter Boyce said. "She's grown up."

"So how old are *you*?"

"Fifty-five. If I remember."

"So," the girl said, "you like had your daughter when you were how old?"

"Twenty-seven, I guess." He turned half toward her to signal this was all right, what they were doing. Burbling away, Mae would've said. She hadn't been patient with it.

The girl took a sip of her gin and tonic. "I'm twenty-four," she said. "So are you divorced?"

"I'm not. No."

The girl looked at him appraisingly, raised her chin an inch, rounded her eyes as if she'd detected something and was about to not trust him. A deceased wife wouldn't mean anything to her. No reason to go on. "What're you doing here?" she said. "Are you, like, on a trip?"

"Renting," Boyce said. "Just the month. Out on Cod Cove." With one drink down, he needed to eat something. He felt slightly woozy. Route 1 offered only the Sea Biscuit and a Vietnamese where he'd gotten sick before.

"What do *you* do for a living?" he said to the girl.

Jenna once more stirred her drink with her finger. "I *wanted* to be a veterinarian. Because. I really like animals. Which didn't . . . work . . . out . . . because I wasn't good at math. *Or* science. So. I help at the no-kill down in Rockland." She looked at him very seriously. Her brow wrinkled. It was a look she'd perfected so people wouldn't think she was dumb. She was older than twenty-four, Boyce decided. Thirty. She was too at home in the bar, telling a stranger her story.

"What do you do at the shelter?" This was just passing time. He could eat at home. The McDowells probably were gone.

"Help find good homes for the little animals. It's fun." She took a smaller drink and lightly cleared her throat. "I have this problem right now," she said and cleared her throat again. She didn't look at him, though her pale lips had composed themselves into an unhappy wrinkle.

"A problem with what?" Boyce said.

"It's embarrassing," Jenna said. "I don't really want to tell you."

"That's fine." It was actually better. It was almost time to leave.

The bartender re-emerged from the kitchen, just his big shoulders and his head, "You two getting along okay? Is this a tender moment I'm interrupting? You're very quiet. I'll just leave. Though I want to show you guys something." In his hand he held a writhing lobster. In his other was a little mottled black-and-white puppy. The bartender knelt in the kitchen door, set the lobster on the floor and the puppy beside it. Instantly the puppy sprang at the lobster, biting its shell and snarling as if the lobster was its enemy. The lobster waved its banded claws and backed toward someplace it could defend—a corner by the kitchen door. Though the puppy kept leaping and growling and biting. "I wanted you to see my new lobster dog," the bartender was grinning merrily. "I still have to teach him to swim. But he has the instincts."

Jenna mouthed something silently to the bartender. The show was for her, which she knew. The bartender scooped up the lobster and the puppy and disappeared into the kitchen. Laughing erupted inside. Sinatra was now onto "I Get a Kick Out of You." ". . . I get a kick though it's clear to me . . ."

"He's *such* a complete asshole. He used to be married to my cousin Cathy. 'Til he discovered he was gay or whatever. He's since changed his mind about *that*."

"What kind of problem have you got?" Boyce asked.

"I'm locked out of my house. Apartment, I mean." The girl stared at herself in the back-bar mirror. She looked tired, and sighed. "It's complicated." She sighed again.

He didn't need to ask questions. It wasn't why he was here. The girl turned her face away and went on talking. "I was living with my boyfriend. Eric. Who's a lot older. He pulls traps, although he went to community college for a semester. He likes books." She tapped her index finger on the lip of her glass as if she was considering Eric. She looked at Peter Boyce so he could see only half of her face, which held a frown. "It's not all that interesting," she said. "It doesn't put me in a very good light."

"It's fine," Boyce said. Again, it was enough.

Jenna shook her head as if she disliked a great many things that were all visible to her. "Okay. Him. And me—him and I, whatever—we had a fight about something stupid. Something I did. And he moved out and took off to Melbourne Beach, where his mother has her condo. He left his boat and his traps for his brother—who does not have a license, or a brain. It was Eric's apartment, but he said I could keep it whenever the lease came due, which is supposed to be Halloween. He said he'd come get his stuff out, and maybe we'd get back together. La-dee-dah. Not very Amity. So. I was, like, living there and working at the shelter. Then two days ago I come home, and the locks are all changed." She fattened her cheeks. "This note on the door said, 'Dearest Jenna . . .' Dearest Jenna. Right? 'Carla and me have moved back in. I took your stuff to your mom's and put it on her porch. Don't come around here or call me. I've moved on now. Love, Eric.'"

She took a good-sized drink and cleared her throat once again. "I don't know who this Carla could be."

Boyce said, "Did you go get your belongings?"

Jenna shook her head. "My mom lives in Ellsworth—with *her* boyfriend. She put my stuff in their fifth-wheel, which she offered to me to stay in. But I was too embarrassed. I've slept in my car for two nights. And I'm not the kind of person who sleeps in his car. I went to Orono, for Christ sake. I have a degree. Or almost."

"What can I do to help you?" Here was a very bad idea. The only thing that seemed remotely humane was also a very bad idea. He felt tired and too old to be doing what he was doing.

"Well." Jenna pressed her lips tight together and inflated them. She didn't have an expressive face—a face like Polly's, in a way. "I really hate to ask this."

"Anybody can get in a mess," Boyce said. "Keeps lawyers in business."

"We don't even know each other," Jenna said. "You're not an ax murderer or anything, are you?

"I'm not. I told you, I'm a lawyer. Maybe that's worse."

"Of course, I *know* who you are," she said. "Your wife died. My mom's boyfriend's stepson's an EMS. They came and got your wife. I probably shouldn't say that."

"It's all right." It was. It was actually fine that things repeated themselves, even here, on this day. That wasn't bad. It was one small adjustment.

"I'm really sorry she died," Jenna said.

"So am I," Boyce said. "She was sick."

"Didn't she kill herself?" Jenna said almost formally.

"Yes. She did."

"Okay," Jenna said. She smiled at him weakly. "Could I take a shower at your place?" Then instantly she said, "If it's weird, I understand. I can ask Byron in there."

Frank was now singing "Make Someone Happy."

"I've got another bedroom," Boyce said. Too quick probably. "You don't have to sleep in your car."

He was now inconceivably offering a vagrant girl to sleep in his rental house. It was the thing old, drunk fools did. In two days, the girl and her Mexican boyfriend are arrested three states away, driving his car, using his credit cards, having murdered several people along the way, including him. How do you become *that* person? Who *was* that person? Was it him, now?

There was a shout out of the kitchen, followed by a clatter of pots bouncing and someone—the bartender—breaking into howls of laughter. "Oh, man," someone said. "I can *not* believe you just did *that*! Michael will shit." More laughter.

Jenna focused her crinkly eyes on him and frowned to indicate she knew he was thinking about something serious.

"I never lie," she said. "I wish I could. It's probably why I get along with animals. They don't lie." She gave him a pretty smile and pulled both sides of her hair away from her face. "Don't worry about my boyfriend breaking in your house and robbing you. He's not that creative. And he's not my boyfriend anymore."

Boyce put two twenties down. "Do you want to follow me home?"

"This is *also* so embarrassing," she said. "My car battery died. It's in the lot at the Shop 'n' Save, where I slept." She widened her eyes again. "Can I just ride with you, if it's okay?"

"Sure," Peter Boyce said. "We'll get your car going tomorrow." This deed was done. Jenna seemed instantly happy and at home—which was the point or had become the point. Make someone happy.

On the drive along the curve of bay, the lighted sky was all but extinguished. Clouds above the trees revealed only a filament of platinum. House lights showed across from the south shore where year-rounders lived. Jenna commented about every road and house they passed. Who lived there, who *had* lived there, where a drug bust had taken place. She told him her boyfriend's apartment—where she'd been locked out—had been handicap-equipped, which was why it was cheap. A person could do fairly well, it seemed to her, without the use of some limbs. She talked about how she wanted to devise yoga for animals. There were poses with animal names, so animals had been involved in the past. She asked Boyce where he'd been on 9/11 and also the Millennium, and when Hurricane Katrina took place, which she remembered being near New Orleans. These events were significant. She told him where *she'd* been on 9/11—alone, with a Vietnamese boyfriend in a cabin east of Caribou. She'd chosen an unconventional path through life, she admitted. But that was fine. She wasn't very ambitious but had attainable goals and could make a contribution by being a good person to people and animals. She asked Peter Boyce if he had any tattoos, and when he said no, she told him tattoos were a sign someone had given up. Then she told him Stevie Wonder had been offered his sight back but had refused. There was no stopping her. Maybe, Boyce felt, driving, you didn't pick up hitchhikers the way he'd done in college, or strike up conversations with strange young women in strange bars. Surely, though, it could be all right.

Their headlights tumbled along the tree-walled road across which occasionally flitted a shape—a bat, an owl. On the margins, a deer then a coyote were glimpsed. North of the highway the forest went on and on and on and on. To the right, the riding lights of lobster boats inching into the night. He was now, just suddenly, paralytically tired. Someone—Mackey at the firm—had said to him: "Whatever you think is the right thing to do" (he was, of course, talking about grief and death and loss), "contemplate the opposite."

This was certainly that. What would he do with Jenna in the house? A woman alone.

When they'd left the village, there'd been a pickup following, and in a while the girl's cell phone rang, though she'd ignored it. "I never answer it," she said. "It's just some car dealer—never who you want." After a while the truck overtook them, accelerated, then turned off on a dark road.

Boyce understood that what he was doing now was attempting to feel different, or feel *something* different. Not be private and sealed away. To open up. A line he'd read this morning on the beach came to him. *Mrs. Dalloway,* again. ". . . She always had the feeling it was very, very dangerous to live even one day." He'd never thought that. He'd believed the reverse. But they could both be true. It would make each day feel different.

The girl grew quiet, occasionally leaning and looking up through the windshield as if she sought a favorite star. When he made the turn on Cod Cove Road, by the red house, the Parkers' windows were lit and cars pushed into the side yard. Their kids were there. Jenna looked at him in the dashboard light and cleared her throat again. It was how she introduced her subjects. She was chewing a stick of gum, the Peppermint smell over-laying her clothing's odor. They were nearing the house. FOR SALE passed through the headlights. The McDowells were long gone. No lights were on. He missed Mae as intensely as he'd ever missed her. It was just sudden.

"Do they let women in combat yet?" She'd been thinking this over, watching off into the underbrush.

"I don't know. I don't think so." He turned into the grass driveway. The house bulked against the lightless sky.

"Me and my sister used to play at this house when I was little." She said "little" as if it were spelled *liddle.* The headlights swept the flagpole and the cistern, the path to the beach, a motionless rabbit. "And here's Mr. Bunny. Hel-lo," Jenna said happily. "My mom, I guess, had some friend who lived here. Mrs. Birney or whatever. We used to play with a kitty she had. Is there still a path to go to the beach?" She smiled at him hopefully.

"There is," he said, shutting the motor off and opening his door quick to get the light on. It was cool near the water, the salt air drifting up. Mosquitoes were a presence. Jenna looked defenseless, alone in her seat.

"You're not picking me up, okay?" she said in the dimness, her yellow gym bag in her lap, her fingers kneading its nylon hand-loops. She seemed as if she might start crying.

"Of course not," Boyce said.

"I'd have to punch you," she said, then smiled her weak little smile. "I smell a little doggy. Sorry." He was exiting the car. Crows made gathering sounds in the trees. "You're very nice," she said.

"My wife's name was Mae," he said, leaning in to look at her.

"That's nice," Jenna said. "It really is. What's your name?"

"Peter. Peter Boyce."

"Peter's my father's name," Jenna said. "That probably means something."

He went through the downstairs turning on lights. Lights kept things orderly. Get her to bed and to sleep. She didn't smell good, it was true. A shower would help.

Fenderson's card was on the kitchen table. The house was cold, the cellar door open, a chill, sewer-y odor had leaked up. Someone had helped him or herself to a coffee cup of the pie and left the cup in the sink. The McDowells wouldn't do that. On a scrawled-on legal pad leaning on the old sink pump handle was a note. "Hi Mr. B, We're your neighbors down the road. The McDowells of Bethesda. Love your beach. Love Maine. We're in the red house. Come visit. Happy summer! Pat 'n Bill, Jeff 'n Naomi." Fenderson had not informed them about Mae. Too much trouble.

Jenna was standing alone in the living room under the floral fixture Fenderson's wife had put up. Her gym bag was clutched to her front. She looked small and uninteresting, her droopy hair half framing her face. In her camo pants and smelly shirt, she looked like somebody who often slept in different houses. She was in his now.

"Are you sure you don't mind me being here." She had a way of starting to smile then frowning. She'd said these words before also. She *was* possibly twenty. Might never see thirty. Things happened to people.

Boyce closed the front door on the night. "No," he said, "it's great." He felt for some reason stern, a way he hadn't been enough with Polly. He'd always kept his distance. "Go have a shower upstairs. You'll feel better. The little bedroom's made up." Polly had not really slept there.

"It's cold." She clutched her bag.

"There's a space heater in the bathroom," he said. The house smelled like the pie and faintly of perfume and the basement. He thought of Pat McDowell in her white hat on the rocks. "A shower'll fix you," he said. Mae would've been amused by black people being the house prospects. She'd maintained off-center views about black people—being Irish. It hadn't helped much in New Orleans. Just some other way she was.

"I don't like the dark," Jenna said, as if where she was was dawning on her.

Boyce stepped to the front foyer—the only grace note in the house—and snapped on the bulb at the top of the stairs. "There," he said.

"What time is it?" She seemed a girl who'd never care what time it was.

"Nine. Little after."

"There's a meteor shower tonight, speaking of showers," she said and smiled. "If you go outside in a while you'll see it in the south." The room's poor light smudged the details of her face. He was more than tired.

"Okay," he said.

"You're so nice to let me be here," she said and began her way up the stairs to the bathroom.

He set the pie in the cabinet where the mice wouldn't reach it. He'd left the car unlocked, but now needed very much to lie down and close his eyes—just for a while. His hands ached. His knees, also. He'd been very tense. But for what reason? In the morning Jenna would be up praising the day and be gone.

He climbed the stairs. Light shone under the bathroom door. Jenna was speaking through the shower noise—talking on her phone, telling someone where she was. Which was welcome. It was hazardous when no one knew where you were. Now someone knew. "You silly thing," he heard her say. "I'll have to deal with you tomorrow. Ciao."

Ciao.

He opened down his covers, raised the window and looked out onto the little patch of lawn, the rhododendrons and the road. A sheriff's car was passing, its inside light on. Another smaller rabbit sat in the grass where the sheriff's lights found it. A dog barked a distance away. He looked up to possibly see meteors, but the window faced north.

Boyce laid on top of the covers, clothes and shoes on. The shower sound was soothing, then the toilet flushing, boards squeaking as Jenna moved about. His mind again floated as it had in the afternoon. What was it he'd needed to decide because it was the anniversary, or something—about Mae completing him, inventing him? Or was that a new thought? He could pay the McDowells a call this week.

"Push over, mister man." Jenna was in the bed, warm, damp, slick under his covers. A strand of moonlight fell on her bare shoulder, a breast she was just covering with a hand. At some unremembered point, he'd removed his shoes, pulled up the bedspread, but still had on his clothes. Beneath the covers, Jenna was bulky, more substantial than she'd seemed. Foreign. *Like a little peasant,* he thought. "I stayed in that other smelly bed as long as I could, where it was freezin'," she whispered.

"You don't have any clothes on," he said, not awake. "No wonder you're cold."

She drew closer. "Pajamas suffocate you. You have to warm me up. I know you're a sad old thing. I won't presume." She grasped him brusquely, the way she'd asked his name in the bar. *Who are you?* All of her was against him—hair, face, knees, her bare back all humid—her little legs insistent. She smelled of the Camay Fenderson's wife had left on the sink. "You're good 'n' warm, aren't you." Her nose pressed his chest, her legs working closer. He touched her breast without meaning to, which caused her to utter a sound. "Mmmm. Ooohhh." Then very softly, "Nothing else. Okay?"

"What?" he said. "What is it?"

"What Muppet would you want to be?" she whispered

"I . . ." he started to say, but knew nothing about that. She experienced nothing unusual being here. She saw everything different from how he saw everything.

"I'd be Janet," she said. "Though in my happier moments I'd be Kermit."

"I don't know," Boyce said.

"Do you want to talk about your wife? You can."

"I don't." He was whispering, too.

"Then we don't have to," she said.

"She would've liked you." It was a lie. But better for her to hear that. It hadn't been a good day for her, except now, conceivably. Mae would have thought she was ridiculous and him more so. An everlasting and embarrassing eejit.

"What's her name?" Jenna said, close to him. "*Was*, I mean."

"I told you. Mae."

"Mae like the month?"

"Yes," he said. He hadn't thought of that recently. They used to joke about it. Something-something brings Mae flowers. "Yes," he said. "Mae like the month."

"I understand," she said. "Okay." Which was how it was in the moments before they went to sleep.

He woke sweating. The girl was a furnace. His left eye wasn't focusing perfectly. His hands were numb from clenching. Jenna's mouth was open, and down inside tiny clicking noises could be heard with her breathing. Her gin and tonics exuded a sour-bread smell. She would sleep hours and hours.

He went downstairs where lights were on, carrying his shoes. He meant to go sleep in the little room once the lights were off. He didn't feel trapped now in some out-of-all-good-sense disaster-in-the-making. This would be fine. Though of course she could be fourteen. "Who of us could stand the innocent evidence of our lives to be placed before a jury of our peers?" It was their joke at the firm. The answer was—*no one.*

He found a tablespoon, got down the pie from the cabinet and stood at the sink in his socks, hand to his chest the way his father used to, left eye un-focused and half-closed, and dippered out a big bite, breathing a heave, filling his mouth—runny and tart and too sweet—swallowing, barely chewing. It was intensely, intensely good—the middle still warm, the crust bitterish, the sugar hardened on top. He took another gulping bite and relished it. He would serve it to Jenna for breakfast before they left for her car.

Unfocusing eyes was a symptom you were having a stroke, everyone knew. The old engine under assault. Blood pressure the obliging assassin. He'd never once thought of his own dying—even in the worst, when Mae was careening around, preparing to depart life.

His death had not been a part of it—a failure of empathy, possibly. Only life had, and carrying on. He heard a sound upstairs. The girl's voice, "Ohhhh. Mmmmmm." Then nothing. A dream. She was deep asleep. Now would not be the time to die. Far too melodramatic, Polly would certainly say.

He put on his shoes and walked outside. Translucent clouds had moved in, the half-moon inching to the horizon. The meteor shower was past. The air had warmed with a wind change. When he'd first arrived to the little house, he'd planned to greet the sun each day, build driftwood fires on the beach, bring a blanket, possibly sleep there. Instead, he'd lain in his bed, listening to crashings in the underbrush, grinding lumber trucks on the highway, moans, voices on the beach, the girdering of lobster boats on the darkened water. He was a born listener, a man who paid attention. Accepting was how you kept the run of yourself. The evolving, small adjustments.

He decided to walk to the beach and not to sleep more. Beyond the privet, the path was almost undetectable. You followed the cooler air to the water. A mosquito pinched his ear, then again. Crows made soft exchanges in the cedars. Skunk stink drifted up. He turned to see if light had come on in the house. But it hulked like a ship at sea, unchanged.

He looked for the side path to the pillbox—the rose briars emitting their faint late-summer rankness Polly had also disliked. And then suddenly he was at the beach—all the way already, its air widening and cool off the nearly invisible water. He climbed stiff-legged over the boulders. The bay sipped and hissed like something being rinsed. Everything seemed to pull outward—the beach sand sour and fishy, the tide to its farthest. Tiny pinpoint lights flickered at the Coast Guard on Schicke Point. A lobster boat rumbled out of sight. He heard gulls shouting in the dark. *Black Magic Woman* played on a boat radio farther out. He was here and nowhere else. Though hardly alone.

He walked to where the sand was damp and the air smelled of sulfur. He had no idea of the time. The lobstermen went at four.

"Okay, then," he said for no reason—perhaps addressing the beach. Everybody must experience—when calamities came down—that it'd been a dream from which you'd wake and things would be as they'd been. He would awaken on this beach, a sleepwalker, turn back to the house—the red house. Mae would be in bed. Means something, means nothing. It wasn't true. Means something, means *something*. You had to imagine what it would be.

Again, in law school—the instant he'd felt he'd grasped something permanent, found a fastness wherein he could reside and hold on, the young professor would flip the page in the case book, grin into the yawing despair of the rows of students, his eyes snapping, and shout, "Next, NEXT. NEXT!" The terror at that moment had been: don't be left behind.

Out on the bay, onto which the moon primly shone, a brief pink-and-green sizzle of fireworks sprouted, commanded the cold stars then quickly faded. What was it the skinny woman said? Life began once the fireworks ended. Everybody had a way of explaining the fix they were in.

"Those are just Coast Guards over on Schicke," the girl said. She'd come along now—not afraid of the dark at all. "They get real bored out there. That was definitely *not* the meteor shower." He turned to make her out. "It's sticky out here. Where'd you grow up?"

"In New Orleans," he said. Both eyes were working again. No stroke. No death.

"You prolly told me that, too. Did you meet your wife back there?"

"I met her in college in New Jersey."

"*Jersey* girl!" She took a deep breath and held it. She

was bored. She'd been nice to him. It had been a novelty. "Did you ever see *Bye, Bye, Birdie* the play?"

He had. With Mae, in a little back-alley revival house in the Village. Nineteen seventy-four. Mae'd loved Elvis. And there'd been a character called Mae. He said. "Yes. With my wife."

"We performed it in high school," Jenna said flatly. She was just talking, seated on a rock in the dark, wearing the terry robe from the bathroom. "'Honestly Sincere.'" She hummed what might've been that tune.

He wished he had something important to tell her. Call upon his years and years of legal experience. But he had nothing. Life, he thought, would now be this—possibly even for a long while—a catalog. This, and then this, and then this, and then this—all somehow fitting together to signify something. Conversations, meetings, people, departures, arrivals. Things passing like ghosts. Not terrible at all.

"I always think I'm going to find a dead person when I come to the beach," Jenna said.

"I do, too," Peter Boyce said.

"Isn't that weird? You aren't down here being all Mr. Gloomy, are you? About your wife?"

"No," he said. "I'm not. I was just allowing the day to begin." His heart was beating regularly, eyes focused in the near absence of light.

"Do I remind you of somebody?" she said.

"No," Boyce said. "You don't."

"Do you know how I knew you were down here?" He turned and looked at her. She was ten feet behind him, aglow in the diminished moonlight, the white robe not quite around her. Being almost naked wasn't unusual for her.

"No. How?" he said.

"Tracks in the grass," she said. "You left me some clues, didn't you?"

"Right," he said. "I did."

"Do you think I'm a narcissist? Some people've told me that." She pulled her robe around her.

"I don't know," he said wondrously.

"So do you think we'll get to know each other better and be friends?" She seemed concerned.

"Yes," he said. "I don't see why not. Do you?"

"No. That's what I was thinking," she said and looked into the sky, as if she'd heard something fly past her invisibly.

And that was all they said for a time while the day made its fresh claim again upon the darkness.

Jimmy Green—1992

They were in a taxi, on their way to the American Bar down General Leclerc, to watch the election returns. Rain had begun blowing sideways, three minutes past midnight. The little Fiat, its windshield dimpled and furred with water, all at once began sliding, veered left and (almost) into the Denfert-Rochereau lion, but swerved again, wheels spinning, then sped all the way around the rotary and half again and stopped, facing up Boulevard Raspail the wrong way. "Ooo-laaaa," the driver said, exultant. "Maximum machine-gun racket effect."

The French woman, Nelli, had squeezed Green's hand ridiculously hard in alarm.

"We're almost there," Jimmy Green said. "He just wants to make it interesting."

"Asshole," the French woman murmured, touching her hair and glancing out the taxi's smeared window. Cars were pounding by, honking.

The tiny driver (unquestionably a Turk) beamed at her in the rearview, a look of delight and rebuke, then juiced it, spun the wheels in the slick, and shot away. Small-scale near catastrophes apparently pleased him.

Green had several times gone past where the French woman worked, on the walk to and from his good little lunch place in rue Soufflot. She was the proprietress, he thought—of the little photo gallery in rue Racine—or else she was the clerk. It didn't matter. He wanted to see her closer up. The gallery sold famous unauthorized, unsigned prints for a great deal of money. To tourists. The faceless couple waltzing on a Paris street (which everyone knew to be staged). Two clochards drinking on the quay. The ubiquitous Lartigue of an upside-down man in a skullcap, diving (so it appeared) into a shallow, shining pond. If you bought one, Jimmy Green thought, you were happy to go home.

Each afternoon, the woman could be seen staring out the shop window at the street, her face mingled in the glass with the lurid Capa image showing Japanese officers in jodhpurs sharing a joke and a cigarette, while a hundred Chinese, trussed and on their knees, waited patiently for what was soon to come.

Green had stepped inside with a made-up question about the Capa. The camera? The film? Where it was published first? The woman smiled at him with her violet eyes. She was older, he now could see. The flesh under her eyes was slightly wrinkled, shadowed, her face longish, eyelids heavy. Thin lips, a small mouth, not perfect teeth. The parts weren't so attractive. But *she* was—the smooth skin, her hands, ankles, her bland expression pronouncing an expectation of being looked at. She wore a flimsy silk shift with blue and pink flowers, and stylish cherry pumps. Her hair was the red-black they all did, with bangs. A look, Green thought, that did not bother about age. She was Jewish, he somehow guessed, like him—though the French were French first. He'd decided he would ask her to go to the American Bar, where he'd never been. It wouldn't matter what she said. He didn't want to sleep with her, just go someplace. He cared almost nothing about the election at home.

He'd walked around inside the gallery, affecting to look at this and that, speaking pointlessly to no one, making himself plausible. Safe. She knew nothing about the Capa, which meant she was the clerk.

She stepped again to the front window, peering at the lycée students coming home wearing backpacks and giggling. It was the view she had of the world. In what he imagined she already anticipated, from the middle of the shop he asked—in English—if she would like to come with him tonight to watch the American election on TV. She half turned and smiled, as if he'd said something else.

"What?" she asked. He said the words again and smiled as if it was a joke. She tapped her red toe lightly on the polished floor, breathed audibly. She was bored. He went on smiling, nodded, felt himself to be extremely American. She shook her head no. "All right," she said. "Yes. I have nothing to do else."

"Nothing else to do," he said. He hadn't yet said his name. But he did. "I'm Jimmy Green. From Cadmus, Louisiana."

"Nelli," she said, and that was enough.

Cadmus was a nice southern town where Jews were allowed to be part of most things except the country club. It was in the northwest part of the state. Oil, gas, and timber. Conservative, but not antediluvian. It hadn't seceded when other towns had. Cotton stopped farther east.

Jimmy Green had been liked—widely—admired and successful. He'd been the progressive mayor for a time, but had friends on all sides. His wife was a lawyer, his daughter was off at Dartmouth, bound for medical school. His father, dead for years, had started a company that serviced cotton gins. Jimmy had been vice president of the bank his father also started to finance his gin business, and before the mayoralty had been offered. Jimmy'd gone to Yale, where he'd been a boxer, studied diverse and widening subjects, which eventually came down to *interdisciplinary.* He was sociable, played golf at the club where he couldn't be a member, got along, had talents.

And then. It had all blown up—fast and faster in spectacular (if predictable) fashion. A bank colleague's young daughter. Some erroneous travel receipts. Sums of money unreported (though repaid). A shocking but needless restraining order. He was required to resign as mayor and at the bank. Being a Jew was naturally mentioned.

"How did you *suppose* this would all turn out, Jimmy?" his wife had said, on the way out the divorce door. "I don't know," he said, trying to smile. "Maybe I didn't think about it." That had been five years ago. Not that long.

He'd moved from Cadmus up to New York where for a time he rented and tried to like it (his father had left him money, which he'd kept track of). Then on to Maine for no particular reason except that he knew people in Camden, and a house by the water had come up. Maine was a very good place from which to begin again, go outward into the world, which he felt he should do. He was only fifty-one. His daughter came up to visit him but cried and was angry. His wife married again quickly, but stayed bitter. He was in touch with a few people who liked and trusted him. A college chum or two.

Nothing, of course, suggested life had worked out terribly well or for that matter that he'd been treated in the least unfairly. Life was still *trying* to work out. Someone (his dead father) would say he was a weak man, but not necessarily a bad weak man. His sister in Cincinnati, who taught at the seminary and had married a rabbi, held less flexible views. Jimmy, though, believed he had some good qualities. He was completely lacking in cruelty. Did not pity himself. Was loyal, in his own terms. Wasn't easily disheartened. Could be patient. Many other people were in his present unwieldy situation—people who understood their fate and circumstances to be not completely who they were.

However, he had no wish ever to go to work again—that was clear—and no reason to. And not one day in life, he found, did he miss Cadmus, Louisiana. Far too small.

In Paris he'd made a few acquaintances—mostly men in his French class at the American Library. From the back of a magazine, he'd found a flat, only for the fall. "Partial rooftop view with geraniums." He took all meals out. Practiced the new language on waiters and taxi drivers, who preferred English. He liked Paris, where he'd been twice as a student and once with Ann, his wife. Somewhere he'd read a sage had said that in Paris you felt more foreign than anywhere, ". . . the thin, quick feminine . . ." something or other. He didn't remember it. But it didn't seem true. He didn't feel very foreign here. What did seem true was that it didn't matter much where one was anymore. Not as much as before. Paris was perfectly fine. Though if someone had asked him why he was here now, in the fall, rather than Berlin or Cairo or Istanbul—wherever—he didn't think he could've said. Those other, ordinary people—who'd had similar life experiences to his recent ones—you never followed what happened to them. They faded. They went on with life, merely outside the blinding glare.

Nelli had said to come to her flat in the Avenue de Lowendal. She had her daughter who would need delivering to the husband, who lived not far. The daughter would be asleep, which would make things easy. She was close to the École Militaire, where the Metro emerged from underground, and you saw the

Invalides, and after that the Tower and the river. His apartment was not far either.

A large, curved Beaux-Arts gate with a vacant *gardien*'s box opened off the avenue into a wide court, like an interior park with four-story connected brick buildings around three sides. Large, leafless trees stood in the dark. Decorative benches were established for when the weather turned and flowers came back. It was almost midnight, lights were on in many of the windows. Cold rain had begun on the walk up, the sky milky with a swarming light from the city. He had his coat and wore jeans and his rubber shoes from Maine.

Nelli's flat was up two flights, a door left ajar as if things were busy inside—people possibly departing and arriving. She greeted him without ceremony, seated on a cushioned hassock, putting on her shoes to go. The flat was spacious—high ceilings, brass fixtures, tall curtainless windows giving onto the garden, heavy floor lamps casting gold, shadowy light onto leather furnishings. All the carpets were Eastern in origin. Rich, Jimmy understood. Many surfaces held artifacts, small human shapes in wood, urns, pottery shards, spears, authentic-looking things. Not a store clerk's pocketbook. He sat himself at the edge of a leather couch and watched her conduct her last, small intimate act of dressing. He hadn't said anything. Only hello, though he was glad to be here now.

"My father who has been an ar-kay-o-lo-zheest," Nelli said, as if she had noticed him noticing. "He kept what he wanted where he went."

She was in a short red dress now, and different pumps with little straps that flattered her ankles. Oblivious to the rain outside. She was even more attractive in the shadowy light. She began collecting scattered things he hadn't noticed into a child's pink suitcase. His presence hadn't changed anything. Whatever they were doing she'd done with someone else. That sensation—of firsts, of things being new—it was fine. Though you began not to want it.

"I'd probably do the same," Jimmy said, almost too long after the subject of her father's deceits had been mentioned. He heard *south* in his voice, which he didn't normally. It meant he was at ease. He'd been in few people's apartments in Paris. The French never invited you. They met you in public places and kept you at arm's length. Here, though, was good. He liked watching her finish dressing, packing her child's clothes. His silence, he believed, would express that.

"I was conceived to this flat," Nelli said. She pointed to a white door that was closed. "In zhat room."

"I was conceived in a car in a cotton field," Jimmy

said. "Following a football game." She produced a quick little intake of breath, as if this was shocking.

A brass menorah hung among an arrangement of African masks. He'd been right, there. She said she spoke English so well because she'd lived in Los Angeles in the seventies with her first husband, who'd aspired to make films but hadn't made any. Her speech came from that time. "No way" to mean "no"; "Soop-air" to mean "good." "Far out," as in "my father removed *far out* antiquities from a country that became Chad." He had not used those words in Cadmus. Her saying them, though, made her seem sweet and unguarded, a way he imagined she wasn't.

In addition to stolen treasures, the flat contained a large rattan cage with two tiny, silent birds inside. There was a map of the London Underground on the little Arabic-looking table. A post-menopausal sexuality seminar circular that was bilingual. And a postcard that showed a teenage Nelli, wearing glasses, sternly facing the camera's eye. It wasn't very flattering. Nelli as a frowning schoolgirl, in a gray, pleated uniform skirt with knee socks and a white blouse, her hair in stiff pigtails. She seemed happier now.

Nelli re-entered through the white door she'd exited. She was wearing a black raincoat and what his mother always called a "head scarf," and was carrying a sleeping child cradled in a pink blanket, the child's body draped across both her arms. In the room she'd departed, a dim light revealed a broad bed with a white duvet, a wall with framed photographs. A black dog walked into the open doorway. Its fur had been shaved, leaving its head and face large and woolly. Like a gargoyle. It stood looking, as if it expected Jimmy to do something surprising.

Nelli glanced at the postcard, balancing her daughter on an arm. A little girl who might be four.

"Do you like this card?"

"I like your picture," Jimmy said.

"Can you take this?" She handed him the pink suitcase she'd packed with the child's clothes. It had no weight.

"My first husband has made this," Nelli said, arranging the blanket around the little girl's sleeping face. The child's hair was dark and curly-thick, her face everted into her mother's shoulder. Rain was now clattering outside. She made a dismissive noise with her lips. "Do you like the dog's *coiffure*? What is it? Haircut?"

"Not so much. He looks sad."

"No. Of course. But she insists on this way." The little girl she was referring to was a well-wrapped bundle. "She thinks he wishes to look bee-zahr. She thinks he feels in-ter-*rest*-ing. He is her puppet."

In the taxi to the husband's, which was behind the Trocadero—an expensive quarter—he began to think that in Maine, where his house was, now was full fall, the longed-for time for everyone. White-frozen mornings, sunny mid-days, nights when the moon slid along as in liquid. The idling time of woolgathering and patient planning before winter. The clock turned back. His house was waiting empty. Once this Paris period concluded, he'd move back. Begin something. His daughter, of course, entered his mind. He'd thought to fly her to Paris—though she was a surgical resident in Minnesota now, and wouldn't come, owing to predictable loyalty to her mother.

Nelli began to speak about apartments, her daughter limp in her arms, a soft, sour aroma rising from the blanket. The child's tiny ordinary face lay composed in sleep. She had yet to speak the child's name, or his.

The river, which they passed over, was already swollen by the rain, the sky hazy white and shining from the Concorde. "I would like to have a new place. You know?" Nelli said softly. "Maybe some country. To have animals. *Une ferme.*" She was leaning against his shoulder and the pink suitcase he held. "Is true that in America there are enormous houses beside the other on tiny—what is the word? Little terrains?"

"Yes," he said. "Tiny lots." His bank had financed many of these before it all went away.

"And where you're living? In Paris."

"In rue Cassette. Near the Sulpice. I rent a place."

"Nice to be there," she said. "Very expensive. Americans like to live where they are not born." With her head over on his shoulder, she yawned, holding her daughter across her lap in the blanket. "My daughter," she said, "would dig *une ferme.* She loves all animals. Do you have animals where you are living in America?"

"I did," Jimmy said. "At one time." He'd fallen into her rhythms of speaking.

The husband, the child's father, was a small, cheerful, bald, café-au-lait West Indian who opened his door wearing a white silk caftan and a gold earring. He seemed pleased about everything. He smiled, shook Jimmy's hand, and accepted the child's suitcase. A young, blond black woman in a leopard leotard was in the apartment and came to the door. Nelli and the husband and the woman talked softly in French and laughed and seemed to be friends—the way it could be, Jimmy thought. Though his wife hated him.

Sammy was the husband's name. He was not the husband who'd made the photograph. They all stayed at the door. No one acted like it was odd to bring the daughter at midnight. The child did not wake up, though Sammy kissed her on the forehead and talked to her as if she were awake. He said her name. Lana. Nelli said Jimmy's name in a partial English way—Jeemy. Green. And lowered her eyes. Then for moments they all four spoke English.

"It's nice to meet you," Sammy said as if it interested him who his wife would bring here.

"Me, too," Jimmy said and felt welcome. The daughter didn't look anything like this man.

Nelli spoke more in French, fast business-y phrases that included the words *demain* and *quinze* and (he thought) *diner.* So many of their words were the same, and everyone spoke too fast. Then it was finished, and they left down the dark stairs.

Outside onto the rain-spattered sidewalk where water was standing, the cab they'd requested to wait was gone. Nelli unexpectedly grasped his arm above his elbow and kissed him hard on the mouth and pulled close. He set his hands on her hips, which were bony, felt her ribs through her raincoat, her stiff brassiere, held her clumsily. Sammy would be watching them from a window. He thought of Nelli—the schoolgirl on the postcard—brazen in her drab school uniform.

His own life, for this moment, felt very far away from him. Which was good.

"I always feel this way when I go away from her," Nelli said softly into his shoulder, her scarf becoming wet.

"How?" he whispered.

"Free," she said. "As if my life was new. It's wonderful."

"It's not what I thought you'd say." He was holding her close to him, breathing in her hair.

"I know. But. Is the truth. I don't ask so often for him to take care of her. I wanted very much to go. With you."

He felt so glad. That she would say such a thing, that she wanted to go with him and whatever it entailed. He looked up the street then for a second taxi's light and saw one.

The long gilt-edged windows of the American Bar blazed out onto General Leclerc. Taxis were arriving and departing in the rain. A few ridiculously young prostitutes waited in the warming light in tiny skirts and knee-high white patent-leather boots, praying someone would invite them inside. Magee, the Irishman he knew from the Library, had told him all prostitutes were Polish now, and had colorful diseases, only they were so splendid-looking you forgot. It was Magee who'd told him about here. Americans came on election night and got drunk. It was the tradition. A hoot. No one cared who won. Least of all Magee.

Inside, the American Bar was enormous and intensely noisy and smoky and full of men, the light was brassy and harsh. The floor was tiny red, white, and blue tiles, which made everything louder. Waiters in long aprons circulated with bottles of champagne. Televisions were on all the walls, and gangs of young business types in shirt sleeves and suspenders were smoking cigars, watching American channels, laughing and shouting and drinking.

An American newsman everyone knew was large on the screen, seated at a desk, with big election totes behind him. It was impossible to hear. Somewhere, a barbershop quartet was singing, and there was for some reason Irish music, as well as the continuous ringing and chatter of the tills. It was meant to be thrilling, but it was oppressive and dizzying.

All the businessmen in suspenders and shirt sleeves were, he believed, Republicans—their haircuts and smooth faces were so well cared for. All were waiting for their candidate to be elected so they could start braying, and run back to their offices when the light came up, ready to print money.

A waiter offered champagne, which was free and tasted vinegary. There was really nothing to do. He and Nelli were pressed against a wall that was all mirrors with gold fittings. Though he was happy to be here, to be with this woman. She stood stiffly in her red dress, her chin raised as if someone were watching. Her eyes were almost black, and in the room caught the light, her thin lips very red and smooth. Red was her color. Her face and its length was her best feature. Unusual. In someone else it wouldn't be.

"Which one do you love to win?" Nelli said through the din. She was staring at a TV where the face of the Democrat and the smiling, older face of the Republican were on a screen together. The results in New York were going to be announced shortly. The young cigar-chomping businessmen were beginning to boo disapproval at what they expected to be the wrong outcome.

"I used to like the Democrats," Jimmy Green said.

"Oh my god," Nelli said, and looked shocked, her hand over her half-open mouth. She then jauntily raised her chin to reproach him. "You're a wacko."

"Sure," he said. He didn't care. Why did he have to now?

"Neexon," she said. "I loved him." Nixon's big, trustless sagging face and lightless eyes re-formulated for a moment in his mind. His father had detested Nixon. "A born Jew hater." It was the only time he'd said such a thing. They'd all watched the funeral on TV and felt solemn.

"Neexon wass so funny," Nelli said. "He wass like a French politician, you know?" She expanded her cheeks and made a grotesque face. How old could she have been when Nixon was president? Living in L.A. with the other husband. Twenty years ago.

Holding his glass and finding it difficult to speak, he started to say how wrong it was to love Nixon. But stopped.

"Eees not so different now," she said. "You think so, but it's not." He didn't understand what she was talking about. She'd thought he'd said something he hadn't.

He watched the square handsome Technicolor face of the Democrat consume the TV above the flashing word *WINNER*. The Republicans staring from below booed and cursed and threw their cigars at the screen.

In a while, Nelli picked out someone she knew, a young, fat-cheeked, pink-fleshed man with a pink balding round head and wire glasses. Like the others, he was smoking a cigar and wearing red suspenders over a starched white shirt his belly urged against. She went to speak to him at the bar, and the man instantly became animated, though he glanced at Jimmy as he hugged her. She patted his round cheek and laughed. She knew people here.

Jimmy scanned around for the Irishman Magee, who was a lawyer for Texaco, but didn't find him. You could barely see through the crowd. No one was speaking French, not even the waiters. It was after one. He felt more dizzy and not entirely well.

In a moment, Nelli had brought over the fat, pink-cheeked young man, who pronounced his name to be Willard B. Burton of St. Johnsbury, Vermont. The name seemed too old for him, like a name he'd made up. Willard B. Burton said he worked "down at Lowndes, Rancliffe in the First." He was a growth fund something-something. His chief claim tonight, though, was to be head of the Young Republicans. He was everybody's host, and soon, he said, when the southern and western states closed, there'd be a reckoning. A "different song'll be playing then" was how he put it.

Willard B. Burton had the palest blue eyes with pink irritated-looking flesh around them, and a fleshy mouth. Someone could've boiled him. He also possessed enormously long feet, encased in shining black wing-tips. He was drinking whiskey and weaving slightly.

"Who are *we* supporting, Mr. White," Willard B. Burton asked, smiling.

Nelli piped up annoyingly. "He likes the pretty one."

Burton narrowed his pale eyes. People were swarming all around. More booing was commencing. More unhappy news.

"Seriously?" Willard B. Burton said.

"It doesn't matter," Jimmy said.

"Well, it does matter. I oughta order you out of here. And don't I hear old Dixie in your voice? You should be ashamed." Willard B. Burton lowered his fleshy chin in theatrical displeasure. His plenteous lips had become damp.

"I'm not ashamed. But you can order me out," Jimmy said. "It's all right. We'll go."

"No. Really," Willard B. Burton said. "We have to put you into a clinic. You're deranged." He weaved a bit forward, fisting his drink, his cigar in his other hand. His lower lip rode up over his upper one so as to express resolve for the clinic idea. This was the expression people at Lowndes, Rancliffe laughed about when he wasn't present.

"Go, go, go now, Burty," Nelli said. "You're being boring. You're bothering me."

Willard B. Burton's eyes caught hold of Jimmy's and grew cold with buffoonish fury. "You really have to get treatment for your mental disease, Mr. French," he said. "You don't know much of anything."

"Go away someplace, Burty," Nelli said and let her eyes wander all around, looking for someone new.

"We'll have to fix you. And we will." Burton was doing his best to be ominous. Jimmy thought someone could slap him, and he'd be better.

"It's nothing to get upset about," Jimmy said and smiled.

"Is that so?" Burton said.

"Of course."

"Well, we'll just see." Nelli had Willard B. Burton's arm where it would've been soft up under his starched shirt. "We'll just see about that," he said, then lurched around with her still holding him and careened into the crowd toward the bar.

For a brief time, then, they stood and didn't speak, their backs to the shining mirrors, which in places revealed a worn black backing. They were at the beginning of a little hallway leading down to the toilets.

People bumped clumsily by. When the doors opened there were the damp smells. Nelli had made no further mention of Willard B. Burton. By tomorrow he'd have forgotten much of this, possibly all. When a waiter passed, Jimmy asked for a gin.

"What makes you like to go in Paris?" she said, using the half-English way. Parees.

"Oh, it makes me feel like I could be something good if I wanted to." Which he believed was true.

"Really?" she was not quite listening, looking around, wrinkling her nose and being a spectator. "I was born to Parees. Do you think this is the good I can be?"

"You're wonderful," Jimmy said. "And you're very nice." This was the thing he said to women he liked when he was drunk. They were wonderful. And they were very nice. He pulled her closer, his back against the mirror. She seemed to want to be kissed again. No one else was kissing.

He kissed her on the mouth and tasted the chalk of her lipstick, smelled a hint of sour baby blanket. Her face was soft, not like a girl's taut, resilient skin. He felt her boniness again, her slightness. Her dry hair smelled of smoke and perfume. He took a grip under her bare arm, into her armpit.

"How old are you?" she spoke into his ear. Her moist breath.

"Fifty," he said and felt drunk, as if the intense noise was the cause.

"Fifty," she said. Some businessmen were now singing to compete with the barbershop quartet.

Beantown, oh Beantown, what a mean, mean town,
Ultimately a rather sad and obscene town
Not at all a serene or a clean town

What did it mean? Jimmy wondered. Something from Harvard, where they'd all gone.

"We should leave here, do you think?" Nelli said. What had fifty meant to her? Possibly *she* was forty.

"Absolutely," he said, then wasn't sure that he'd said that.

She kissed his ear, sent a shock into his thighs. The word *WINNER* was again announced on the TV, followed by great shouting.

"I think your friend's candidate didn't win," he said.

"He's not my friend." She was looking around the room.

He peered into the large room for Willard B. Burton—to determine what he might be doing at this moment of abject loss. The round, unhappy face wasn't to be found.

On the way out he saw Magee at the copper bar looking drunk and perspiring. A tall blond girl was beside him in a skimpy silver skirt. Magee was wearing a ludicrous western suit with pockets the shape of arrows. He'd sweated through his shirt, and his trousers were half unzipped, his brown eyes red and un-focused.

"It's become a bleedin' wake, now," Magee allowed.

"Just as well," Jimmy said.

"You should stay. Some shite from your embassy's givin' a speech about American democracy. It'll incite a fuckin' riot."

"We're leaving," Jimmy said. He had Nelli's hand behind him. He smiled at Magee, who touched him lightly on the shoulder.

"Good man," he said. *"Qui est votre cocotte?"* The tall blond girl turned away. Jimmy didn't understand the last word, something Magee had got wrong. He moved Nelli toward the heavy leaded doors and the street.

As they stepped out onto the sidewalk where raining had ceased and a file of taxis was at the curb, their drivers standing outside their vehicles, chatting up the whores, he became conscious of footsteps—behind him—the sound of the bar's doors having opened again, warm inside air brushing his neck. Some instinct said *Move, stand out of someone's way.* He gripped Nelli's hand to pull her aside.

"You're the silly fuck who needs to have a lesson taught him?" a man's voice said.

An American.

Jimmy turned to see a man not larger than himself, but dressed as they all were. White shirt sleeves, bright suspenders, dark hair tousled, but with his fists balled, shoulders squared, turbulent, small eyes. "Could be you've . . ." Jimmy said.

The man hit him, in the face two times. First in the right temple, then on the side of his other eye, almost in the same place. The blows made hollow, *sucking* noises inside his ears and didn't particularly hurt. Though they were stunning blows and made his knees watery, while the young man who'd hit him—there were stars and stripes on his suspender bands—began instantly to recede, suggesting to Jimmy he himself was falling, hands reaching behind, fingers toward the pavement. Like being on a seesaw.

What he fell against was not pavement, but the yielding side of a taxi, painted to portray a zebra's stripes. His fall was further cushioned by the hard ass of one of the prostitutes, who was in the way. "*Incroyable,*" he heard someone say, as he sat down more than fell onto the wet sidewalk, not feeling hurt, only very, very dizzy. Though he did feel he should get up right away.

The man who'd hit him was already walking back into the crowded bar. People were looking out at Jimmy through the open doorway. He heard music, the noise of bottles clinking, the barbershop quartet singing "Auld Lang Syne," people laughing. At him, he supposed. Though it was really not so bad.

Nelli was kneeling beside him, they were all—the prostitute, another prostitute, a female taxi driver—helping him up. The seat of his trousers was soaked. His head was booming. His knees were uncertain. He seemed to have twisted one little finger on the taxi door.

"Cocksuckers," Nelli said.

"It's fine," he said. He felt drunk, more than hurt.

The prostitutes had begun drifting away down General Leclerc, looking back warily, their patent boots shining in the car headlights. He could smell the woman driver—mealy, sweaty hotness. To vomit seemed inevitable.

Other men were now leaving the bar wearing business suits, striding into the early dark. They looked at him and smiled. Though the night was now in jeopardy of being sad. Not what he'd wanted. He'd wanted the opposite. A happy outcome. His gaze roamed the misty, yellow-black sky. Pigeons wheeled above then disappeared beyond the building tops.

Traffic lights swam across the taxi ceiling like film frames. Jimmy let his head loll against the plastic seat back. This particular taxi smelled of apples. *Les pommes.* Getting busted up really felt not so bad—almost pleasant. His jaw, though, was swelling, both sides, the flesh tight to the bones. His skull throbbed. Possibly his little finger was broken. It could all be tolerated. He only needed to go home.

The driver, as she drove, spoke French softly to Nelli, who was directing them to a place she liked. Brasserie Grenelle. She was hungry.

"I'll just go home," Jimmy said.

She sat beside him, staring at the streets at one A.M., busy and attractively bright. She was not eager to touch him or address him. Some not-good quality of his had become apparent. Something that disappointed. Distance from him was needed. Their brief closeness, when he had kissed her in the bar, had been extinguished by being knocked down.

"But if you want to eat something . . ." he said. She looked over, her crisp, tinted bangs making her face heavy and serious. "I don't want your whole night to be spoiled." He smiled in a way that made the bones in his face be painful. She seemed not to want to pay any attention.

Outside the taxi, in front of the Brasserie Grenelle, which was closed, he vomited into the curb gutter, hands against the taxi's side, while the driver explained to Nelli through the window that they were no longer allowed to be her passengers. "*Desolé, madame, mais non, non.*" Jimmy wished to say something. Take command. But when he stood the taxi departed, its roof light quickly growing dim. Nelli watched it without speaking.

"I really should go." He was very sorry to have drunk gin, sorry to be sick for her to see, sorry she was no longer glad to be with him as earlier she had been.

"Where are you living?" She put on her head scarf and was irritated. She'd forgotten he'd already said. Waiters were putting chairs onto tables inside the brasserie. No one was walking on this block. It had begun to be colder now that the rain had finished. Across the street a small truck with lawn mowers in back had paused at the curb. A man in green coveralls climbed into the truck bed to re-arrange things.

"Near the Sulpice. I'll walk." He could smell terrible breath in the air in front of him. In his dream of boxing, you didn't lose, couldn't possibly. You were hit but felt nothing. You rained down blows.

"You are stinking," she said, beginning to walk away down the boulevard, much as she'd done in the gallery that afternoon. It was what she did. "But come on. I am close to here now."

"No. I'll walk home," he said.

"Yes," she said, departing. "Maybe someone won't rob you in one minute."

Her pumps made little detonations on the pavement. He thought again of her kissing him in the downpour, in front of her ex-husband's building, before any of this had gone the sad little way it had. As if he'd dreamed it.

The flat in Avenue de Lowendal was lightless and silent. Heat had come on, the air close and stuffy. Out the windows the sky still hung yellow with mist, the little park dripping. Only two lights were on in other flats. Earlier, there must've been noises—voices behind walls, water falling through pipes, music, floating sounds from elsewhere. Now all was still, though the tiny birds fluttered in their wicker cage. The dog who believed he looked interesting stood in the bedroom doorway, sniffing.

Nelli became business-like. She would be going to work soon. As she moved about in the glow of a table lamp, she began to disrobe, as if no one was in the room with her. She made a call to hear messages, then entered the bedroom. He could hear her shoes drop, the scrape of hangers, the sound of talking softly to herself.

He was wet to his skin, hair slick, his body stiffening, as if there'd been a car wreck. The flat had a smell it hadn't had. Something in a sink, or a pail, not completely disposed of.

Nelli re-entered barefoot, wearing only white underpants and a black brassiere. She was pinning her hair back for a shower, wearing glasses, as she had in the postcard picture of herself as a girl. Her body didn't attract light, but he could see how slender and elongated were her hips, thighs, shoulders, arms—younger-appearing than he'd believed. Nothing of childbirth.

"Could you take the dog to do a pee, please?" she said, hairpins in her mouth. She opened a coat closet and produced a leash. "When my daughter is no here . . ." She started to say more then stopped. The black dog began wagging its tail and looking at Nelli. It had assumed a position beside the door. Nelli put the leash on the table. "You can bathe when you are back. I'll put a bed for you on the *canapé*." Her face looked puzzled. "I don't know canapé? What is it?"

Canapé meant something else.

"Okay," he said. His feet were numb, his back and shoulders and jaw slowly seizing. The dog produced a sigh as it sat. Nelli went back to the bedroom, turned on the light, and shut the door.

In the garden, air was frigid. His clothes had warmed indoors, but now were awful again. He couldn't stop shivering in his coat. The dog nosed the wet grass, unhurried. In a window opposite, a man stood in the dark beside a blue-lit aquarium, peering down as if Jimmy were an intruder. Rain demarked the season's change. Now would be the famous Paris winter commencing. He would stay longer, he thought. Perhaps he would see this woman again. All didn't have to be ruined. Better was possible.

They were celebrating in America now. Willard B. Burton of St. J would be in his bed, doubtless alone. He, Jimmy Green, could rightfully say he'd paid the price of victory on a foreign shore. Though being *here,* in the freezing night, this bit of misery—he could never have imagined. *Here,* of course, was never precisely the point you'd attained (a view he often reminded himself). *Here* was a point you'd passed already but didn't realize. Was that what optimism meant? Or was it pessimism? Seeing where you find yourself as inevitable and past? It made him recollect his partner's young daughter. He hadn't thought of her recently. In California—or had been. Working in TV. Patricia.

None of it should've caused what it caused—all the calamity. The embittering loss, the disassembling of life. Though that had possibly been inevitable also. He'd even thought it at the time. It had happened before it happened.

Above, in the cold plane trees, unseen wings fluttered. The dog didn't look up. His finger was throbbing, as was his head. Another light opened in the flat he was soon to return to, as though a door had been pulled back. Nelli stood with light behind her, wearing a white bathrobe and making a beckoning gesture. Her lips were moving.

How long had he been in this dark garden? He'd lost the time. It was the moment to return inside, however. Behind the low clouds, sky was lightening. He turned to go.

Leaving for Kenosha

Louise had the dentist at four—a cleaning and her night guard adjusted—then the two of them were off for early dinner at Cyril's, the place she liked out the Chef Highway, a higgledy-pig roadhouse-on-stilts the hurricane had comically overlooked. Later on they'd head back to Hobbes' condo for homework and later still a Bill Murray movie before bed. It was the great storm's second anniversary.

Tuesday was Walter Hobbes' day with his daughter Louise. Her mother was driving out to appraise some subdivision plats over in La Place, then sleeping at Mitch Daigle's across the lake. Ultimate mojitos, a big doobie, and some boiled shrimp. Walter and Betsy had been divorced a year. Betsy'd "fallen in love" with Mitch while showing him a house—a present he'd planned for his wife that hadn't quite come off. Now and then Hobbes bumped into Mitch's wife Sissy at the Whole Foods. Once a great, auburn-haired, husky-voiced Miss Something or other at UAB, she'd grown sturdy and caustic in young middle age. In the Whole Foods she'd frowned at Walter as if he'd dispatched his now ex-wife to commit espionage on her already-less-than-perfect marriage. He'd turned unexpectedly, and there Sissy was, in front of the lettuce and fennel. He'd instantly smiled, and a silly, dauntless smile had begun on her face, too. Then her shoulders sagged. She'd pursed her lips, shaken her head, chin down. She put her ringless hand up like a traffic cop. Keep away. Then she'd pushed her basket along.

"We observed a moment of silence today for the poor flood victims," Louise was saying as they crossed Prytania, past the French consul's residence, the drooping tricolor in front and the big black Citroën in the circular drive. Outside was ninety-eight, but with the a/c it was pleasant. Kids with their uniform shirttails out were pranking along the steamy sidewalks, whooping and laughing. Privileged kids from another school. The dentist was close. "Today's the second anniversary of the terrible hurricane," Louise said officiously.

"Yes," her father said. "Did any of your classmates lose someone?"

"Of course." Louise was in the sixth grade and knew everything about everything. "Ginny Baxter—who's black. She and I opened our eyes at the same time and almost laughed. It was like praying, but it wasn't. It was weird."

"Did you remember your device?" She'd begun grinding at night, and daytime, too—when night guards weren't socially welcomed. Francis Finerty, her dentist, believed "broxing" was a result of the divorce when Louise was exactly ten years and two months old. Louise believed it was the result of the hurricane and wasn't such a big deal in contrast to what others had suffered.

Louise sighed a profound sigh, placing her small hands atop her green plastic book bag and began twiddling her thumbs. She ignored her father's question as if it were too mundane to discuss. "I have two requests," she said, staring out at the last of the school kids.

"The court will entertain two only. As long as one of them isn't skipping the dentist." Hobbes was a litigator.

Louise sometimes liked her dentist, though not always—the jowly round-belly Irish jokemeister who went on silent Catholic retreats, read Kierkegaard and Yeats alone in the woods, and thought about Thomas Merton. Louise felt this was pretentious. Finerty was likewise divorced—from a pleasantly round-faced Presbyterian woman who'd returned to County Down somewhere in the past. Finerty always complimented Louise on her perfect white teeth, praise she preened over.

"Ginny's family is taking her out of school. They're moving away tomorrow. I want to take her a card or whatever."

"That's very considerate," Walter said. School had been going only a week. Louise had her hands deep in her bag, digging out the plastic case that held her night guard. They were on the dentist's street already. St. Andrews, off of Magazine. The old Irish Channel, appropriately enough. An apartment block. A Chinese takeout. A Circle-K. "Why're they leaving now?" Hobbes was angling into the curb. He intended to wait in the waiting room, read *Time,* then chat up Finerty about fishing off Pointe à La Hache (something they never did together but talked about).

Louise had her night-guard case in both hands. "Her father works for UPS."—she said it like "ups." Versus "downs."—"He got transferred. To Kenosha. Where's that?"

"In Wisconsin. If it's the same one."

"Ginny said that. I forgot."

"It's on Lake Michigan." He'd gone across on a ferry once with some students when he was in law school in

Ann Arbor. A million years ago, though only twenty. "It gets cold."

"Do you think there're a lot of black people living there?"

"There're a lot of black people living everywhere. Except Utah."

Louise was silent. This was enough to know.

Louise was getting out, or starting to. "Would you go buy a nice card? For me? Please? While I'm inside dying, because of you. Then can we go out to her house, and I can give it to her."

"Where does she live?" The afternoon was being diverted—which could spell trouble, since Louise liked routines but said she hated them.

"I have the address." It was in her book bag. Louise said the name of the street—out St. Claude, where the most houses had been destroyed two years ago. It was like farmland now. "She'll be surprised." His daughter had long, rather mousy brown hair and wore glasses that made her look business-like. Sixteen rather than twelve. She was wearing her plaid school kilt and standard wrinkled white blouse and white knee socks. To Hobbes she looked perfect. Was perfect.

"We can do that," he said.

"They have cards at Walmart. Gobs 'n' gobs," Louise

said. She liked saying that. "I bought one for you this year." Her mother took her to Walmart for durable play-wear, book bags. And cards.

"What would the right card say?" Hobbes asked.

Louise looked in at him gravely, from outside the door. She'd been thinking about this. "We'd love to have you come back. Love, Louise Hobbes."

"I doubt I'll find one that says that," Hobbes said. "You'll have to write in a message. I'll get you a plain."

"Get an extremely pretty one. No flowers. No birds." Gasping afternoon heat swarmed into the car. Louise was staring in at her father as if he needed better instructions. "Maybe one with a New Orleans theme. So she'll remember me and be miserable." Louise had the night-guard case in her small hand. Her nails were painted a similar green. Nothing frightened her or seemed impossible yet. "Watch after my book bag," she said. "Please." She closed the car door.

Often on summer nights Walter lay awake, his bachelor apartment high above the swank curve of the river—containers and tanker ships at anchor, running lights smudged in the dense darkness. It hadn't seemed at all necessary for Betsy to divorce him. Mitch Daigle wasn't a bad fellow, but not someone to leave a life over. He'd known Mitch in the Young Barristers, been friendly for at least one summer at the River Bend Club. Mitchell from Mamou, suavely handsome, nervous-eyed, come to the city the way Hobbes had from Mississippi—for a big lick in the oil and gas exuberance, now long finished. There'd been a slew of them—boys—ready to make their stand and get rich. New Orleans didn't require old family ties for that. He and Mitch had gone into staid, white-shoe firms, then drifted to smaller outfits on the money tide. Betsy had found Mitch a suitable Greek Revival on Palmer Street, then, in the come-back showing, fucked him in the client's bed. Betsy explained she'd read a book in college about lost children caught in a cyclone on a South Sea island. All the island animals—lizards, birds, fuzzy creatures—had gone crazy before the storm. It was fashionable to blame bad things on the hurricane—things that certainly would've happened anyway. As if life weren't its own personalized storm. You needn't think too long about why things happened, Hobbes believed. It was enough to admit that things *did*. Still, you tracked back to the cause of harm out of habit, lived in your head. Even Louise Hobbes did it.

Betsy was living alone in a condo, a part-time mom, spending evenings on a hot screened porch, drinking rum, staring out at the distant city lights, becoming bored all over again.

The Walmart parking lot was hotter than any place he'd been so far today, the paper-strewn expanse buttery with fumes from the river. After the hurricane, it had been looted, then looted again for good measure and not been re-opened long. Ants swarming a cupcake. A large black woman in tight fuchsia shorts trailing three tiny kids and a muscular young man in jeans and a Saints jersey—were strolling out the exit, navigating shopping carts.

He got out fast and hurried in, where it was instant, cold relief from the cooking heat outside. He was dressed for the office, not for Walmart. No one looked at all like him. The general feel, once inside, was of vast, unboundaried space, stretching farther than you could see. Families, shoppers, grannies in wheelchairs, abandoned kids, bored young-marrieds in from the country—making a late afternoon of it, letting Walmart be what the day offered. The size of the room made it feel empty—which it wasn't. He hadn't been here in a while.

He asked a checker where greeting cards could be found and went straight there—between school supplies and the discount wines—where no one was around to help. The air here was freezing and chlorinated. Hobbes had sweated along his hairline and shirt collar. There was no reason, of course, to make a complex assignment of this. What he'd choose wouldn't please Louise anyway. Left to herself, hours would be expended finding the perfect card, which would be rejected later.

Most of the tiered offerings, Hobbes found, were for conventional occasions—graduation, birthday, anniversary, confirmation, birth, sympathy over a mother's death, illness, other events requiring good humor. But no messageless cards, except two with sex themes—one, a wit had written on and drawn in a picture of a large penis with a mustache.

Lots of cards depicted black people—tan, clean-cut men wearing chinos and oxford shirts, and pretty women smiling out at fields of bright cornflowers, wearing gold wedding bands, with children who looked like they'd done well with their science projects. They weren't like the people in Walmart today. Ginny Baxter might conceivably resent a card designated for her race. It was because of her race that she was moving. Tempting to ask one of the red-smocked associates, a person of color, if she'd be offended by a well-meaning white child giving her child a friendship card in which the humans depicted were more or less "black." Would it be insensitive? One more thing white people didn't get in the advancing cavalcade. It was exhausting.

Here, though, one said, "Have a Wonderful Trip!" A bright red minivan full of waving, smiling tan children, pulling out the driveway of a blue suburban home with a leafy oak tree in the grassy front yard. Festive balloons rose into a clean blue sky. The message said, "We won't be happy 'til you're back!" Louise would think it was queer and also "inappropriate." The people pictured were also obviously headed to Orlando, not Kenosha. This task was past his capabilities, Hobbes realized. Louise could've easily made a card of construction paper and written her own clever but tender message. Only she'd have been unsure, then mortified. A father's job, this was. Louise never asked for much.

When he first knew Betsy—he was a new lawyer in New Orleans—he'd given her cards he'd customized. Walter specials. "Sorry to hear you've been in the hospital." To which he'd hilariously add "mental." "It's your birthday!" "100th" written in. Betsy loved "funny," or thought she did. Usually they made her say "You're a weirdo," or, "Pretty wild, and likely dangerous." None of which was accurate. He was Walter G. Hobbes from Minter City, a skinny, good-natured oil and gas guy who wore Brooks' suits with loafers and occasionally loud bow ties and argyle socks, voted Democratic and simply hoped all this meant she would marry him. Which she did for a while.

He plucked a card with a big cartoon goose on the front with its orange beak taped shut and its big goose eyes bulging in exasperated excitement. "It goose without saying . . ." Opened up, little red hearts were floating round the inside, where the goose was pictured smiling, its beak un-taped and ". . . I miss you" splashed across in big electric-yellow letters. On the drive out, Louise could add something personal from her bag of colored Sharpies—once she got over hating the card. Ginny would forget all about Louise in two days. Her card wouldn't make it to Kenosha. Which Louise understood. There were no ready words for Ginny and Louise's loss.

Francis Finerty was standing outside his little dentist's office—a comfortable, 1920s, Mediterranean family home converted to an office when he and Mary came in the 1970s. A fresh go, away from bombs and soldiers in the Bogside. He was talking animatedly to Louise on the front steps, still in his pink dentist's smock. Louise was the day's last patient. He wouldn't want her waiting by herself. Finerty was Walter's dentist, too; and Betsy's dentist. Possibly Mitch Daigle's dentist. He was round and exuberant with drooping blue eyes and bushy hair, and a predilection for laughter that made you like him, if not quite warm to him.

He enjoyed telling disgraceful stories from his youth when your mouth was propped open. He didn't tell these to Louise.

"I was on about explaining the concept of the phantom limb to your young medical scholar, here." Finerty came down to the car, his brogue all re-ramped for Louise's sake. Louise had no conception of what Irish was. She *had* explained to her father on previous occasions she intended to be a doctor. Finerty was holding open the door for Louise to climb in with her night-guard container and plastic bag of dental supplies. He smiled to indicate something had been established as collusive between them. Finerty had grown daughters his wife had left him with, and who were Americans. They frustrated him by living in the Bay Area. Finerty enjoyed forging connections between dentist practice and the priestly vocation he'd chosen against—possibly unwisely. He had a fleshy flat nose, a rucked forehead, and thick Groucho brows he could make cavort during off-color *paddy* stories from behind his dental mask. Sometimes he closed his eyes when he spoke—to denote pleasure.

"Are phantom limbs part of night guards and teeth grinding?" Walter ducked to see Finerty through the open door space. Blasted tropical air was crowding in.

"Along in the general thesis of loss, yes," Finerty

said. His eyebrows jinked up as his dark eyes widened. Finerty had a gargly voice and stiff, curly hairs on the backs of his thick, skillful hands. "Apropos this somber season of remembrance."

Louise frowned up at Hobbes in case he was about to say something disallowed—about her. Louise had constructed her "look": studious, often stern, implicitly skeptical, and—in a way only she understood—sexy. She abruptly smiled to exhibit her new shiny-clean teeth, her smell faintly medicinal.

Finerty liked engaging in mock philosophical palaver at the conclusion of appointments. To him, a spiritual dimension haunted all tooth extractions and restorations. Francis, Walter felt, was a man fully engaged, and the loneliest man he knew. Going fishing with him would be a trial.

"Precisely," Walter said to the issues of loss and the somber season. Eyes closed, Finerty laved his soft hands like an undertaker. "A loss becomes its own elemental presence, which is the essence of Beckett, if you don't mind your dentist being a reader."

"How're her teeth?"

Finerty smiled. He had small, blunt teeth of his own, carelessly spaced. "Entirely lovely. She knows it only too well."

"And I know how to take care of myself, too," Louise

said, for some reason rudely. She smiled again, garishly at her father and revealed the yellowish, translucent Lucite guard she'd just snapped in place over her perfect incisors. "I have to wear this all my life," she said.

"At least until the tension in that very life relents." Finerty pulled a face of mock dismay.

"'Til I'm sixty," Louise said.

"We're working on that," Hobbes said. Louise would never be sixty.

"If we knew what went on between women and men, we likely wouldn't need dentists a'tall, would we?" Finerty pushed the door closed and stepped onto the curb in a dainty, little hefty man's hop.

"He's a creep," Louise said. Finerty was only twelve inches from her, sealed off behind the cool window glass, still talking.

"No," Walter said. "He's not. He's a good man, and he likes you."

"Everybody . . ." Louise was starting to say, "Everybody likes me," but didn't, her night guard bulging inside her lips as Walter eased them away from the curb. She knew better. Finerty was waving. She waved back.

"This is ***SO QUEER*****!"** Louise had the card open, studying it menacingly. "Why's this idiot bird got tape on his stupid mouth? What's 'goose without saying'?

I said no birds. 'I miss you'? It's disgusting." It made Walter disheartened. Now Louise would be resentful and unapproachably misunderstood for hours. Their evening was cast adrift. He hadn't considered a goose to be a bird, it was true.

They were driving out St. Claude, the wide, rubbish-cluttered boulevard through the once-thriving all-black section—now littered with shut-down schools, caved-in, looted appliance stores with white goods scattered on the sidewalk, a boarded-up Hardee's. A boarded-up gas station. A boarded-up ramshackle bar with an inert neon roof sign. *Mars Bar.* People were on the streets—mostly black people—observant, missionless. Every other traffic light wasn't working. The city had yet to restore itself here.

"I thought you could use your Sharpies and customize it," Hobbes said.

"And say what? It's stupid. I don't have Sharpies." Louise promptly tore the goose card in half and in fourths and in eighths and threw the pieces on the car floor. "Now I don't have anything to give. Thank God."

"You still have your winning personality," Walter said. "That'll definitely make Ginny change her mind about leaving. After I risked my life at Walmart."

"Fuck Walmart. You didn't risk your life. That's racist." Louise turned toward the spent cityscape and put her bare knees together tightly. Finerty would've had a more novel approach with Louise. His Irish-American daughters wouldn't comport themselves thusly in times of turmoil. Hobbes felt he lacked a novel approach.

"How old are you?" Walter said, steering cautiously through a signal-less intersection. No police around to save you. People were in an unforgiving mood.

"Old enough to say 'Fuck Walmart,'" Louise said. "And a lot more."

"Well, try to save back something nice for Ginny." Louise had pronounced the address on Delery Street shortly before going ballistic about the goose card.

"I'm not going without a gift. *That* goes without saying." Louise had righteous anger always at her disposal.

"You'd better concoct something to say, then. It's the gesture that counts. Or would've."

"What am I supposed to say?" Louise sniffed, as if she might cry a little, or try. That was *not* one of her assets. Dry eyes were her redoubt.

"Let's see," Walter said. "How about 'Dear Ginny, I'll miss you when you're gone.' Or, 'Dear Ginny, I hope your new life in Kenosha is wonderful.' Or, 'I hope I see you again.' Those seem serviceable."

"They're pathetic."

Louise was working her teeth and did *not* have her device in.

"No, they're not. They're things that *shouldn't* go without saying. This is a part of your education."

"Why did you get divorced?" Louise said blazingly. It had been her default defense for some time—always from ambush. A mean rabbit out of a pretty hat.

"I forget," Walter said, seeing the Delery sign—a paper placard stapled to a telephone pole, the regular sign hurricaned away. All around were other handwritten signs, in Spanish. "Demolición de Su Casa." "Reparos." "No se siente sola."

"No, you don't," Louise said. "Was it your fault?"

"I'm sure," Walter said.

"Why did you do it, then? You were bad."

"Nobody was bad," Walter said. "Not even you." Again, he felt profound fatigue. "It's always easier if somebody's bad."

Louise looked at him contemptuously, blinking her small, intense eyes behind her glasses, fists clenched, her dental supplies still in her lap. Louise had gained weight in these months. She now had an adolescent pimple on her forehead near her hairline. She was leaving it untended to out of malice. The torn goose card pieces were scattered on her school shoes.

"I don't understand you," Louise said. She was now twenty-five, he was her poor-communicator boyfriend, they'd just broken up, possibly for the last time.

"I know," Walter said, slowing to turn alongside a great many-windowed, weather-beaten, brick high school now deserted. "It'll have to do though. It'll make an interesting subject for later life."

"What *later*?" Louise said victoriously. "There won't be any later." She liked the final word in all arguments. He did not.

Delery—long, straight, potholed, refuse-strewn, going toward the lake—was a street of wreckages. Where the flood had churned past, homes were flattened, floated away, had their roofs removed. Others—compact brick ones—were scoured out, their walls surviving staunchly. Weeds thrived where concrete slabs had held houses. A sleek sporting craft had been miraculously hoisted and deposited atop a white frame bungalow. An ancient Studebaker had been pushed through the front door into someone's living room. All magical achievements of the water. Most houses bore a dark water stain above their casements and the messages of rescuers. "No Pig Found/9-10-05." "Dog in house/10-8-05." Another simply, "One Dead Here."

Farther down beneath the baking, white sky, a crew

of shirtless, aspiring young black men was busily loading usable timbers and shingles onto a sagging pickup bed. No one was remaining in the surrounding blocks of battered streets. All was becoming fields. A few surviving trees. A long view. It was the submersible land everyone knew about. It had always been mainly black and poor, but still a place to live. Louise's school had made a field trip, and later written moving poems about it, painted gaudy landscapes, written letters to kids in faraway cities, predicting better things. Come back.

Louise was possibly cataloguing complimentary phrases she could address to Ginny when they got where Ginny lived, and had sunk into silence. The fell weight of destruction—grammarless, attractively foreign—had yet to fully impress her. Some uniformed white men were up ahead—utility workers in yellow helmets and white jumpsuits—gathered around a light pole, connecting, disconnecting. Two wrecked houses behind them had little trailers parked in front. A black-and-white spotted dog stood in the grass, staring.

"This is horrible," Louise said, as if she'd never seen any of it before. She pressed her nose to the window, her glasses frames ticking the pane. She had a better reason to be here now.

The address numbers on the few standing houses led them to the place they were going, which was not far.

"Ginny lives with her grandmother." Louise sighed, emitting a small cloud onto the window glass. She had found a new course to being resolute—affect competent ennui.

Ahead, in the next emptied block, was a collection of vehicles none of the other houses had out front. A man was in the street, lifting household articles—a chair, a small table, a lamp—into the back of a red-and-white U-Haul that had a mountain scene from the state of Idaho on its side. "It's not just potatoes!"

"There's Ginny," Louise said, buoyant, no longer bored. She now knew everything she needed to say.

A child dressed in exactly Louise's uniform stood on the side of the street opposite the man loading household articles. Two cars were parked in the weeds where a house had been but now was a concrete slab. She was just watching. A chain-link fence recollected a back yard where a mangle ironing contraption sat marooned. Everything around Ginny was open ground with different squares where houses had been. A steepled white church rose in the distance. Gulls soared, singing out. The character of destruction, Hobbes thought, was quite diverse.

Louise was out before Hobbes could get stopped. Ginny saw Louise, knew her, but didn't move. Louise marched straight to her and began talking. It was an official visit. She took Ginny's hand and waggled her arm until Ginny said something and smiled. Louise and Ginny looked alike in their uniforms and tortoiseshell glasses and long straight hair.

Across from where the girls were, stood a remarkably new but small house, raised to a man's height on concrete pillars, everything freshly painted bright blue with white trim. A new concrete driveway had been laid, azalea plantings set against the base of the pillars, bright plastic geraniums in window boxes, a thick carpet of St. Augustine fresh off the truck. On the elevated front porch, a desiccated, elderly black woman in a long skirt watched the man loading boxes and suitcases into the square trailer—all things brought from inside.

For a moment the man didn't acknowledge Hobbes in his car. Then he stopped loading and looked first at the two girls and at the car and Walter Hobbes getting out. He was moderate-sized with short, neat hair, and was wearing a tank top he'd sweated through, plaid Bermudas he'd also sweated through, and black basketball sneakers with white knee-highs. His skin was the same light-brown color as Ginny's—just like Louise's color mostly matched Hobbes' own. The man loading the U-Haul stood a moment, then came across the street, wiping his hands together.

"Louise wanted to say good-bye," Walter said. Everything was knowable.

"All right," the man said. He was thirty-two, smooth-muscled, compact. He might very well have *been* a UPS man—mannerly, implacable, thorough.

"They're in the same class," Walter said. "My daughter."

"Okay." The man regarded the girls. Ginny and Louise were locked in a fast privacy. "Ginny," he said, interrupting them. "Louise's daddy." Louise and Ginny both looked at Hobbes, who waved. Ginny waved back. Louise turned away.

A second woman appeared on the porch of the blue house, beside the elderly desiccated woman. She was very dark skinned and statuesque, her hair braided in rows. Her face, even from the street, was reproachful.

"I'm Walter Hobbes." Walter extended his hand.

"Miller," the man said and shook Walter's hand with a not-firm grip. He was almost featurelessly, smoothly handsome, his face shiny with sweat. He had a small gold stud in his left earlobe. On one bicep was a tattoo that said "Cher" in ornate script. He wore a wedding ring.

They both stood then in the unmoving heat and looked down the street of remaining ruined houses and emptied lots in the direction of the lake. This was the girls' visit. Nothing need be said about how it was to be a UPS man, or a practitioner of the law, or what it felt like to leave for Kenosha in the white heat of August.

"What do you do?" Miller said. First name? Last name?

"I'm a lawyer." It sounded quaint to say that, out here.

"I get that," Miller said. "I'm with UPS."

Hobbes smiled, nodded. The best company ever. Best benefits. Best work conditions. Best customers. Not even like working. "Is that your house?" Walter looked at the bright blue shotgun with the women on the porch watching him as if he was up to something. Louise laughed and said "Oh *you*. You're so funny." The skinny spotted dog that had been up the street trotted past and on into what had become empty fields.

Miller motioned at the women and nodded. "It's my mother-in-law's."

"It's pretty," Walter said.

"It's where her old house sat 'til the storm come through. Some people showed up from a church. Told her they were going to build it back. And did. She didn't even ask. She just moved back in like nothing had happened. Nothing really surprises her. She's from the country."

Anything he could think to say now, Hobbes understood, would be insulting. He lived in an apartment overlooking the river.

Miller regarded the house as if his thinking was along those lines. "We moved in with her when our house got ruint'. But. I took a transfer up north. I ain't turning that down. My wife wants to stay here. But . . ."

"How does Ginny feel?"

Miller ran a hand down his bare arm where his Cher tattoo was. The sun was burning straight onto them from behind clouds. Walter's jacket was wet through. "It's just a game to her. A big adventure." Walter looked at the girls together. "Tell me something good about Wisconsin," Miller said. His brows raveled as if he would take whatever was said seriously.

"It's on a lake," Walter said. "It gets cold. The Packers play there."

"I'm starting to be worried about that cold," Miller said.

"They have seasons," Walter said. "We don't have those. You might like it."

"Okay," Miller said and paused to let this idea cycle past. "I went through Chicago in the Navy," he said. "But it was in the summer."

Then they were silent while their little girls walked

a few yards farther down the street, arms around each other's waist. They had their little girl things to impart, more private than earlier. "So, how're *you* doin'?" Miller said. The two women on the porch turned and walked back through the sliding door. One of them had laughed, and said, "You know how *he* goes . . ." An air-conditioning unit hummed, noise Walter hadn't noticed. Miller's question meant, ". . . since the hurricane happened . . . What's been doing? You're a human being, apparently."

Walter looked down the street at Louise Hobbes, her kilt, her knee socks, her glasses. She was caressing a lock of Ginny's hair—the spidery tips.

"I'm doing all right," Walter said. "I guess that's how I'm doing."

"You livin' good?"

"I guess so," Walter said.

"There you go," Miller said, smiling. "That's what matters." He, too, looked down toward the girls—lost now in each other's past and present.

Walter observed Miller's hand extend, ready to be shaken again with the same un-firm grip.

"Good to meet you," Walter said.

"All right, then. You be careful," Miller said.

"Absolutely," Walter said, taking the large, soft hand

in his. Behind him his other hand found the warm door handle of his car. He smiled back. Miller. Last name, first name. Someone no longer living here.

"We're leavin', quick as I'm loaded," Miller said, walking back to his trailer, carrying on talking. "Make it to Memphis. Be to Wisconsin tomorrow. Work the next day. You know how it is."

"I do," Walter said. "Safe trip."

"I'm a good driver, if it ain't already snowin'."

"It won't be," Walter said.

"There you go," Miller said.

Far down Delery, where the workers in yellow helmets were collected around the light pole, a police cruiser turned onto the street and began slowly inching their way. It had been satisfactory here. Better than it might've.

Louise sat in her seat with her legs crossed, hands in her lap, pleased. She'd achieved victory. "She's lucky to be moving away," she said, watching the demolished neighborhood glide past. They were on St. Claude again, where it was possible to view the city's center at a distance, as if from a desert floor—tall bank buildings in the gritty haze, hotels, office towers not ruined by the hurricane. The city—the middle, where Walter worked—always seemed to rise up where it shouldn't be. Once, flying in from somewhere, the plane had banked west so he could gaze down the river's course to the old quarter—the part the tourists knew. What a mistake to put a city here, he thought. A man from Des Moines would tell you that. Nothing promised good from this placement.

"Did you do okay without a card?" Walter asked. They were bound for their hilarious early dinner at Cyril's. Ginny and her family were now sent on their toilsome, hopeful way. Bill Murray was on the horizon. Louise's mother was comfortably across the lake at Mitch Daigle's. Walter Hobbes would be at work tomorrow. All was as good as it would be.

"I definitely did," Louise said. Vivid sunlight sparkled through the windshield, the kind that could give you a headache.

"It's good to know you can put things in your own words," he said. "It's hard sometimes, but it's better."

"Whatever," Louise said. "Or buy a better card. Or not go to Walmart, which was my idea, which I'm sorry about. Or never have any friends." Her jaw was working, grinding. He knew it without seeing it.

"One at a time," Walter Hobbes said.

"Do you think possibly *I* could maybe move?" Louise said. The goose-card clutter lay under her shoes, the dental supplies sack on the seat between them.

"Well. You could move to Wisconsin and live on a glacial lake surrounded by stately conifers, go to a country school and learn to canoe and memorize the legends of the Chippewa, and have your classmates say 'holy cripes' and 'Jeez Louise.'" He looked at his daughter proprietarily, reached across and touched her shoulder to indicate he wasn't making fun, only trying to tickle her. Many things would be possible for her in time. Not even much time. Some of them would surely be good.

"I'm thinking about going to Italy or maybe China. Or Ireland. And never seeing anybody I know now again." She withdrew her laptop from her book bag but didn't turn it on, just looked ahead.

"Would you include me?" Hobbes said.

"And Mother, too," Louise said, and gave him a look of anguish. A look that saw a fearsome future. She turned her laptop on and waited.

And for that instant, Walter Hobbes experienced a sensation of something being about to happen. A feeling of impendment—not necessarily bad or good, just something in the offing. Though he knew that if he only paused in his thinking, as he'd recently learned to do, didn't follow his thoughts all the way to where they led, or came from, then this sensation of impendment could subside, or even develop into something he liked. Louise was a smart child beyond her years.

In her life she would go to these places and to many others and learn many things. And she would be allowed, also, to forget many things. There was nothing he needed to rebut—only to let her words pass away. He drove on then. They were going out the Chef to Cyril's, the center of the city still a remarkable feature in the evening's steamy distance.

A Free Day

Eileen Lewis had taken the bus down from Ballycastle to spend the night with Tom Magee at the Maldron at the airport. Tom was off to Paris early, and Eileen was planning a day in Dublin. Not really to shop—though there were the arcades, and the nice little jewelry boutiques in Johnson's Court, where she'd bought small things when she was at university, and still occasionally would step in. She'd bought some pretty garnet earrings two years ago, though she'd no occasion for them and hadn't seen them in some time. The day, though, was just to be a free day. A day in town.

Tom had married her old Queens' roommate, Marjorie Stearns. They lived in Westport, County Mayo, where he was in the off-shore services business. An engineer or some such. Eileen was an integrated primary teacher. Marjorie was American—from New Hampshire. "Live Free *Then* Die"—was her joke about that. She was "fiercely independent" but otherwise humorless. A barrister. Tom and Eileen had had this arrangement under way for four years, since a night on the town—the four of them—at Pep's, when Eileen was still married to Mick and the kids were little. Mick was long gone. The kids nine and eight. Eileen was thirty-six. In Ballycastle now, she'd been "seeing" (the awful word) a good man named James Bowen, who fished and whose wife had died. With James she could perceive a possibility. He was mirthful, kind, liked music, had almost gone to Queens but for his father dying—the boat at risk of being abandoned. The familiar story of staying. James knew nothing of Tom Magee. Marjorie *apparently* knew nothing about Eileen. There wasn't any long-range plan to be anything more. Only this. Three, four times a year, when Tom flew out—sometimes to America for seminars—and Eileen would come down on a pretext. "Extra teacher training." Extended ed. Not that James would've asked. No great wrongness to it, Eileen felt. Marjorie was a bit on the mannish side and probably didn't afford Tom her full attention. Whereas Tom was artistic in spite of the engineering. He played coronet in the city musicale, went to the ballet, liked sailing, had been at Trinity reading English when the thought occurred to him he'd need to earn a living.

Far, indeed, from great wrongness, Eileen believed. Far from guilty sensations, or of some reckoning needing eventually to be faced. Instead, there was a great exhilaration of rightness. Tom's life imbalances being put easily right without a grain of harm visited on a living soul. And her own. A kind of tonic. Tom was certainly no one she'd choose for life. Quite dry. He had a boyhood limp and a professorish beard and was losing hair. She'd likewise put on a stone cooking for the boys and felt her drive not as strong as once. Fucking Tom Magee in the airport Maldron, then having a free day in town while he flew away to wherever, was just a thing you did. The same way being a single mum raising two boys in a shabby little one-street seaside town, where there was pitiful to do but go to work and to the bank and the pub with her fisherman beau, was a thing you simply did. Couldn't *not.* It wasn't the sex. That she could get any day, and did. It was the lark of it. Tom was the smooth and occasionally pleasing way in for that. A portal.

In Dublin she did very little. Took the airport coach in. Had a late breakfast at Bewley's, when it was still open. Took a walk through Trinity—Tom's college—

where she'd once hoped to go, herself, but lacked the funds. Inside the walls was especially charming. She could walk about and never know where she was apt to come out. Plus, the little shops in the old part. A pint at O'Neill's, or the Duke, where the professors drank. Sometimes something would be on at the National Library—a talk or a recitation. Then that was that—the walk across the river to the bus, then the long trip north, when she'd sleep as the miles poured past. Friday (her flexi day) over to Saturday. Sunday rest. School Monday. On the bus, she'd glance at the various riders and think they were all engaged in some similar escapade—only in the details were they different. She used to think—when there were still the red phone boxes—that when you saw a woman talking in a pay phone you'd be certain something was in the works. Solo on the bus, the same. But again, you couldn't *not.* It was such a small thing. Whereas to live (and die) on others' terms was giving life away cheap. She wouldn't do that.

The logistics had become simple and customary. Change in Ballymena to Europa station, then the Translink to the airport—climbing down amidst the other travelers going on to Galway and Cork. Take the courtesy van the short distance to the Maldron, walking in as though she owned it, with only a largish handbag. Tom would've phoned already with his room number. The occasionally heart-pounding walk down the clean-smelling corridor, past the nodding, Philippine cleaners with their carts. Fingernails on the door. Then everything was commenced. If familiar, it was no less consuming and occasionally even frantic, coming close to violent, which she cared less about but Tom apparently needed as a measure of the ardor. He was forty-five, did the elliptical and free weights, in addition to sailing and the coronet.

Later—in bed—they would talk about subjects that were allowable and didn't tread into the sensitive. She always asked politely about Marj, whom she hadn't seen since this all took up, and felt she would likely not see again. His work interested him still—being off-shore; his company being bought by a good firm in Norway. He did not inquire about James, of whom she said little except that he existed and golfed. Some talk arose about her boys and their difficulties with the father who lived now in Derry and saw them infrequently, which Eileen resented, if only for the time lost. Tom and Marjorie had no boys *or* girls, and there was sometimes fitful, insincere talk of how one got old, etc. Eileen did not give much thought to growing old—only to being forty, which was coming up fast. And then what? They laughed about it.

Sometimes (not always), they would make love again. Though, if the residuum of their separate journeys worked to induce sleep instead of passion, they skipped it. Tom slept soundly and silently. She merely dozed, thinking about him in the highly restricted and fractional ways she felt were appropriate but not preoccupying. She knew him only a little when all was said, whereas Marjorie she knew better. They'd traveled to New Hampshire from university one fall break, met the educated, welcoming New England mother, the stern Antrim father, the special-needs sister; saw the family's tall log house in the primeval woods. Once she and Marjorie kissed and caressed on a walk along a forest trail, where the light was bright and crisp. She'd liked it; they'd both liked it—but never did it again or spoke of it, could never precisely meet each other's gaze again, though they tried. Yes, there was a tedium to this business with Tom, the tedium of a long affair. And a betrayal. Though she liked him, would touch his back, his bum, his thin hair while he slept. She could easily know him better, step into more serious questions (his fears, his dissatisfactions, his illnesses, his feelings about Marjorie) but would never be more intimate with him than this. Exchange of personal data wasn't intimacy; in fact, it could be intimacy's death stroke. Her life with Mick had proved that beyond a shadow. Listening to Tom breathe, hearing his soft snores, the noises in his stomach, hearing the occasional—well, yes. And fucking him—in ways she enjoyed. This was as intimate as she cared for, and in large measure as much as she'd ever wanted or missed.

By seven P.M.—dark in the winter, light in summer—they'd been in the room four hours. Tom always brought Chablis and put it on ice. Dinner was proposed by him as a relief. The city, of course, was miles away—a sixty-euro cab ride there and back. Though there was Malahide, even Swords, nearer places they could go and "dine." An Indian, an Afghan, and two pastas—northern and southern. A taxi took you, a taxi brought you back. Never once did they fail to make love on re-arrival. Usually for longer, often languidly with an appreciation for different details, a sense for the other that might've got lost in the earlier flourishes.

And then straight off to sleep, sometimes still "united," often without good night. Just falling in, with silent consent. Tom would rise early, dress in the dark as she slept or pretended, and depart (his limp audible) after kissing her in the warm bedclothes. Once he'd whispered "I love you." Though even in sleep, she knew he'd mis-thought her for Marjorie. He never said it again. The last was the door softly clicking shut.

Eileen awoke startled, thinking it must be ten or more. The blackout curtains deceived the time. Tom was in Paris already. The empty Chablis bottle a shadow beside the TV, the only remnant of him, other than the obvious. The day seemed to spring at her.

Though she saw it was only eight. She could hear the rumble and gathering thrust of the jets queuing not far away—the curtains muffling that, too. A peek through the gap revealed the roadway full up with cars off the roundabout. She herself could be going somewhere. Lisboa. Even America. A pleasing thought. James has talked about a trip at half-term. Nothing decided. It was only late January. There was time.

She had, however, a terrible thirst, and a genuine hunger, as well. With Bewley's shut, breakfast in town wasn't the thing it'd been. There were the posh hotels—which were too pricey. Buswells was less but was too small and closed in. Plus the unlikable feeling that one was in with a tour, some coach huffing outside, heading south. In Bewley's she'd felt a local, knew how the ordering scheme went, could read the papers 'til the shops opened.

Better to take breakfast here—as she and Tom had

done twice, when his flight was delayed. They'd stayed in bed, made love, though the cleaners had knocked, and the noise of the planes was distracting.

First a shower, though, then the blue wool slacks with the new jumper she'd bought at Debenhams, when she'd taken the boys up. And the still stylish yet reliable boots in case the weather turned bad. *And* the Aquascutum. James' present at Christmas, which she didn't like. "You remind me of a spy," he'd said when she put the thing on. "It must be how you think of me," she'd said. He'd laughed. She had not. It wasn't entirely fair.

She'd eaten little at the Thai in Malahide the previous night. Picked at her noodle dish, been quiet. Just an odd bit of a vacancy. Postcoital. Hormones. The lot. The winter yaws. Plus Tom feeling "in total command" after lovemaking. Banging on about the new bosses from "Norwegia"—his joke name for it. And Paris, where he had his favorite "little restaurant" no one knew about. And of course Marjorie. She couldn't remember much of those parts. Some court case Marj was arguing.

Now, though, was Saturday. Hers. Her free day. After breakfast, possibly take a taxi to the bottom of Dame Street if the road works were finished—which they probably were not. Pity a tram wouldn't serve the airport. What a breeze that would be for such occasions as this. Which, she believed, would not be ending any time soon. Why would they?

At eight forty-five the breakfast room was all but empty. A slow day—Saturday. All the cheap package tours departing early. Tom, whom she's scarcely thought about, would be back tonight, driving himself west, while she'd be on the bus with something right for James and for Frank and Bob. Computer things she knew about only because they'd submitted a list with the names of stores they'd read up on.

She took the fry-up with the trimmings. And a latté. Tom had ordered a Bristol's the last time; but that would wooze up the morning, take away the keenness for things once she got to town. Plus, it was inevitably chilly—she hadn't been out; a buzz would intensify the cold. Last night had been quite brisk nearer the sea. She hadn't liked it.

In the *salon de thé* was only a man having breakfast with his teenage daughter in her school uni. And two Africans—a small man and a large woman in their pretty tribal garb. They were laughing softly, though the room was still and otherwise silent. A bit cold, the light slightly insufficient, the staff taking down the buffet, and noises coming through the kitchen porthole doors. It wasn't unpleasant. The eggs properly poached, the tomatoes crusty, warm-through and sweet on top. The sausages popping. All very convenient. The staid English-y feel of things seemed right, even here, as the day commenced. Not Bewley's, by any means. *Tempus omnia revelat,* or some such.

She had a thought, just for a twinkling—a strange thought. All of them in a queue—Marjorie and James and her sons, and loss-leader Mick and Patrick French in Ballycastle, with whom she'd had the brief dazzle just before (and just after) Mick had left, and who still occasionally rang up. It wasn't a thought meant to tweeze out what they all might be thinking just at this moment. You wouldn't know, and no matter. But that they were all in the full throes of whatever they were up to on a Saturday, wherever they were. While she was, unbeknownst, having a fine breakfast in complete serenity and seclusion, without a thought (or almost) for any of them. Such motionless moments—being in this less than splendid room with utter strangers—were hard to come by, and precious, and needed to be demanded, even at the cost of . . . well, the cost of it all. Tom did not enter into this—this queue of faces and lives. Tom and his coronet was the wild card that filled out the hand, and needn't be all that much considered. What she'd said. A portal.

She paid with her euros—Tom had certainly closed

out the room account upon leaving, the room being on the firm. Eating "in," without Tom, was new. Normally, he'd hang the *Please Let Me Rest* card outside on the door, so she could sleep in—though it wasn't so relaxed being in the room alone when she wasn't officially supposed to be. Except, she couldn't leave when he left in the dark. To do *what* once she alighted in Dame Street at half six? Still, she'd always gotten up and chain-locked the door once he was gone as precaution against the cleaners. Then got back to sleep.

The young woman with her cart was already in the corridor when she got off the lift, though not outside room 119, which had the *Please Let Me Rest* on its door handle. What was the Spanish word she so liked the sound of—soft and lotion-y to one's tongue? *Huespedes.* Guests. And some French story called that. *L'hote.* Odd, the things flooding back when the mind finds its ease. *Huespedes.*

The key card Tom had left now didn't work for some reason—the tiny bead on the lock going to red didn't change to green. No familiar click or soft buzz to signal entry. Possibly she'd kept it in her pocket close to her phone the way you weren't meant to, but had never happened before. She turned the shiny little card over so the arrows were down and the magnetic strip up. Nothing. She rubbed the card on her jumper sleeve as she'd seen shop clerks do. And which had worked. But the light stayed red. Tom had said, and James had remarkably said much the same once in the Canarys, "They want to make it clear to you the fuckin room's not about to be yours. You're in their custody. You need to keep proving that you haven't pilfered the key, slipped a deft hand in someone's coat pocket, and gotten up here ahead to hijack the diamonds." Once, when the card had failed coming from dinner, it'd been necessary to return to reception, present it and have the key re-programmed. As if, Tom had said. Meaning, *as if* he'd be up to anything inappropriate on the firm's nickel. A royal pain. Gone, he'd remarked, were the days of real keys, real locks and real people.

Back down the corridor the cleaner's cart sat outside room 124, the door opened, lights inside. Eileen stepped down and tapped lightly on the door jamb using the defective key card, not wishing to cause alarm. A smiling, pretty Asian face popped out from the bathroom, yellow earbuds both sides.

"I'm so sorry to disturb you," Eileen said, "but my key's gone cranky. Could you possibly let me into room 119? I'm about to leave." Could the young woman even hear her? Eileen held up the card, the no-good key card, as her evidence. No funny stuff afoot. The girl had the master on the cord around her gray uniform waist.

The little face instantly brightened, a look of alertness, recognition, sympathy, immense willingness to give limitless assistance.

"No English," she said, earbuds still in. In a display of contrition, she pushed out her lower lip like a child about cry. "Key no good. Go reception. They fix."

"If you understand that much," Eileen said, "*you* could let me in. It's just my things in there. My purse. My passport with my picture. My driving license. I can prove I'm me. It's a matter of a moment. I promise. I won't tell a soul. It's our secret." She now held out a ten-euro bill. "It's the least. I'd be so grateful." There were of course security cameras. Gone were the days of necessary secrets.

Eileen's heart for some reason went pound, pound, pound. Something that didn't exist an hour ago, when she was safely *in* room 119, peeking out at the traffic queue to Terminal 2—something that didn't exist *then,* did now, but really hadn't needed to exist if she'd merely stayed in the room as she'd always done 'til it was time to leave. Oh, the knowledge had been there—cautionary knowledge. One simply hadn't observed it, hadn't chosen to see it, had chosen instead something more agreeable. The *salon de thé.* The nice breakfast.

The mind's ease. Marjorie—the barrister—would be the one to tell her all that, were she to have the chance.

"Go reception," the young woman was saying. She was pointing toward the lift alcove, or perhaps the stairs at the end, with the green exit sign portraying the man appearing to flee. "They fix for you." She smiled as she had already. "Very easy. Be okay."

"Are you very sure?" Eileen said, brightening herself. The things that now presented (but hadn't before) offered an odd appeal. A fresh discovery. Her heart slowed. This would be fine. "I could go a hundred," she said. Once it was a sum of money. A hundred. So much you could buy.

"Yes," the girl said, beaming. "Reception. Have go to work now."

"Yes, definitely," Eileen said. "You go to work."

"Have nice day."

"I'll try to."

There was a moment at the reception—the moment she'd have happily had elude her—the burly Sikh with a bright green turban behind the shining counter, much more than well dressed, his lacquered face also shining. Wonderful teeth. Polished nails. A brilliant smile. Aftershave. You simply couldn't not *try,* though—not *try* to save the day at whatever expense of one's dignity.

"Oh, no need," the big clerk said and inserted a blank into the little magnetizer box. A look of complicity. "Absolutely no worries." She'd mentioned her driving license.

"The things are all mine, inside," she'd said. "My passport. A brown purse, some black shoes, an empty bottle of Chablis, some underthings." This, to be engaging.

"Where has your husband flown off to to-deeh?" the clerk said cheerfully. She'd said Tom was her husband; they'd kept their names, all very modern; just sometimes a bit bumpy. Like now.

"To Paris," she said brazenly.

"Ah," the clerk said. "I have never been. But someday."

"I've never either," Eileen said. Which wasn't true.

"So, we'll see each other there," he said, handing her the fresh little key card, ready for use.

"I'll look for you," she said.

"I've been to America," he said with pride.

"Still awaiting my moment there, too," she said, ignoring New Hampshire. "Someday, someday."

"So. I'll see you there, as well. *Out* to America. Is that how you say?" He was gloating, she knew.

"I suppose," she said.

It hadn't been so difficult, once her mind was put to

it and she could let go of how such things can make you feel. It'd been quite simple.

The free day had not turned out so well. It *was* chilly. She had gotten cold. On the uneven pavement on Nassau Street, she'd turned an ankle in front of Eason's. Then it had snowed, just a little, but her old boots got damp and her feet felt numb. The little estate shop was shuttered and padlocked for Saturday. The latté she had in Powerscourt arrived weak, though the carvery at O'Neill's was entirely acceptable. She'd sat at the snug window and watched it snow 'til it quit. She found a scarf for James in Brown Thomas; two shirts and a bird book for the boys (no games); a sheer silk blouse for herself—which James would like. She thought of buying something for Tom—something nautical and funny. But where would he wear it?

A further stroll through the Green in the damp and cold began to feel excessive with her achy ankle, though she made it to the top of Grafton Street and around down into Dawson Street past the smart men's shops and the fancy restaurants. The tram works were still up. Luas. Lewis. Someday you'd ride to Phoenix Park, but not—it seemed—to the airport.

Ultimately, she walked, ankle and all, across O'Connell Bridge and onto an earlier bus—a direct one, lucky enough. It had all commenced with a startle at eight, and not got better. The next time she'd factor it in, be more prudent.

In her seat, by herself, she thought a thousand things, letting the day climb up and off. When Tom was later driving back by himself, she would be home in bed. They never spoke on the day of. What was to say? I miss you? So, so funny, though, for her heart to go racketing just because she'd got locked out. As if the whole spindly edifice could go up in flames. The grisly details. Some feral creature staring back at her as from a dark cave, eyes burning. What was the shite poem? ". . . What the hand, dare seize the fire?" And yet, how nice the bearded, turban bloke had been. He'd had it all figured. Came with the yob. Such improvisations made it all interesting. Still, he could've been pissy.

But now. What was *supposed* to happen as consequence of just such an indelicate moment as had passed? Some new and sudden and fiercely clear *understanding* of one's self? A stern new caution—like a new key? What was the French word? An *aperçu*? That wasn't right. But it was all rubbish. Everyone was an adult—excepting of course the boys. If one was expected to learn something, there was nothing. Nothing at the moment, at least.

She was exhausted, as the fall and rise of winter

landscape—Dundalk, now—wore past. Almost the sea view from the right side, snow commencing again but gradually changing to rain. There was so much time to be alive; then you weren't anymore. It was little enough to ask. The ankle throbbed on a bit, 'til she let her eyes give way, allowed the bus—its steady rumble—to soothe her out, so that in a while she fell asleep.

Second Language

Jonathan and Charlotte were divorced but had stayed friends. Charlotte Porter believed that if you married a second time, you had the right only to expect "pieces" of what the first marriage had contained, though you had to be certain the pieces you got were the good ones. Charlotte had *had* a long marriage—to Francis Dolan, the architect—tall, craggy, handsome, black-haired, dark-eyed Irishman she'd met at NYU, and who'd made his career designing steel and glass corporate cubicles of the kind you passed on the interstate near where they'd lived and raised their children in Goldens Bridge, north of the city. At age forty-five, Francis Dolan had announced he'd like to give northern Maine a try; learn about wooden boats, restore one, sail it to Ireland, later possibly sail around the world. Would Charlotte care to come along?

Charlotte had given this some thought, since she knew sudden, spectacular deviations from the marital norm could be perilous. Francis had always been an agreeable but affectless husband—typical Kerry-man, he believed. He didn't mix cheerfully with people, including other architects. He treated his and Charlotte's two children with affectionate but distant regard, yet loved Charlotte—as she loved him. (Though he often acted toward her as if he was slightly surprised he knew her.) The year was 1998—the year of Monica Lewinsky. Charlotte had three years before achieved a broker's license and done well (instantly) in residentials. Unemployment was down. Housing was brimming. There was no war. Money was to be had. She was forty-four, a tall, easily smiling, lanky, intelligent beauty with a sharp sense of humor and a degree in finance, who felt confident about most everything she did. In her middle twenties she'd been a second-tier runway model at Eileen Ford while working on Wall Street. House hunters often did double takes when she hauled "those legs" out of the car to present a property.

Charlotte, therefore (she felt, entirely in character), decided *no.* She would stay on in Goldens Bridge for the period Francis was away at sea. She'd look after the children—eight and nine—and pine for him like a seafarer's wife, sew quilts, make bees' wax, keep a diary, stand on a widow's walk, etc. until their life resumed. She knew when Francis came back, he would likely be changed. But she would be also. The children would be. These changes would entail challenges to each other that would require adjustments, new decisions, and lead them (and the children) in new directions together, which everybody understood marriages needed but sometimes could not achieve any other way. She had lived by herself only a little since college, but looked forward to it now. Francis Dolan's ensign would rise again from the horizon. Then they would see. Nothing seemed to her irregular.

Jonathan Bell had met and married Charlotte Porter all in the space of three months in 2002, during which time Jonathan bought an expensive loft on Watts Street for which Charlotte was his broker. (She'd reclaimed "Porter" after she and Francis were divorced, when Francis didn't sail home.) Jonathan had fallen gaspingly in love with Charlotte, showered her with museums and concerts and dinners in the *then* top-drawer places. He took her to the Columbia–Yale game (he'd played for the Lions in '71), bought her diamond earrings at Harry Winston, drove her up for the autumn color tour to the Green Mountains, where he slept with her for the first time in the Woodstock Inn and proposed to her at breakfast—to which she surprisingly accepted. They were married at Christmas, three months before hostilities commenced in Iraq and just as the housing market started (though no one realized) to go south.

Johnny Bell was from Chicago. He'd come out of college in the early '70s with a degree in petroleum engineering, burning to get into the oil business. At the Latin School he'd been the unusual boy—big, unwieldy, soft-muscled but an intense athlete, who performed enviably as a stoutish soccer goalie, but also read history and the Romantics, wrote an excellent paper on Charles Beard and the dispute over economic origins of the Revolution—which won a prize—and also played the French horn. He loved reading. But the idea of world oil exploration, he realized, was his great and guiding passion. He believed if he got rich fast—and he would—he could read all the books he wanted, go back and get a Ph.D. in something, and end up teaching big, cumbersome, innocent-but-smart kids like himself in some good New England prep school, where teaching counted and people came out well-rounded—the way he was. He had no doubt about this.

He'd married a girl from his North Shore neighborhood. Mary Linn (Hewlett), who'd gone to college at Champaign-Urbana and trained to be a grade-school teacher, was a year older and waited to marry big Johnny Bell the moment he graduated. Johnny'd gone to work for an obscure wildcatter company in east Texas—on the lease end (which was his plan). In five years he learned enough about seismology and mineral rights and leveraging, about how to talk *to* people, not down to them, and (importantly) when to step up with the money. By 1980, he felt he was experienced and savvy enough to go out on his own and had commenced roaming about Texas buying up small leases the bigger companies would later decide they needed but that he (inexplicably, so it seemed) now owned.

It turned out to be a good idea. He and Mary Linn had spent a year in Houston, established a nice life with one daughter. Johnny kept a small office in Manhattan and worked to keep his operation manageable when everything in the oil patch was going crazy. In 1998, at about the time Francis Dolan was sailing away to Dingle in his restored Nordic Folkboat, Johnny and Mary Linn retired early to the dream home they'd bought the land for and built in Idaho—where Mary Linn believed she might teach school (possibly on a reservation), and which Johnny (who was only forty-six and worth a shitload) felt he could use as a staging ground for a next phase of life, which still theoretically included a Ph.D. in a more useful science that would secure a better world for everybody. He and Mary Linn were Democrats.

All of which would very likely have taken place if one spring morning at breakfast, with impeccable mountain light streaming in over the meadow, and snow still on the peaks, Mary Linn hadn't sat down with a cup of tea, looked across the table at Johnny, smiled curiously and remarked that she'd probably feel better if she would just lay her head on her folded hands a moment, which she did. And died before Johnny could reach to touch her. She had cancer—the Idaho doctor said—something deep, deep within her limbic lobe. Dying was likely the only real symptom she'd experienced.

The next year. The next year became, of course, the year of deep, furious, and murky shadows, of wandering, of unbridled confusions, of panics of such helplessness that Jonathan thought he could not survive. He no longer believed he had any right to have his own plans—Mary Linn's unfinished, preposterously unfulfilled life and dreams (teaching Indians) represented such a greater, un-solaceable loss than his life could ever rise to—though he still had years and years. For all his oddness and schoolboy calculations that had worked the way he'd mapped out while still a large, studious, self-consciously-driven kid at the Latin School, it had always been Mary Linn who imagined and oversaw their life's rationales, and who seemed more completely to experience it. Their love. Their intimacy. Their confused fears. Their shared intelligence about most everything. All he'd done was move comfortably into her kind and beneficent world—even taking credit for much of it, since Mary Linn didn't mind, even liked it that he would. All he'd *really* done was make money and pay for things. Now that that infallible, magical, irreplaceable world was gone (like a star plucked from the firmament, causing the sky to go black), he had no idea how to manufacture anything resembling a life.

When he met and in short order courted, flattered, wooed, romanced, and impulsively married the glamorous, spirited Charlotte Porter, Johnny Bell had been in town not quite a year. He'd sold his Idaho house—furniture and all—and folded his assets, in excess of twenty-five million, with a Columbia friend who promised to keep him rich and getting richer, in exchange for the use of his money for a fund the friend had cobbled up. Jonathan was in New York only because he had his small office there and, once he'd sold the Meadow House, couldn't think of anywhere else to be. He hated

California, where his daughter was. Texas was not a place he could go anymore. Chicago was over with the deaths of his parents. He considered graduate studies, but found he wasn't interested in anything and wouldn't qualify except as an oddity. New York made sense in the way it did to many people—because (but only because) no other place else made any sense at all. Elimination. His understanding of history—Charles Beard—told him this was the course many things followed.

In the city he took a sublet in the East Thirties and put out feelers for someplace permanent. He got interested—which was how he heard about Charlotte—in a school in the Bronx where adult Spanish-speaking immigrants were being taught to speak English and to have a new chance at life. He and Mary Linn had served on boards for similar projects in Houston. Mary Linn had taught in one. This seemed like a fitting tribute. As it happened, the Bronx school was seeking a new board president with business savvy, who could step in if need be with executive skills and run things. Teaching in a private school, which is what Celia, his daughter, was doing in California, was forgotten.

When Charlotte Porter came to pick Jonathan up in his Murray Hill apartment in September 2002, she'd been in the city for two years—serving clients who'd found themselves empty nesters and wanting to leave

Brewster, Katonah, and Lake Mohawk for a Gotham victory lap before packing off to Jupiter and Hobe Sound. Charlotte had not considered getting married again, and many times had wondered whether, if she hadn't met the charmingly remote and handsome Fran Dolan at a NYU student function and hadn't smoked a powerful joint, she would *ever* have married anyone. She liked men, had had two relationships since her divorce. One with an intense but too-diminutive brain surgeon, and one with a burly cop who'd wanted her to relocate to Staten Island. Charlotte also felt she liked women as well as men. She'd never slept with a woman and didn't see any reason she would. But she imagined a time when she and some likable, open-minded female might decide to go in, share expenses, move to Rhode Island, buy a shingled house by the ocean, and start a business selling lampshades. Nothing seemed out of the question. Having her two now-teenage children, Cormac and Sinead, still at home was cumbersome but could be worked with. Though then surprisingly they'd asked to move to Dingle to be with their dad, and had become less conscientious about calling. Which she understood. She had been that way, too. Life changed. They would come back to college. Or possibly not.

Lately—it was around the time she met Johnny Bell and showed him a loft and in three months married him—lately, she'd seen the movie *When Harry Met Sally* on TV. The whole long thing everybody howled about—the fake orgasm and how cute Meg Ryan was. Walking through her house, the one she'd shared with Francis Dolan and the children, holding now a glass of pinot, turning off lights, closing the house for the night—she'd thought, "That was 1983 (the year they'd married). I remember that very well. Life had its proper ground then. You knew more or less where you were and what, and what you would be later. But now. What word," she thought, "would you use to say what life was even *like* now—much less later?" It was an interesting question. Life now *seemed* to be composed of some strange, insubstantial paper she couldn't quite keep hold of. Standing at the back screen, peering into the dark yard beyond which were woods where feral animals still roamed, the word "surface" was all but written against the night. Life was that and only that. A surface. That was what you could rely on it to be. Which was all right, since she'd never really thought of it as being *very* different, even though she'd tried to apply other words. "Proper ground," for instance. And not that this fact was perilous or depressing or even anything you'd need to change. It was just not the way she'd tried to think when she was married—that life is a surface. Now, though, it seemed very, *very* true. She was rather sorry she didn't have Francis here to talk about these things with.

At the splendid Watts Street loft, which she would soon sell to Jonathan Bell, the two of them stood side by side on the landscaped roof deck, facing the direction once dominated by the Twin Towers—now a sunny vacancy. Charlotte assumed the client knew what he wasn't looking at and saw no reason to be more specific about the place, although in other showings of the flat, listed at four-two, clients had wanted to talk all about *the day;* where they'd been, who they'd known who died, how you could've lived elsewhere in the city and never known anything was happening. They *all* said that. That terrible morning, Charlotte had been on the phone with her mother in Alpine, in New Jersey. Her mother had seen the first plane pass over and mentioned it as strange, then gone on about something relating to Charlotte's younger sister Nika, who was a movie producer and considering getting her head shaved. Charlotte had been at home.

Jonathan Bell didn't mention the disaster. Instead he stared straight off into the newly emptied air as if being here on this warm, breezy rooftop above the busy city made him happy in a way he hadn't expected, and wasn't sure what to say or do about it. He'd talked to

Charlotte—as they walked through the vacant, sunny rooms—with affection, but in no particular detail, about his dead wife. He mentioned his former dream house in Idaho—and that he'd thought he'd miss it but did not. Strange. And how not missing it made him feel both guilty but also unexpectedly free. He mentioned his daughter, teaching in California, and about the school he was involved with and hoped would provide new and decent lives for people who had no reason to expect a new life. He quoted the poet Blake on the subject that fools should persist in their folly to become wise, which was what he'd done to be successful in the business he'd not long ago given up. He asked Charlotte how long she'd done real estate, and where she was from—Alpine—and what her husband did. These were the things people talked about. Men always asked you about your husband as a way of finding out if possibly they could sleep with you at some hazy time in the future—a time that would never come. Though it was Charlotte's habit to answer all questions with candor, and to permit the client to believe she might also envision a day, a moment in a taxi or an elevator, when an unplanned touch or unexpectedly intimate look might indeed change folly into some form of knowing. The goal was to draw the client nearer to you and make the sale. Male clients understood this and didn't mind if nothing happened later. It was probably a relief to them if nothing happened. Which with Charlotte Porter nothing ever did.

Jonathan Bell, however, seemed somehow not to be your everyday rich oil gazillionaire. A large, apparently ruminant man in khakis and deckers, a blowsy green polo and faded blue "C" cap from college. He was substantial and attractively needy, and certain about himself. Talkative. He definitely wasn't handsome in the way she'd always wanted men to be—was too bulky and an audible breather. And though she knew that the Blake quotation was his way of impressing her and of determining if she could *be* impressed, she didn't mind; thought it was nice. Better than the way most things happened. She even liked the measured, throaty, chin-down way Jonathan Bell talked, which—Charlotte guessed—must've been the Chicago way. It had character and was new to her. So that just in one moment, out on the terrace in the sun and warming breeze where she'd been many times with different sorts of rich clients, she felt unexpectedly good—just being around this man (and understood why his wife had loved him so). Something had happened when she wasn't noticing. What was it? Perhaps only she was aware of it—since Jonathan Bell in all likelihood wouldn't be. To her complete surprise she was thinking:

"Could I ever imagine myself in the arms of this big, sweet, preoccupied, grieving and probably, finally distant and frustrating man?" To which the answer seemed, oddly, "Yes. Without a doubt or a second thought. Why didn't I know it when I first saw him?"

Jonathan Bell was looking at her when she brought her sparkling eyes to him. He had small brown eyes and seemed puzzled, even concerned, as if he'd been speaking then realized she wasn't listening. He feared something unpleasant had happened. The normal fear, Charlotte supposed, of a man whose wife had put her head on her hands and never looked at him again. He was a challenge. But she might possibly be up to it.

She instinctively smiled. Jonathan had taken off his Columbia cap and was holding it at his side like a schoolboy who's been ordered to do that. He had a large square head and thick woolly hair which (to Charlotte) denoted *Middle West.* "I'm sorry," Charlotte said. "For a moment my mind just fled from real estate." In his eyes now, she thought, she looked like a pretty young girl.

"It's fine," Jonathan said and smiled back with relief. "I was just wondering. If I buy this apartment, will you have dinner with me tonight?" At that very moment, a small hawk—or a falcon or a kestrel, some raptor in any case—soared out into view in the rising air above them, staring down as it did into the peopled vastness. Jonathan had heard of such creatures living in the city. It had a wildness still.

"I *would*," Charlotte said. "Even if you don't buy the apartment. I was going to ask you if you hadn't asked me." In only three months they were married.

In the relatively brief time they turned out to actually *be* married (two years, give or take), Jonathan felt he and Charlotte Porter were extremely happy. To him, the best part was that he could never have imagined getting to marry *anyone* like Charlotte—so pretty and spirited and unpredictable and clever and independent in ways Mary Linn wasn't (not that that mattered at all); ways that always made him feel glad and eager to be around her. Charlotte was much more glamorous than Mary Linn, who was more a handsome 1950s-style wife and mother he had profoundly loved and inexpressibly still missed. Charlotte seemed contemporary, fast-paced, glittery and unpredictable about all the things Mary Linn had taken seriously, worked patiently in behalf of, puzzled over, returned to, and always, always finished. And yet because he *was*, remarkably, *married* to Charlotte Porter, it seemed all sorts of new things, ideas, involvements, passions, unthought-of outcomes to the mere fact of being himself were now possible—though insisting on knowing what these things precisely were seemed unnecessary. It was an article of faith that they existed and would continue—even if Jonathan felt he would likely never alter his clear view of himself. He was down-to-earth, not so sophisticated at day's end, a big, nice guy from Chicago with some brains, who'd made it in the oil patch. Being the lucky man who'd made Charlotte Porter fall hopelessly in love with him would never change any part of that.

Charlotte, it turned out, liked "doing things." So they did things. Many. They went to St. Petersburg. To Bhutan. And to Morocco. All in one year. They went to San Francisco and New Orleans. They went to Idaho to visit Jonathan's memory-encrusted, former dream house—owned now by a movie agent. (Charlotte didn't particularly like it but praised it.) Charlotte, it seemed, had few close friends—who all, however, adored her and were thrilled to see her walk through any door and gained joy just from being around her. There were two gay decorators in Westport—Byron and Tweedy, who they drove to see and spent a wonderful night with. Charlotte had worked with them in the early realty days. There was an aged post-expressionist painter and his aged wife—Jess and Bella—who they visited in Bucks County. Byron and Tweedy had their summer place in Tenants Harbor, where Jonathan and Charlotte also visited—not far from where Fran Dolan had restored his boat and sailed it out of sight forever. Jonathan found a rental near there the first summer, and they'd gone kayaking and hiking and eaten lobsters off the boat and drunk martinis with "the twins" until the sun sank below the forest's perimeter and the islands, and it grew cold and they had to put on sweaters.

Jonathan himself had only a few friends in the city. (Just the odd sectorings and re-sectorings of life.) There were people at the school he'd assumed an interest in. Plus, a few classmates he kept contact with. Acquaintances and neighbors from Texas and Idaho sometimes visited New York, but he didn't always see them. And Bailes, the Columbia hedge-fund guy, who'd been his and Charlotte's witness at City Hall, and with whom they'd gone out for dim sum to celebrate. (Jonathan's fortune, that night, said, "Today you are the luckiest surgeon in America." Charlotte's had hilariously said, "Curb your lust for revenge.") Jonathan had also kept in touch with one of his old history professors, and he and Charlotte had traveled up to 120th and Riverside one evening and engaged in a long-winded dinner with Sol Hertzl and his young Swedish wife, during which they talked about the new war and what could be done to stop it before the world was consumed. They were all of one mind, although Jonathan did not feel, given his experience, that oil was really at the heart of all that went on in the Middle East. It was much more complicated. The history needed to be consulted—the Ottomans, etc. It went on very much like that.

Charlotte seemed to like everything he liked and everything they did. Marriage seemed like the same good idea to both of them. Every place he took Charlotte and every place she took him they were both enthusiastic about and Charlotte was charming and vibrant and pretty and kind and generous—though sometimes she had a tart tongue when she'd had one too many gin and tonics, and also sometimes a sexy sense of humor when she was among people she knew—men, especially. All of which Jonathan felt was precisely what he'd have wanted, and a thousand times better than he'd ever have bargained for when he'd come to New York mired in grief with his dreams in ruins.

Not that everything was perfect—a fact that gave life measure and a testing ballast. Jonathan's school in the Bronx suffered a weekend fire that nearly destroyed the building, badly injured a janitor, and was unquestionably set by a former student—a fact that caused dismay among the board regarding the wisdom of rebuilding on-site rather than someplace safer. Everything was finally restored, but the school had had to close for a time. The real estate market, meanwhile, began to show signs that the downturn was at hand—though mainly in the out-suburbs, not in the city where Charlotte still worked and was unfazed, feeling she was likely even to do better.

After a year of being married, Jonathan had begun to realize that as happy as he was, and as happy as Charlotte seemed, he had not quite developed what he would call a category or idea or a system that being married to Charlotte seemed to operate under and fulfill. They went everyplace together. Being around her made him blissful. There was nothing about her person he didn't like. She was reliable, neat, very passionate, respectful, observant, fastidious, not dependent, and seemed not to lie about anything or have much of a temper. But there was a sense he detected—which hadn't been true there on the roof garden when they'd first met—that some part of Charlotte was not easily reachable. Not that this shouldn't be true. They were both adults with dense lives behind them. It simply *was* true—which had not seemed the case with Mary Linn. Though he conceded possibly he was wrong about that. One day, not long after their first anniversary, he was sitting in the spacious, sun-shot Watts Street loft, reading *A Portrait of a Lady*—a chapter near the end that begins, "It was not with surprise, it was with a feeling of which in other circumstances would have had much of the effect of joy, that as Isabel descended from the Paris Mail at Charing Cross she stepped into the arms, as it were—or any rate into the hands—of Henrietta Stackpole . . ." It was just at that moment—unexpectedly—that Jonathan found himself thinking the words, "I'm not feeling very married for a married man."

Immediately he thought again, as he often did, how his life had been with Mary Linn; that it had all along been Mary Linn who'd invented the workable, reliable mind-set for their (his) whole life—even though they pretended as if they'd both fashioned it. This was a truth about himself he did not admire. In fact he felt disappointed about himself.

And he might well, Jonathan believed, be doing the same thing again—expecting Charlotte to create a sense of what being married meant, what it felt like, what its essence should be. Possibly he lacked a talent for this, or else was lazy and self-preoccupied and possibly even too old.

Charlotte certainly gave no sign of wanting or being remotely able to furnish the categoricals of (their) marriage—which seemed to Jonathan at least provisionally understandable. She'd given no apparent thought to changing her name to Charlotte Bell. She'd said Jonathan could move into the Goldens Bridge house if he pleased, though she meant to keep it. He might not, she realized, wish to do that, might choose to stay in his all-but-new loft. They could therefore keep two houses—one in "the country," she said brightly (though it was hardly the country), and one a stylish town residence for when that was convenient. She had a freer sense about being married than the conventional.

Jonathan, for his part, had not liked the Goldens Bridge house at all—a flat-roofed, glass and board 'n' batten deck house perched on a woody, ledged overlook in sight of a polluted stream where nothing lived. The house had tiny rooms, high crank-out windows, low, dim ceilings. It was a cave. It reminded him of cheap, remote Houston suburbs where people drove for hours to get to work and never saw their families. What kind of architect had Charlotte's first husband been that such a wreck had seemed acceptable? Irish, he supposed. Jonathan preferred the idea of selling both properties—hers and his—buying a mansion overlooking the Hudson in Riverdale, and having that be where they lived.

Charlotte had happily said no thank you. She liked the deck house. She'd lived in it thirty years. She understood precisely why Jonathan might not like it. But she intended to live in it because even though she'd raised two children there and been married to another man she no longer loved within its inadequate rooms—it was paid for, was hers, she felt protected there. It was the perfect size for one. Plus, she liked working from home.

None of which did Charlotte explain to Jonathan with any tone of inflexibility or ultimatum, but in fact with the same smiling, sparkling-eyed, teasing spirit she'd discovered as her way of making Jonathan happy, and that had so far proved successful in all her other exchanges with him. These conversations also included her insistence about going on working (because she gained validation from selling things); the possibility that they might not see each other every single night; and also her conception that their new marriage would be a "do things together" union, which was when Charlotte revealed her view about second marriage and the need to get the best parts of the first long one, while missing the bad and boring parts that drove people crazy—even if, she granted, Jonathan's first marriage to Mary Linn had never driven *him* crazy and could have lasted on forever but for her untimely death.

It was this (Charlotte's) array of attitudes and fervent, positivist beliefs that made Jonathan—alone in his many-windowed apartment, reading *Portrait of a Lady*—believe that Charlotte was not going to invent a more close-fitting conception of marriage than she already had with the do-things-together and spend-odd-nights-apart scheme. In all likelihood, if there was ever to be a better-functioning, full-enfolding *conception* of marriage between him and Charlotte—not at all like the one Mary Linn had valiantly, successfully applied herself to for decades, but different—then he, Jonathan, was going to have to supply one for them or (basically) live without. Which seemed something he could possibly even do—since living with (or mostly with) Charlotte Porter was the best life story he could imagine for this stage of life.

In May, when Jonathan and Charlotte had been married a year and almost a half and were going many places but living not really together but only partly, Jonathan began to take note of the fact that he had put on weight and was up to two forty-five, but hadn't particularly worried about it or felt different in any way. His weight had always drifted—two twenty-five to two forty. His blood pressure was completely reliable. He explained this bump by the fact that he was less active, went to the gym less, read more—precisely the way he wanted to—and to the fact that he was now so happy with his life that he'd begun saying yes to everything. Charlotte didn't seem to mind or notice. He was a big man. She liked that and told him so on their initial trip to the Woodstock Inn. "You're a big old boy, aren't you, Jonathan?" she'd said their first night together. The subject never really came up afterward, although the word "big" was often in her depictions of him. "You're a big reader." "You're a big sauvignon blanc enthusiast." "You had a big life before I knew you." Charlotte, of course, stayed sleek and slender and fabulous. There was just more of him to love, Jonathan thought.

But on his yearly visit to Doctor Kramer, there was a callback saying there were troubling signs in Jonathan's blood work, indicating there was possibly disease in his thyroid, plus also a marker for high triglycerides, both of which would account for his weight gain but also to more ominous portents. They should look further—more thorough diabetes tests. There could be cautionary surgery down the line, ahead of more serious episode eventualities. Cancer didn't seem in the cards.

The whole flurry of events happened at once. His tests came back uneasily inconclusive. Jonathan went to Albert Einstein the next Thursday. His thyroid was removed with some minor surgical complications owing to his weight and (now) blood pressure. The histology was done and proved to be negative (though a big cyst *was* found). Jonathan came back home—or "home" to Charlotte's deck house in Goldens Bridge—on Saturday afternoon, determined to rest up a couple of days or three, after which they were flying up to Owls Head in Byron's plane for the holiday weekend. It would be Memorial Day.

Charlotte turned out to be a wonderfully tireless, skillful, enthusiastic and somewhat severe nurse. She cooked healthy meals for him—savory soup and organic meat loaf that he loved. She helped him change the dressing on his neck, standing beside him, supervising, as he—grumpy, a bit saggy and unshaven—did the re-wrap in the bathroom mirror. She made him a place on her living room couch where he could nap, watch the Cubs, and see out to the newly leafing trees and the dry streambed and the high suburban sky, and where she could sit beside him and do the analysis on her realty comps. She'd brought movies from Blockbuster and driven him down to the city to have his incision inspected and declared to be healing nicely, the sutures dissolving as expected. Charlotte looked after him, Jonathan thought, in a way he could only have dreamed of. It was just for three and a half days, but Charlotte never grew impatient or bored or distracted or dismissive of the fact that because he didn't have cancer he wasn't up and around and back to his own place so she could carry on listing and cashing in on high-end co-ops, condos, and town houses. Charlotte walked around the house, dressed, Jonathan thought, like a movie star, her golden hair sleekly back to emphasize her sharp chin, her perfect, cultivated nose, her small ears, her cheekbones that had turned the heads of people at the Ford Agency. She was tall and lithe and long-gaited and, barefoot in pale blue sweats, seemed to roam the house ever in search of more things to do for him that would assure his recovery.

For his part, Jonathan stayed mostly on the couch, wearing his blue-and-white-striped pj's from Paul Stuart, eating homemade whole-grain bread and olive tapenade (and the meat loaf), staring out at the revetment of oaks and beeches and cedars down to the squalid stream, wondering what *actual* appeal this place could possibly have for Charlotte and why marriage and the new life with him, in which there were no money worries, wouldn't make a big new house on the Hudson irresistible. Through the sliding glass, Jonathan could make out where Charlotte's kids—or someone—had built a large tree house in the arms of a big copper beech. This construction had three levels and steps nailed to the thick trunk bark, with Tarzan ropes hung down for swinging. It, however, had been allowed to deteriorate over years. The children were in their twenties and in Ireland and didn't come home much. He'd met neither of them. It all seemed odd. The thick ropes were wispy and gray and weather-worn, and some of the steps had fallen off. A few of the tree house timbers were rotted through. It was a hazard. The whole of the appurtenant grounds had in fact fallen into disrepair—from disuse—the beds and plantings and the retaining wall that separated the yard from the deep gulley and the woods. There were dead branches in all the trees that could fall and do damage. The house itself was showing signs. Gutter straps, he'd noticed, needed tending to. Soffits in need of venting. An old TV antenna should've been removed long ago from the chimney. The flat roof almost certainly needed re-sealing with acrylic. In the dining room ceiling corner there was a scabby-looking brown water spot like a cancer, which Charlotte had had patched but didn't seem to care about. She, after all, looked like a million bucks, could sell sand to Bedouins, and charm the pants off the Pope. She was, though, letting many other things go but didn't want anything to change—in spite of having invited Jonathan (sort of) into her life and liking how that was turning out. She liked *him*. Liked who he was, liked the big oversized, middle western metes and bounds of him, which he'd once thought only Mary Linn could truly love. It was incongruous. In her way, Charlotte was too.

They had agreed—the two of them—about Jonathan's money. His daughter got a fat trust fund that could easily see her through an entire life without working—unless the world turned upside down. Charlotte would receive a cool four mil if and when he died, though she didn't want it, she said. Jonathan kept five million as walking-around-town money—living expenses, travel, doing things together with Charlotte. The rest he kept in Bailes' technology fund where it seemed it did nothing but grow, grow, grow. Eventually the lion's share would transition to charities—including his school, which Jonathan was considering re-building from the ground up out of his own pocket, since the board had turned fractious, with members resigning. He could very easily stand the repairs on Charlotte's crumbling house—and would, if reluctantly—but that seemed not something she wanted him to do. So, he determined, he would simply forget about all of it and knew that after not even very much time this would not be difficult.

On Monday evening when he and Charlotte had returned from the city with the good news about Jonathan's incision (in two days they were to fly to Owls Head), she'd fixed him a martini (the surgeon allowed one only) and herself her favorite gin highball, and had taken a seat at the picture window, facing the twilight, the woods changing shapes in shadows and the big tree house no longer visible. A balming breeze from the north had invited her to open the sliding door and to turn off the window units. Jonathan was back on his couch, coddling his martini on his belly. Charlotte was sitting so as to face away, her lovely silhouette against the light remaining in the spring sky. Peepers were peeping in the woods where there was a secret pond. It was, Jonathan felt, magical. Even here.

For a long period he lay saying nothing, though the pain below his Adam's apple where they'd gone in, throbbed dully. Cubes tinkled in Charlotte's glass. The fine, slick surfaces of her silk trousers shifted as she crossed her long legs. A bracelet rung fell lightly against another bracelet rung. She sighed—a very deep and profound suspiration. A sigh he'd never really heard—from Charlotte or from anyone. Not even when Mary Linn had died in front of him at breakfast. It was a sigh you could imagine someone sighing in a novel. *Tess of the D'Urbervilles* or some such gloomy book. A sigh that was, there in the descending spring darkness, more eloquent and plaintive and heartfelt than anything he'd ever heard. It made him feel terrible, for just that instant, alone and in need of something for which nothing was commensurate, and completely inadequate—to Charlotte, his wife, whom he felt he loved. Though he *wanted* to be adequate even if nothing could be commensurate for him. He wanted, with the great fund of feeling he contained, to give to Charlotte each and every thing she might need. He considered rising off the couch, walking across the empty space between them and laying his hand on her thin shoulder. Nothing more. No words. Though that didn't seem the right thing to be doing. Possibly there *was* no perfectly right thing to be doing. Except here was a moment, a magic moment for the two of them together. So that what he did, trying not to sound alarmed, and taking a drink of his still-cold martini, was to say, "What's going on in that dreamy head of yours?"

Charlotte smiled in the shadows. "Oh. Nothing. There's usually not much going on in my head, Johnny. Sometimes I just have a feeling and let myself completely feel it. Don't you do that?"

"I do," he said.

"Well . . ."

"I usually try to find words to match my feelings, though," Jonathan said. He half remembered something from college, something Archibald MacLeish had written, but he couldn't say it. Something, something, "but equal to . . ."

"Well. That's just you," Charlotte said.

"They don't have to be the right words," he said. "Sometimes wrong ones can be as good. Sometimes better."

"Uh-huh," Charlotte said.

"So. What words would you put opposite the feeling that just made you sigh?"

"Ah," Charlotte said and shook her golden hair as if to shake off confusion, then ran both her hands back through her hair—in a way that made Jonathan feel not even in the room with her, someplace high up in the ceiling if the ceiling had been high. Someplace from which he could not communicate with Charlotte. "Let's see," she said slowly. "I would say . . . that the words . . . that go with the way I felt . . . and that made me sigh are . . . Ummm . . . that I never have bad dreams anymore. Specifically . . . the ones about being enrolled in some class in college and having to take the final, only I haven't been attending all semester, and I'm panicked. I don't have that. Francis used to have those, too. He told me. He felt it had to do with being taught by Jesuits. Though I was never taught by Jesuits. So that's it. Is that what you wanted to hear? Did Mary Linn ever sigh?" Charlotte kept staring out into the trees' silent reticule.

He was looking intently at her in the all but vanished light. For an instant he saw a bat flicker past the window then disappear. "No. I don't remember Mary Linn ever sighing. She wasn't a sighing sort of girl, I guess." He expected this would prompt Charlotte to say something. Something like, "Well, that should prove something." Or, "That must've meant she was very happy." Or, "Nobody's the same, I guess." But she said nothing—at all. He lay uncomfortably on his side, holding his martini glass that had grown warm, the gin in it flat and metallic. Charlotte sat, no longer in silhouette, but very still, staring into the new night. He could not hear her breathing, could not hear the ice in her glass or her bracelets touching down her arm. She seemed to have come to the end of whatever thought she'd had that had caused her to sigh and now was happy to have no other.

"How does your poor neck feel, sweetheart," she finally said. She shook her golden hair again as if she'd waked herself.

"Good. Pretty good," Jonathan said. "I'll live."

"I know you will," she said. "We'll have a good time with Byron and Tweedy. It's always so nice to be up there. Maybe we'll go for a sail."

"That'd be great," Jonathan said and thought about sailing fast with a mounting breeze behind them.

"It'll be cold at night, it always is," she said. Charlotte stood then and stretched in the shadows. Moonlight filtered in through the sliding door, reaching the angles of her long body. She yawned and walked out of the room without speaking more. He heard her bathroom door close, heard the light click on, heard water running from the tap. And he heard Charlotte humming, then singing. A Doobie Brothers' song she always liked. "This is *it,* make no mistake where you are. Your *back's* in the cor-ner."

On the Owls Head flight, during which the map of the New England coast floated blandly underneath—its not-quite-greenly settled shores, the big Narragansett, Boston and the Cape on toward the adamantine coast of Maine, Charlotte in the back seat thought intensely and exclusively of Jonathan, a large, neck-bandaged figure in his tan poplin jacket, squeezed into the "co-pilot" seat beside Byron, and enthusiastically talking about English as a second language.

Encased in the engine's noise, Charlotte was realizing through these moments that she was not the most perfect person to be married to Jonathan Bell—even though she *was* married to him and liked him very much. Jonathan was a man who apparently believed in greater and greater closeness, of shared complications, of difficult-to-overcome frictions leading to even deeper depths of intimacy and knowledge of each other. Whereas she really didn't, was simply not that kind of person and had never been. This discrepancy, she felt, was likely going to make them both very unhappy, since it meant that something immensely important to each of them was always going to be missing, or be far too present. And this (this absence or if you like, *presence*) would make Jonathan feel unappreciated, make him distracted and too insistent and wrongly misunderstood, which would then make her extremely unhappy. It occurred to her—too late, though she'd certainly thought it before—that the distant Francis Dolan had likely been the perfect match for her, as Mary Linn had been the perfect match for Jonathan. How often it must turn out that the first marriage was the best. Most people misunderstood that.

Out the airplane window, Charlotte saw other tiny planes taking off from Logan Airport, nosing slowly upward then disappearing. It was possible, she thought, she should never have gotten married again at all—and worse yet married poor Jonathan. Since what had foreseeably happened was that she—Charlotte—had turned out to be simply the woman she'd always known herself to be, including when she was selling Jonathan the loft on Watts Street and been so charmed by him on the terrace that sunny day. For some reason she had simply lost sight of herself, stopped paying attention, or even stopped believing in Charlotte Porter from Alpine. She'd wanted Jonathan to like her for being that—adore her, even—but not consider her as being anything more or less. Certainly not *penetrate* her. Not explore her. Not hope to find her out and *learn* her—like a second language. Just let her be. Only . . . what? She didn't know. It was too bad.

Whatever she didn't provide Jonathan—and she could say the words, but didn't really understand them—obviously the kind, loving and obedient Mary Linn (whom she didn't really care about) had provided perfectly. They'd been young and everything had been new. The world had been nothing but surprise after surprise. Then time passed. The surprises had stopped being a crucial feature, and they had grown accustomed to each other (Jonathan had said none of this), which must've been normal and good in its way. Even deep—the thing he liked. Yes. All that caused Charlotte—high above the Atlantic's pearlescent curve—to realize (for the first time) how unthinkably terrible it was to lose a spouse. She and Francis had been lucky not to lose each other but merely to fall out of love. Europeans possibly understood this better than Americans. The two of them—she and Francis—hadn't conceived of a point in life where a lack of new stimulus became a state of being so that you had to go deeper—whatever deeper meant. Just something you invented to pass the time that was otherwise passing too slowly. Neither of them had needed such inventions—at least she hadn't.

None of which was any of Jonathan's fault. He was a generous, kind, intelligent, loving, needing man—more loving and patient and decent, in fact, than she'd expected. He liked people to feel good around him—which she did. She was exactly the same way, at least in this last regard. Though their goals were different. She felt as accommodated to him as she first had on the terrace garden, in sight of the missing towers, of what was now his building. Nothing had really changed from that point on. But Jonathan—it was the engineer in him, she supposed—Jonathan was ever on the way to somewhere. For a moment, she supposed, it was that that had excited her, caused her to want to go, caused her to forget who Charlotte was.

Divorce, Charlotte felt, would be a much better and easier state to maintain than marriage. It took being married to a nice man like Jonathan, offering her the desirable things he offered her, to make this clear. She had been divorced from Francis Dolan for four years and didn't feel they were forever banished from each other's lives (though they'd never seen each other again and never spoke). She and Jonathan would do this better. There would be no anxieties, no sense of always, puzzlingly letting someone down. If they stayed married (which she now understood they wouldn't) she would end up saying words she did not want to say—

harmful things she'd heard other people say. She would grow somber and stop being gay and unpredictable and beautiful. Marriage would change her, and that she didn't want. Jonathan was only fifty-three. He could find someone to be deep with. Or not. And in that way, as the lighthouse on Owls Head rose below them, and the whitely shimmering sea with tiny sails upon it stretched eastward, where there were green islands and what seemed to be a mountain—in that way, the matter of her marriage to Jonathan Bell was decided.

Charlotte told Jonathan her news during their weekend in Maine. She hated telling him so soon after his surgery, with the padded bandage still wound round his neck. But she had it in her mind all Thursday, and then on Friday morning she woke up feeling wretched and cruel and deceitful (though she wasn't). Plus, she knew about herself, that when she thought something important she could never sit on it.

She and Jonathan had walked up to the Tenants Harbor country store to buy sandwiches and cold wine, with the thought to eating lunch in the cool sun on the seawall where the lobster boats unloaded. She felt she could tell him in a sweet way, even though she knew it would be a shock.

Jonathan was happily seated with his lobster roll

un-wrapped, opened across his bare knees, watching two ospreys transporting sticks to the top of a tall spruce across the little harbor. They were repairing their nest. It had not been possible to go kayaking due to Jonathan's incision. But they had had a strenuous walk in the late morning that had led them to the store. Tweedy and Byron had driven into Rockland for dinner supplies and package-mailing. It felt to Charlotte that she and Jonathan were alone enough on the seawall for a serious talk—they were conspicuously alone, which she found unexpectedly stressful. It was as if she had already told Jonathan what she intended to tell him, and he was—in his sweet way—pretending not to react just to make her feel better. Jonathan was wearing pink walking shorts, a white T-shirt, and a porkpie made of green toweling. He was very pale and looked, she felt, ridiculous with his new extra poundage and his bandaged neck that showed a tiny bit of bleed-through.

"Jonathan," she said.

"The larger of the ospreys is the female, I believe," Jonathan observed. Store customers were trafficking in and out behind them, piling into SUVs with their lunch and driving away. It was a lovely noon. They had a half bottle of cold Pouilly-Fuissé and plastic cups.

"I have to tell you something," Charlotte said. "I hate to. But I don't think being married is working out well for me. Us. I mean . . ." She repressed an urge to lay a hand on his wrist, and instead clasped her own hands tight together and pulled her elbows in. She did look at him and smile, but felt it was the way a nurse would smile at a dying patient, which Jonathan Bell was not. It was actually a smile of forgiveness—for herself. She made herself stop smiling.

Jonathan, his sandwich on his knees on top of the wax paper, looked at her beside him—only glancingly—then stared at the birds he'd been so delighted to watch and tell her about. "Oh," he said. "This is not working."

"No," Charlotte said. "It's not."

"Why?" Jonathan said. "Is that a possible question?"

"It is," Charlotte said. "I've been thinking about this for a while." Which wasn't true. She was not the kind of person who thought about things for a while. She didn't really believe anybody was. When Charlotte thought about something once and very intensely, as she had about Jonathan on the plane ride up, that was then what she believed, which hardly ever changed. She almost said, "Why, Jonathan? Because you have an interest in some *unknown* you're willing to invent, and I don't." That, though, seemed insulting and wasn't really true. So she said, "I'm going to make you unhappy as a wife, Jonathan, and I don't see any reason to do that."

"Do you have another lover?" Jonathan said, continuing to eat his sandwich.

"Of course not," Charlotte said.

"Not that *that* would be the worst thing. I guess," Jonathan said, then sat silently for a time. Two big gulls landed in the rocky shallows in front of them and began eyeing them eating their sandwiches. Jonathan tore off a piece of his bun and tossed it, which set the gulls shouting and flapping, which attracted another gull.

"I'm not sure what you observe about me," Jonathan said, now very formally. "My history. My age. My temperament. It could be very little." They had never, she knew, had this kind of conversation, though he'd tried. She knew he liked it—no matter what its devastating subject—because it promised to search deeper into whatever he thought the conversation was *really* about, but that she didn't think needed searching into. "I think you might be underestimating me."

"What part?" Charlotte said. "I think you have a good temperament." She took a tiny bite of lobster—the claw meat. She'd now said the hard words. There was no claiming them back. They could talk on like friends. Their marriage was over.

"My ability to love," Jonathan said solemnly.

"Oh, no," Charlotte said. "I don't underestimate

that." She wiggled her pretty painted-blue toes at the gulls, causing them to paddle closer. "You're very, very loving."

Jonathan breathed audibly in and breathed out, and began folding the butcher paper over the remains of his sandwich, still in his lap. She smelled a tiny scent of perspiration—on one of them or the other.

"A wife should make her husband happy and feel good," Charlotte said, feeling much better about everything, as if a heavy iron door had opened, then closed, but then opened surprisingly again. The sun was warming her legs.

"I think you have to make *yourself* happy, not wait for someone to do it," Jonathan said.

"I know," Charlotte said. "That's true. And that's what I'm doing by saying this to you. I'm trying to make myself happy. But you, too."

Jonathan nodded. His sandwich had become a neat, white parcel in his large hands. The sun was on them. A nice new smell now—a scent of clean clothes, starch, and soap—arose from somewhere, released by the sunshine. Charlotte realized the two of them looked like people having a fine time sharing a sandwich, feeding the gulls, basking in sunlight. Nobody would think they were putting an end to a life together. There was nothing fine about it. Though she was glad to feel not horrible, and not required to do it all over again. Jonathan was never horrible. He was anything but that.

"It's a skein, isn't it?" Jonathan said in his measured way.

"What is?" Charlotte said. This time she did willingly smile her forgiving smile—for him. He was forgiven for being left behind.

"Getting married, being not married, getting married again, getting now un-married. All of it." Jonathan touched his finger to the upper edge of his gauze bandage, beneath which was wounded flesh where there'd been a defective thyroid gland. Charlotte hadn't liked looking at the scar. "It's all a skein. There's probably no reason to concentrate too hard on any single part of it. You need to see the whole thing to understand it. And of course we can't yet."

"No," Charlotte said. "We can't." She had no idea what he was talking about, but for some reason—goodness knew why—she felt irritated, and gladder than she *had* been that she was leaving him.

"I do like to be around you. I like it very much," Jonathan said.

"I like being around you," Charlotte said. "Maybe we'll be able to do that better when we're not married."

"May *be*." Then he said, "I think it'd be better not

to tell Byron and Tweedy about this. Don't you? They can find out later." He'd said this suddenly. It seemed unlike him. But he was embarrassed, she supposed. It must be, Charlotte thought, his way of expressing shock and loss.

"Absolutely," Charlotte said. "I'd been thinking about that." Though she hadn't. "We'll tell them sometime. We can have two nice days together."

"Yes," Jonathan said. "We certainly can do that."

And that was all they said that day on the subject of their divorce.

At the end of the summer, a year after their divorce, Charlotte called Jonathan to ask if he would drive with her to Yonkers to visit her mother in River Mansions, where her mother was living and which Charlotte had worked hard to arrange. The summer of their divorce Charlotte's mother Beezy (Beatrice) had suffered a sickening, debilitating stroke in her home in Alpine, and Charlotte had moved her across to the Mansions, overlooking (almost) the Hudson. It was a nice clean facility run by Lutherans, and easy for Charlotte to stop off if she took the Saw Mill up. Jonathan had visited there once to be polite but had stopped coming once their divorce was official.

Since arriving to River Mansions, Charlotte's mother,

who'd turned eighty, had precipitously declined and was no longer always lucid. Though when she was, she talked enthusiastically about death and nothingness, and Charlotte complained to Jonathan that visiting her (three times a week) had begun eroding her—Charlotte's—sense of personal vivacity, leaving her frequently feeling distressed. Charlotte feared, she said, that this could be moving her toward depression, since by the time she got home from Sotheby's (even on the days she didn't see her mother), all she wanted to do was pour a big glass of chilled Tanqueray and go to sleep watching TV. Most weekends, if she wasn't showing houses, she just stayed home and slept. She'd also sometimes found herself crying for no apparent reason—which she thought was "not like Charlotte," who didn't have a depressive personality.

Jonathan had seen Charlotte only two times in the year they had become ex-spouses—an expression he detested, since it was glib and quite cynical, and missed important facets of human experience that couldn't be glibly erased. A texture in things. Once, he'd seen Charlotte at the Loew's on Second Avenue, as he was coming out of *Other People's Lives.* Charlotte was with a tall, stern-faced man who looked to Jonathan like a lawyer—wide, clothes-hanger shoulders, angular like an eagle, with shiny, slicked-back dark hair, aviators, and a tan. Very different from himself. Charlotte had looked beautiful—lanky and loose-limbed in a pair of wafer-thin blue sandals and some kind of short, spangly Mexican dress he'd never seen her wear. She seemed surprised but happy to see him and introduced him the way you'd introduce a new friend to an old friend—not how you'd introduce your former husband to your boyfriend. At least Jonathan felt this way, but was cordial. Jake seemed to be the man's name. He seemed indifferent.

The second time he'd encountered Charlotte was on his own block on Watts Street, a chilly morning in late October when he'd been for a walk to the river. Charlotte was seated on a building stoop, wearing a long green wool sweater, writing onto a clear-plastic clipboard, obviously awaiting a client. Jonathan wondered if the client was the raptor/aviator guy, but supposed not. When he approached, Charlotte seemed tired and kept looking him in the eye from where she stayed sitting on the stoop, as if she didn't know what to say or why he was even here. Jonathan didn't know what to say either. In Chicago, you wouldn't have said anything, would've crossed the street to avoid contact. Which of course he wouldn't do. Something about seeing Charlotte, though, made him think about his parents, dead and in their graves downstate, near Springfield—where they were from. Guy and Betty. Fifty-one years together. Divorce hadn't been in their vocabulary, as Jonathan didn't think it was really in his—though it was now. In his dream, they were sitting in a car, an old Ford, laughing. Thinking of them—which he didn't do often—was like a strange, vivid but pleasant dream. He missed them.

Charlotte brightened, gave him her glorious, warming smile and overcame her fatigue and brief dislocation. She asked to know what he'd been up to, and if he was "well." She blinked flirtatiously, the way she had when she'd shown him the loft, nearly three years ago. He told her—awkwardly—that he'd become more deeply involved in his school. He'd experienced some luck with the hedge fund, had fresh capital, and was adding an arts wing to the previously damaged building. He told her he was going up to Columbia for an *extended ed* class in European intellectual history, something he'd always expected to do. He'd been to Scotland fishing with Bailes (though he didn't tell her he'd had a sorry time). He was about to tell her he'd met someone he liked—a woman who worked for the Metropolitan. But Charlotte's phone began ringing inside her purple NYU bag. She'd frowned and said, "These things are the ruin of my life. I'll get rid of it quick."

Whoever was calling, though, caused Charlotte to stand up off the step and walk slowly down the sidewalk, her voice going softer, changing in resonance to something private. Jonathan stood a few moments, waiting for her to come back and let him tell her about his new friend—Emma—or to signal this was a longer call than she'd thought. After a minute, Charlotte had put her hand against a lamppost and lowered her head, going on talking, her back to Jonathan. And he'd just walked on toward his building, since she seemed to have forgotten him. When he reached his entry, he turned and looked at Charlotte, but she was still talking, her head lowered. He had gone along inside.

After that, he did not bump into Charlotte again, as if it had been completely inevitable to see her two times, and completely inevitable that it never happen again. Once—it was only for an instant—he thought that he saw Charlotte in O'Hare. The tall woman he'd glimpsed going up an escalator as he was going down had had Charlotte's thick, golden mane and stood on the escalator in a hip-thrown, sidelong way Charlotte often stood. But he quickly realized—when the woman noticed he was staring—that it wasn't Charlotte, and thinking it *was* only meant she was on his mind not far below the surface. Which he didn't expect was true, but still was natural, he thought, though not important; a human reflex that would fade with time, even if it never disappeared forever.

Still. He didn't quite understand how one could be married to Charlotte Porter—or to anyone—for part of only two years, be happy with her, believe she was happy with him, and then get divorced as easily as you stepped off the #1 train at Canal Street. Or for that matter, as easily as you'd gotten married in the first place. And more. What he *really* didn't understand was how it had all been not very difficult *for him*—given his traditional views, his previous long marriage, his parents' extremely long and devoted marriage, plus his positivist thoughts about the enfolding rationales for marriage—which he'd believed he and Charlotte had mutually begun to fortify, but about which he'd apparently been entirely wrong. Charlotte's views stressed spontaneity, discouraged complication and the examined life, while favoring a more immediate, simpler, low-hanging fruit mentality. Many people were that way, he knew. (This, he realized, was somewhat oversimplifying Charlotte.)

But how had he adapted?

Perhaps, quite possibly, Jonathan thought, even though his old system of proper knowing, learning, developing, penetrating didn't comprehend what he was now experiencing, it was perfectly possible *he himself did comprehend it*—in the way, more or less, one comprehended by instinct that an oil well was about to pay off, in spite of much evidence to the contrary. Possibly there was a gap between his old belief system and himself. The fact that it hadn't been all that terrible not to be married to lovely Charlotte was arguably proof of a more genuine, up-to-date, if wordless, awareness of himself. Which (conceivably) was why he'd said to Charlotte, on the sun-warmed seawall in Tenants Harbor, when she'd told him she wanted not to be his wife anymore, that everything was a *skein.* (He had otherwise not made much sense that day.) It was a whole new way of seeing the world—something Charlotte did fairly naturally. He and Charlotte, by this rationale, were divorced, but still together in a way that lacked a positive vocabulary but was genuine and more reliable than marriage because it left each of them free—he wasn't sure what the correct word would be. *Autonomous,* possibly, something he'd never placed that much value on—always preferring commitment, duty, and responsibility. It was, however, as if divorce could be a new and better version of long marriage—something he'd never thought of, but would.

Jonathan's daughter Celia, who had been visiting from California, told him that in her view her mother's death had brought about a "mini-nervous-breakdown" in him, and that Charlotte Porter (glamorous, winning, and mysterious—to him, at least) had just been a symptom. Someone who bridged denial and bargaining. Celia'd studied for a degree in public health at SMU. It was, she believed, healthy that it had ended congenially with Charlotte—good for the next stage of life—whatever that was to be. It was probably even good that he'd *married* Charlotte, and that she was the kind of alluringly impenetrable woman for whom longevity was never a reality. Celia used the expression "scar tissue" somewhere in this context, which caused Jonathan to speak sharply to her, to the point that her facile grad-school terminology diminished him and disappointed him that she could say these things. She was not seeing his life as complexly as it should be seen. To which Celia offered no argument, merely hung around for a long weekend in the city, went out a lot, then flew back to Tucson where she taught in a Montessori and lived with her husband.

The morning she left, however, Jonathan had waked in a tumult and a sense of jarring surprise at being where he was—alone in his apartment on Watts Street—and not somewhere else. Where, he didn't know. This sensation seemed to have something to do with Charlotte, though he certainly didn't want to call her up to ask what it could be, as if she might be feeling the same way. Which he was sure she wasn't. A dimension of his intense but brief life married to Charlotte was that in addition to each of them seeming to have few friends, he knew virtually no one who knew her. And Charlotte knew virtually no one (apart from Bailes and Celia) who knew him—which didn't matter to Charlotte. But this sensation of being jarred (frustration and disorientation, really), suggested he needed, or wanted, to know something he didn't know from someone he didn't know—about Charlotte. He couldn't imagine what it was. Anyone might've said—Celia—that this was all just a veiled expression of loneliness.

Likeliest, Jonathan felt, the person (the *only* person) who might know what he was talking to himself about would be Charlotte's departed former husband. In Ireland. The mariner/architect. Dolan. There'd always been a connection (at least Jonathan acknowledged one) between Francis Dolan and himself, which Dolan might very well respond to empathetically if offered the chance—even though Dolan had totally abandoned Charlotte to ply the seas, whereas Charlotte had abandoned Jonathan for no reason other than that she wanted to and seemed not to regret.

In mid-February, just after Valentine's (in complete violation of his bold new understandings about marriage and the *skein* of life), Jonathan called Francis Dolan in

County Kerry, where Dolan conducted his architect's practice and lived with a Polish wife and his ungrateful children. It was not at all hard to find the number. And there would be no need to reveal the call to Charlotte, who (he realized) might not have objected, but would've made him feel strange just by knowing.

Francis Dolan was coolly polite when Jonathan spoke his own name into the phone and identified himself as Jonathan Bell, who'd married Charlotte, after he (Dolan) had been married to her, but was now also divorced from her just as he (Dolan) was . . . and was now calling from overseas, wanting exactly what? "Ah-ah-ah, yes. Right, right," Dolan said, sounding surprisingly Irish. Jonathan hadn't expected that. It was nine in the morning in New York. It was two where Dolan was. A place called Dunquin. By the sea. Francis Dolan would be in the middle of his architect's work day, drawing up something on a big table.

"I'm sorry to call you in the middle of your work day," Jonathan said, feeling stupid, as if the time was not his own choosing.

"There we are. Okay," Francis Dolan said. "Has something got the matter with Charlotte?"

"No," Jonathan said. "I mean, I don't know. I don't think so. It's not why I'm calling. I don't mean to alarm you."

"Well. Good then," Francis Dolan said. "What is it I can do for you? Is it John?"

"Yes," Jonathan said. "Jonathan Bell. In New York."

"What can I do for you, Jonathan?"

Francis Dolan was now a certifiable person, standing probably before a huge, mullioned window confronting the sea, possibly wearing a heavy woolen cardigan. Francis Dolan was fifty-two. Jonathan had seen a picture with the children at Charlotte's—tall, lean with a scrunched Irish face and curly black hair—in just such a sweater. Suddenly, however, wishing to say what Dolan could do for him, all the brash, tumultuous, jarring alarm and disorientation that had caused Jonathan to believe he needed to know something about Charlotte went abruptly still. He'd expected a question to simply formulate in his mind the instant he was on the line with architect Dolan—as he now was. But it did not. Instead there was only silence. Which was not a question. He felt cripplingly embarrassed and childish.

"I wanted to ask you a question about Charlotte," he managed to say to Dolan—eliciting another silence, a sigh, then the sound of something being poured into something else. A glass. Water. A glass of water on a desk.

"What would that be?" Francis Dolan said, his voice sounding as if he'd cast a glance out the window. "I've not spoken to Charlotte in quite a while. I'd say years.

The children barely have contact though they love her well enough, I guess. Are you not married to her?"

"No," Jonathan said. "We divorced. Last year."

"Ah-ah-ah, yes," Dolan said. "You mentioned that in your leader. Sorry. What is it you want to know, then? I don't know anything anymore."

Jonathan suddenly then *did* know precisely what he wanted to ask of this man whose life he'd intruded upon with no warning, had never met and would never meet, and with whom he had no connection whatsoever—in spite of idiotically supposing he might. "I wanted to know how you feel about Charlotte," Jonathan said. "I'm having a hard time knowing how *I'm* supposed to feel, being divorced from her." The possibility that he *was* having a mini-nervous-breakdown now seemed completely plausible. He stared out his own window toward the great airy sky-space that the World Trade Center once dominated.

"Say again," Francis Dolan said. From Ireland. "How I feel about her?"

"I realize it's . . ." Jonathan said.

"Well, that's completely out of line, isn't it?" Francis Dolan said. "Have you been drinking, Jonathan? How do I *feel* about Charlotte? How does *anybody* feel about Charlotte? She's totally self-consumed. And totally irresistible. You have to survive her. You don't know that? That's why she has no friends."

"No," Jonathan said, only about the drinking.

"Is this a hoax of some kind?"

"No," Jonathan said. "But this call's out of line. Like you say. I hope you can forgive me."

"Forgive you. Well. Grand. Of course," Francis Dolan said.

"I'm sorry. I'll just hang up," Jonathan said. "You won't hear from me again."

"Well. That'll be grand then, too," Francis Dolan said. "Cheers."

"Cheers," Jonathan said and hung up the phone and felt—though he did not succumb to it—the gasping, cringing, gut-cramping urge to shout out. He wasn't sure what he would shout.

Charlotte drove them—in her '92, cream-colored Mercedes estate wagon with three hundred on the odometer and Sotheby/Charlotte Porter realty signs stacked in the back. She picked Jonathan up after a showing, and they drove up the West Side toward Yonkers, where Charlotte's mother was in River Mansions. It was Labor Day. Little traffic. That would come when the weekenders swarmed back and all the bridges and parkways clogged and things got hellish. The shining river beside them formed a steely mask in the late-morning sun, tidal currents working barges against the flow. The sky above New Jersey was flat summer white behind the rows of apartment towers and the big planes settling down to Newark.

As they drove up toward the Henry Hudson Bridge, a dog—a big loping saddle-brown hound that looked to Jonathan well cared for, a sporting dog—ran across the highway, stopped at the median fence and sat down to watch the cars whiz past. It was contemplating the other lanes. Not a good chance, Jonathan thought. He and Charlotte would see this dog again on their way back to town.

Charlotte didn't seem the least depressed or concerned about her mother. She seemed happy. She was thinner and wore a pair of jaunty yellow-framed glasses and had shortened her hair and colored it darker. From weight loss she now had deeper smile lines, which made her look older than he remembered. He hadn't seen her since the day in the street. A year. She was still radiant and spirited and engaging and lovely. He'd remarked to himself as he waited for her in the lobby, that he no longer had any interest in being married to Charlotte (for all the good reasons he'd schooled himself in); but he knew he *would* marry her, which was possibly exactly what they should do. It didn't seem any less likely than that they wouldn't. Those old, mossy congruities were long over with. Good riddance. It had made him feel pleasingly satisfied as he waited for her.

Riding through Riverdale where he'd once hoped to buy a grand house and make her deliriously happy, Charlotte talked about whatever popped into her head. Not one shred of awkwardness after the full year of silence. Charlotte felt completely happy around him. She was wearing the same wafer-thin blue sandals she'd been wearing outside the movie, though this time she had on what she called "my peasant outfit"—beige with fine red stitching, showing her slim, bare shoulders and tanned legs. Charlotte asked about Jonathan's health. She thought he'd had an operation, which was the one he'd had when they were married. She pointed out he'd lost some weight, and was wearing jeans, which he hadn't before, but she thought was a good choice—though his seemed baggy and ought to be, she said, traded in for nicer ones. Charlotte told him that visiting her mother was something of a burden and she'd started taking a friend with her. Though now, since she had so few friends, she'd used them all up. She said her mother suffered congestive heart failure and was retaining sodium. She also had uremia, which made her have amazing waking dreams and say hilarious things—which she might do today, and he should not be bothered. Charlotte said this probably meant kidney failure and wasn't a good sign. There was also a "laundry list of other ailments," too, which signaled her mother wouldn't be around much longer. One cure cancels out another cure. Her mother didn't want to be "fixed," anyway, and had proclaimed she was looking forward to a long blissful period of being dead. Charlotte also talked about her sister, who'd visited but now was gone, which Charlotte said was a relief because she didn't like her sister, who had recently "gone forward" with shaving her head bald and begun intensive training to become a spiritualist. Nika had caused a lot of trouble in the hospice wing, before getting on a plane and going home. Nika had explained to anyone that when someone dies the room fills with pressure—the nurses denied this—and that she (Nika), due to her training could feel pressure already building in her mother's room. Charlotte thought Nika was irresponsible and should just grow her hair back.

Charlotte told Jonathan she had experienced a "few setbacks" recently, though she didn't say what these were. He thought possibly a breakup, possibly with the raptor-ish lawyer, or conceivably that she wasn't selling her quota high-end properties. She said she had gone on medication and was feeling better about things.

Indeed, she said, her life would soon be empowered "to move outside usual contexts" and that she would then "allow certain things to rise up while permitting other things to recede and vanish." She didn't say what any of these things were, and Jonathan didn't care to ask.

Jonathan noticed as they drove that Charlotte wasn't wearing the three thin silver bracelets she'd previously worn all the time and that showed off her pretty wrists. She *was* wearing a big emerald-cut emerald ring as green as a traffic light—a gift, he supposed, from an admirer. Though possibly her mother had given it to her, in the run-up to a dignified death. When he commented on the ring and its brilliance, Charlotte looked over at Jonathan and smiled a teasing, equally brilliant smile and said she'd sold the diamond earrings he had bought her at Harry Winston, during the time of their courtship. She wasn't really the diamond earring type, she (now) told him, though she'd said before that she adored them. She told him she loved the emerald ring—an antique—and he (Jonathan) should think of it as being an indirect present from him, which was how she thought of it.

Jonathan watched the emerald ring sway back and forth on top of the steering wheel as Charlotte drove up the Saw Mill, left, then right in the mid-day traffic. He pictured the twin diamonds in their blue-leather *HW* box, remembered his infectious, reckless feeling when he'd had the box in his coat pocket on a cold November evening in 2002, when he'd walked up to Sixty-Seventh to give the earrings to Charlotte at dinner. If he'd ever given Mary Linn a pair of diamond earrings—and he *had* given her an almost-as-lovely dinner solo (not from Harry Winston, it was true)—she'd have worn them in her coffin. Which she did with the dinner ring. She'd asked Jonathan to put it on her finger if she should suddenly die. Good as his word, he'd slipped it on just before the coffin lid was closed.

This, like everything else with Charlotte, was not expectable. New rules of behavior. Gestures not retaining the original significance. Promises implying different outcomes from the historical norm. He thought a moment about Charlotte's practical provisos for a second marriage—to get whatever good was left—and how easy it still was to be with her, even now. How little unhappiness she occasioned. He didn't care about the goddamned emerald—which was a revelation in itself. Though what he did care about was still not easy to put into words, but wasn't nothing. This was what he'd wanted to ask her other husband Dolan but could only muddle around with words that humiliated himself. He didn't care a fart about what *he*—the first husband—felt about Charlotte. He cared about what he himself felt.

But that required a language he hadn't yet mastered. Though she was not insubstantial. He was sure of that. When Charlotte had told him, sitting on the seawall, a year and a half ago, that their marriage wasn't working, what she seemed to want was for them to become much better accommodated to each other—accommodated in a way marriage wouldn't permit. For her, at least. She might've thought Jonathan would never be able to do that, though she didn't seem to fault him. Only now, Jonathan thought, he *was* able. He *was* accommodated to Charlotte and their situation. Totally. He felt, in fact, as empty of unexpressed desire for Charlotte as she apparently felt for him. Which, he guessed, was the idea.

"You're cross at me, aren't you, Mr. B?" Charlotte said, driving and smiling.

"No," Jonathan said.

"You got pretty quiet for a minute. I didn't want to hurt your feelings about the earrings." She put her hand, the one with the jawbreaker emerald, lightly over onto his that held his bulky class ring.

"You didn't," Jonathan said.

"But you have to tell me if I ever do," Charlotte said brightly. "I apparently do it to people without knowing. Is that a deal? I intend to know you for a long time."

"It's a deal," Jonathan said. Then he added, "I *hope* you know me."

"There's no hoping about it," Charlotte said. "No hoping at all."

River Mansions was not a mansion at all, but a boxwood-hedged, '40s-era redbrick, medium-low-rise apartment rectangle that had once been a place where citizens who weren't old and dying lived normal lives. Scrubby, third-growth trees blocked any view of the river, and across a wide boulevard, Yonkers carried forward its normal industry of dispensing acetylene products, selling custom plumbing fittings, making burglar alarms, and the development of solvents for resolving toxic accidents. Charlotte's mother hadn't liked the Mansions when Charlotte moved her out of Alpine and across. "It's a dry dock for old wrecks," she said, then added, "Not that I'm not one. I was certainly married to one."

Charlotte's father had been a mid-level patronage appointee in the city of Paterson—a mild, reliable man who did things in the comptroller's office and wanted sons instead of two beautiful daughters. Charlotte's mother—who was Romanian—had been, she said of herself, "the gypsy spirit in their union." A small-time theatrical agent who loved actors and escapades, who drank and smoked and cracked jokes and paid little or no attention to her family, her mother had encouraged

Charlotte and her sister to quit high school and tour Europe—to learn. But they'd each gone to NYU and chosen to learn nothing instead. Charlotte's sister had tried for a while to be an actress but failed.

Since it was Labor Day, families were arriving at the Mansions to visit their impossible, aging relatives—bringing flowers, cards, magazines, jigsaw puzzles, baby photos, and candies the elderly shouldn't eat, all to celebrate with a declining loved one a long life of toil on earth. Jonathan had brought a potted blue hydrangea plant because it seemed to match Charlotte's mother's exuberant personality—even in hospice. Though Charlotte said on the way in that Beezy might not notice his gift, and he shouldn't feel bad. She would've adored it earlier. Charlotte had brought nothing with her but Jonathan.

Charlotte's mother was propped up in her adjustable bed, wearing a curly champagne-colored wig and a pink short-sleeved T-shirt that had WILD THING . . . I THINK I LOVE YOU and a little cartoon devil printed on its front. Her small brown BB eyes moved toward them when Jonathan and Charlotte slipped in the room, the single window of which gave down three floors to the River Mansions campus lawn, where patients and their families were having holiday outings on the grass. Yellow flowers outlined the entire grounds. Across the wide boulevard a small refinery installation you didn't see when you drove in had its escape flame flickering into the Monday sky. A sign on Beezy's door read OXYGEN IN USE, but Beezy wasn't wearing her nosepiece, and there were no monitors or cylinders or wall outlets to suggest she should. Beezy was possibly past these. A young priest wearing a cranberry-red collar and a short-sleeved black shirt sat at the foot of Beezy's bed, holding a guitar he'd just been playing. On the covers was a booklet that said *Life—A Staging Ground* on its front. The priest had brought along a silver Mylar balloon with the words *Up, Up* & *Away* printed on it, also in pink, and which he'd tethered to the head of Beezy's bed. It was all part of his priest kit.

"She likes torch songs," the young priest said smiling, standing to leave. "Or she did when she got here. She doesn't enjoy much of anything now." He looked dotingly at Charlotte's mother, who was now asleep, or at least her eyes were closed. The priest's plastic name tag said he was Father Ray, SJ. "Do you?" he said to Charlotte's mother.

"No," Charlotte's mother said emphatically. And surprisingly. Her eyes snapped open at the sound of her own voice. Charlotte gave first the priest and then her mother her most appreciative smile but seemed at a loss to say something. Charlotte's mother was attached to a drip sac, the tube of which disappeared ominously underneath her T-shirt. Her right arm now sported a green plaster cast with yellow smiley-face stickers all over and a lot of people's Magic Marker signatures. Jonathan saw that Beezy's flesh, above the cast and below, was yellow and blue and scrunched. She'd suffered a fall (at some time), which everyone knew meant the end was probably near.

"Charlotte's so lucky to be married to you," Beezy said either to Jonathan or the priest. Her small head was sunk into her pillow like a bird's. "Her last husband was a shitty Mick nobody liked."

"That's not true, my darling," Charlotte said. "His children loved him. Still love him." Father Ray was nodding and smiling, not wanting to say more, just leave. Charlotte's mother had no idea who he was. Charlotte took possession of Jonathan's hydrangea, moved to the far side of her mother's bed, set the plant on the bedside table and began gathering up tissues that had accumulated and putting them into a shiny metal waste can. She pulled the curtains farther open for better light. "We thought you'd be sleeping," she said. "Jonathan brought you this nice plant."

"My eyes are open," Beezy said. "If I'm asleep, they're closed."

"I'm the same way," Charlotte said cheerfully. She

picked up the plant again and put it in the middle of the window ledge, where it looked more cheerful though not exactly pretty.

"What is that?" Charlotte's mother said, her eyes tracking the plant's movement. "Is it a big zinnia? I don't like 'em. They stink."

"It's a blue hydrangea," Charlotte said gaily. "Which you *do* like. Supposedly." She began smoothing the surface of the white hospital blanket, glancing up at the wall TV. Sound was off, but Oprah's big shining face filled its screen. Jonathan hadn't come completely in, but thought the room needed to be disinfected. He unconsciously for an instant pinched his nostrils closed.

"Back when I was alive I did," Charlotte's mother said, relative to her taste in flowers.

"That's right," Charlotte said and looked to Jonathan and smiled. "You're dead now. I don't know why we even come to visit you."

"Your sister liked Dr. Kamasutra," Charlotte's mother said weakly. "I think the bald pate might've queered that deal, though." Beezy wheezed, and Jonathan heard the clatter of her breathing. Tussive, slow, strained, contained within. Breathing that had nothing much to do with anything going on inside her body.

"Mom calls her doctor Dr. Matsui, Dr. Kamasutra,"

Charlotte said, still peeking at Oprah. "Nika liked him, apparently."

"*Apparently,*" her mother said.

Jonathan felt too large inside this room, and too male, as if some male odor were emanating off him. He wanted to speak; to insert a positive word into the awful goings-on. However, Charlotte and her mother were an entity that didn't really require him to speak. Charlotte's mother was completely different from when he saw her a year ago. What she seemed now, in this room where she was soon to die, was definitely human but unsustainable, as if right in front of him she was growing smaller at a rate Jonathan—large, bulky, towering over her—could actually *see.* Like a balloon deflating. Could this be pressure filling the room? Someone had applied rouge to Beezy's cheeks. But her skin was more the color of her pillows, her champagne-bonneted head ready to disappear into their plush. It struck Jonathan to silence. He was relieved he'd never had to see Mary Linn in such a condition. Seeing her dead was bad enough. This, though, was worse.

Beezy was now staring straight at him. Her mouth had pinched up tight and inward and frowning, as if she was experiencing a terrible effort to express something. Jonathan wondered what Beezy was seeing. "So. What do you have to say for *yourself,* Varney," Beezy said.

Her tiny eyes blinked, then blinked again. "You're never overestimated by people who know you, are you?" She smiled a pitiless smile for whoever Varney was. Charlotte could smile in this very way. Beezy took a deep, difficult breath. Then her mouth gapped and went down, and her face relaxed from smiling and looked lopsided, as if the vitality that made it a face had subsided. Her eyes were still darting, but then they, too, closed as if a cloud had paused above them. Below the green cast of her wounded left arm, her fingers were working, working.

The room smelled sour but also sweet at the same time. Jonathan heard what sounded like a jackhammer juddering somewhere deep in the old building's works. He'd said nothing, had been asked nothing since he'd arrived—except as Varney. They hadn't been here long.

There was a soft knock then the hiss of the door opening. A woman's smiling face appeared. A nurse. She leaned into the space. Crisp white cap. Her nose pointy, her eyes blinking, her mouth red with fresh lipstick and big. She looked at Jonathan and then at Beezy and then at Charlotte.

"How're we doin'," she said. "Do we need anything?" She had an accent.

"We're doing well." Charlotte spoke on Beezy's behalf. "Thank you."

The nurse smiled her significant smile. "And how

are *you*," she said this to Charlotte. "Are *you* doing well, too?" They knew each other. The nurse advanced, exchanged a fresh water beaker for the one on the bed table and started out again.

"Yes," Charlotte said, wishing to be engaging. "I'm doing just fine too."

"O-*kay*." The door slid smoothly back and closed.

Labor Day visitors to the Mansions were now filtering back to their cars in the late-summer warmth. Elderly inhabitants stood at their windows, watching. Some waved or wept, others just stood. The warm lush grass had a fresh chemical odor, though you could smell the river close-by. It was ninety out.

They'd stayed in the room for a while, saying little, Charlotte occasionally looking at TV. They were not waiting for anything. Jonathan went to the window and studied the streets. Yonkers. Was it a city? He'd heard about it but never been to it. It was some man's name. Yonkers. A Dutchman. Beezy's breathing evened out in time and was calm. She said things in her dreams. "Well, if I did *that*, I'd be crazy. Wouldn't I?" Charlotte had answered to make her not be lonely. "No, Mother, you wouldn't." Another time, but less clearly, Beezy said, "Yes, Tom. Yes, Tom. Yes." Tom had been her husband, the girls' father.

Charlotte, for a while, leafed through *Life—A Staging Ground,* which the priest had left. She read something out loud to Jonathan—softly, so as not to wake her mother. "The new millennium, lashed by winds, etched in blood." She looked at Jonathan who was across the room. "What is it that's 'etched'?" she said.

"I don't know," Jonathan answered.

"That's very strange, isn't it?" she said. "Etched in blood."

After a while the nurse made another appearance, all shiny face, clean-smelling, crisp. She was bringing something for Beezy. Yellow custard. She went to her bedside, put her hand on Beezy's wrist, waited as if listening, then said. "Well, then." She must've been Swedish. Lutheran. "I believe she's left us all behind now."

"Oh!" Charlotte said and seemed very surprised. "My goodness. I really wanted to be here."

"Well, you are here, dear," the nurse said, beginning to straighten Beezy's covers. "You're right here. I'm so glad."

There were all the things to be done, and the River Mansions people were there to do them efficiently. Arrangements had long been agreed to. It was not an uncomfortable time. Charlotte turned off the television, then made an effort to cross her mother's hands. But the plaster cast was bulky and made it not easy. And there was the drip, which eventually was removed by someone. In time, two black men in blue scrubs came with a gurney and clean sheets. One, an older man, seemed very solemn. The other, who was younger, was not solemn at all. "She peaceful now," the younger man said.

Then it was time to go. Nothing else needed supervising.

All along they had planned to go for sushi. A place Charlotte liked far downtown, with little boats that delivered California rolls and miso soup and unagi on a stream of water that ran in a channel around a circular bar. It was hard to envision, Charlotte said. It was Charlotte's treat for Jonathan's coming with.

Outside, though, on the hot River Mansions sidewalk, Charlotte had turned and looked up at the old, low brick edifice. Elderly people were staring down at her from rooms. The blue hydrangea was still in her mother's window. She began to cry. She cried without drama, Jonathan thought, tears rolling freely over her cheeks, her mouth wrinkled, trying to smile, breathing through a stuffy nose. He stood beside her. Families were walking by, paying no attention to someone crying. He put his hand on her bony shoulder, where the fabric was cool from when she'd been indoors. He simply waited, attended her, let her do what she wanted or needed. He didn't imagine she would cry very long. He remembered at that moment and for no reason that Charlotte had wished for no money in their divorce. He'd authorized the four million—without her permission or knowledge. They were still married then. But divorce was her idea she'd said. Money wasn't owed. It wasn't as if he'd done anything wrong. He thought, though, he should settle the money on her now. Ease her life. It would keep them bound by something of substance. She was a woman who needed very little.

"I really wasn't thinking about my mother, just now," Charlotte said, when she'd almost stopped crying. Jonathan had handed her a green-and-red silk handkerchief, and she had blotted her eyes and blown her nose. "I'm sorry about my nose," she said and smiled smally. The sun was dazzling heat up off the sidewalk. He'd begun sweating—the thing he did and hated. A big-man's thing. "I was thinking about my sister and how much I don't love her, how I'll hate calling her and hearing her yak and yak about spiritualism, as if it meant a fucking thing. You know?"

"I think I do," Jonathan said. He had never met the sister. And he had never seen Charlotte cry, though he'd been married to her almost two years. Neither of them had cried.

"You didn't feel the room get full of pressure, did you?" she said. "I mean . . ." She cast her gaze back toward the window, where at one time or another she, her mother and Jonathan had stood, and where the hydrangea plant had now been removed. Charlotte shook her head as if she were rejecting things too numerous to consider.

"I didn't feel anything," Jonathan said.

"No." She looked at him in the sweet way she'd looked at him on other occasions. Occasions he remembered. "But you were so good. You were so good to come with me. You took charge. I just couldn't navigate, wouldn't have known what to do if you weren't here. I'd be lost."

"Well, that's good," Jonathan said. He hadn't done anything, but felt now a stirring, a feeling close to sexual, rising through him but not lasting. "Are you hungry?"

"I'm not," Charlotte said. "I'm really not. I know I said sushi."

"It's fine," Jonathan said.

"It wasn't a bad way to die, was it?" Charlotte said. "She just went to sleep. Just let herself go. Wouldn't you want that to be your fate?"

He'd felt different about it. He thought Beezy had actually clung to her life, had held on to it fiercely. Charlotte simply hadn't noticed, had noticed other things. Though Beezy's was not a death he would want. Some crappy room with sour aromas. A balloon. Oprah mugging on TV. There were better ways. Mary Linn's not being one of them. Hers had not been awful, but had been too abrupt. He hadn't been prepared. "I can't say," Jonathan said regarding his dying preferences.

"Oh. I suppose you're right." As though he'd complained about her mother's death. She shook her head as if she'd been in a daze, touched her cheeks with his handkerchief, her emerald ring catching the afternoon sun.

Jonathan then realized that the question of "what is desired of life?"—which was, in his view, the next most logical question—would not come up. Not at this moment. Possibly it never would come up in Charlotte's thinking. This was the thing he knew.

"I'll tell you what," Jonathan said. Charlotte smiled at him weakly. She liked sudden new things, had no idea what he intended. "I'll take a taxi home. It'll be easier." More people were going past. He and Charlotte could be talking about anything. About the great and drastic commotion now loose upon the earth. Or something smaller. Across the boulevard from the River

Mansions, the refinery flame licked the sky. A police siren was heard in the distance.

"But will you walk me to my car?" Charlotte said. She leaned into him, put her warm head against his chest as if she was listening to his heart beat-beat, beat-beat, as she had other times. "I'll just go home and go to sleep. Okay?"

"Yes. We'll both do that," Jonathan said.

"We'll talk tomorrow, won't we?" She breathed deeply, breathed him in, he was so close.

"That's right," he said. "We will." And that was all they said and did together where these particular matters were concerned. There would be other days, as Charlotte said, when he would see her. Definitely. Things would go on for them until whatever was desired of life was clear and accommodatable, as though they had always wanted it that way. All these things, these separate things were really connected, he felt.

Acknowledgments

I wish to thank my dear friends Cormac Kinsella, Fergus Cronin, Gerald Dawe, and John Banville for their valuable counsel; and my friends Joseph O'Connor, Daniel Victor, Joanne Sealy, and Kenneth Holditch for their good guidance through terrains not known to me. I'm grateful to Deborah Treismann for sensitively editing "Leaving for Kenosha" and "Displaced," to Emily Nemens for helping me finish "Nothing to Declare" in style, to Miranda Collinge for taking pains with "Jimmy Green," and to Megan Lynch for thoughtfully working through the rest of the stories included here. My thanks to Sonya Cheuse, Dale Rohrbaugh, and Sara Birmingham for deftly pushing this book into the world. I'm grateful to my colleagues in Trinity College,

Dublin, for taking me in; in particular my thanks to Terrence Browne, Stephen Matterson, Eve Patten, and Orla McCarthy for their friendship. I'm grateful to Gill Coleridge for happy decades of motoring around England, to Simon Williams for his many and amusing generosities, and to Christopher and Koukla MacLehose for a great, *great* deal.

I'm grateful to Emmanuel Roman and to Barrie Sardoff for their trust, and to my colleagues in the School of the Arts at Columbia for offering me time to write most of these stories. Eudora Welty and James Salter are lively in my thoughts as friends and inspirations. My thanks to Alexandra Pringle for her astute encouragements. I've been lucky for most of my life to know and learn from David M. Becker, who once taught me real property and (almost) how to be a lawyer, and became my great friend. Amanda Urban has seen me through a lifetime, keeping what's important in at least *her* clear sight. My thanks to Daniel Halpern for generously supporting the writing of these stories.

And finally, my much more than thanks to Kristina Ford for being her dazzling self. RF